Haldimand County Public Library
CALEDONIA BRANCH

A BOOKMARKED DEATH

OCT - 2021

Holdimand County Public Library
CALEDONIA BRANCH

By Judi Culbertson

A Bookmarked Death
A Photographic Death
An Illustrated Death

A
BOOKMARKED
DEATH

A DELHI LAINE MYSTERY

JUDI
CULBERTSON

WITNESS
IMPULSE

An Imprint of HarperCollinsPublishers

Haldimand County Public Library
CALEDONIA BRANCH

This is a work of fiction. Names, characters, places, and incidents are products of the author's imagination or are used fictitiously and are not to be construed as real. Any resemblance to actual events, locales, organizations, or persons, living or dead, is entirely coincidental.

Excerpt from *A Photographic Death* copyright © 2014 by Judi Culbertson.

A BOOKMARKED DEATH. Copyright © 2015 by Judi Culbertson. All rights reserved under International and Pan-American Copyright Conventions. By payment of the required fees, you have been granted the nonexclusive, nontransferable right to access and read the text of this e-book on screen. No part of this text may be reproduced, transmitted, downloaded, decompiled, reverse-engineered, or stored in or introduced into any information storage and retrieval system, in any form or by any means, whether electronic or mechanical, now known or hereafter invented, without the express written permission of HarperCollins e-books.

EPub Edition MARCH 2015 ISBN: 9780062365149

Print Edition ISBN: 9780062365156

10 9 8 7 6 5 4 3 2 1

Dedication

To the memory of Ignatz—because a cat is never just a cat.

Chapter One

ALTHOUGH I RARELY garden, I was conscious of spring that May because of the winter we had just endured—the worst on Long Island in one hundred years according to the *New York Times*. I watched the daffodils push out of the earth, crowding each other like shoppers at a Black Friday sale. I cataloged every flame and crimson tulip as it appeared. The ice on the pond had melted quietly away, and walking out to my Book Barn that early morning I caught darting glimpses of orange and gold fish.

It promised to be a beautiful Sunday, though there was no slacking off for people with a small business to run. Mine was called Secondhand Prose. The more used and rare books I could describe on the Internet, the more I could almost make a living. Tracking down unusual volumes, investigating their origins, then finding the people who wanted them had never lost its charm. I captured books as rare as Siberian tigers, common as barnyard kittens, and found good homes for them all.

Delhi Laine, Book Rescue?

The barn and the farmhouse closer to the street had been bequeathed to the nearby university in the 1970s and offered to us as a rental since my husband, Colin, taught there. On rainy days the barn still held the comforting odor of cows, but the animals were long gone. The rough-hewn room now held a long library table with my laptop, a landline phone, and piles of books to be listed for sale. The floor was covered with threadbare Oriental rugs from the Methodist parsonage where I grew up, and I had tacked René Magritte and Frida Kahlo posters to the walls. About seven thousand volumes waited in cartons and on bookshelves.

That Sunday morning I brought a carton of vintage children's picture books over to list on the Internet. But before retrieving *Nurse Nancy*, a Golden Book with the bandages miraculously intact, I clicked on the *Newsday* Web site—a familiar delaying tactic. Although Long Island has hosted such sensations as the Amityville Horror, relatively little happens in Suffolk County. But today I stared at the lead story:

FIRE DESTROYS SOUTHAMPTON MANSION: TWO DIE

The fire had started in the early hours of Sunday morning on South Main Street, the fashionable thoroughfare that led from the village down to the Atlantic Ocean. By the time the police and fire department arrived, the house was too badly burned to save the owners, Dr. Ethan Crosley, an archeologist who taught at Brown University, and his wife, Sheila. Evidently they had returned from their estate in Barbados to attend the college graduation of their daughter, Elisa.

The white letters on the blue background waved and bounced like schoolchildren vying to be chosen. What I was reading was impossible. I closed my eyes and waited for the typeface to settle down. Then I looked again and scrolled down the page, disbelieving, snatching at words. *Gasoline, torched, arson.* There had been another fire in the neighborhood in April, a vacant house, as many of the homes on South Main Street were before Memorial Day when the season began. The Arson Squad was focusing on individuals with a known compulsion to set fires.

I was staring at the photograph of the large, once-beautiful clapboard house, now a lopsided ruin, when the phone rang, jerking me in my chair. I saw by the caller ID that it was my youngest daughter, Hannah, and picked up the receiver quickly.

"Hey, Hani." I kept my voice easy though I was sure I knew why she was calling.

"*Mom?* Mom, the most terrible thing happened." Her voice was shaky, and I knew she was fighting not to cry.

"You mean the fire, the Crosleys? I know, honey, I just saw it online."

"But how could something like that happen? How could Elisa's parents just be dead? They said it happened in Southampton." There was a trace of accusation in her voice, almost as if I had lured them to Long Island and struck the match myself. I knew she didn't believe that, she was just struggling to make sense of the tragedy. Still, it was well-known that the Crosleys were not my favorite people.

"But why were they in Southampton?" I asked.

She snuffled. "She said her grandparents had a vacation house there and they left it to her father. She spent summers there. Imagine, she was here on Long Island too!" Then she remembered the present. "Mom, it was so *awful*. We were just going out to breakfast, joking around about the weird pancake flavors at IHOP when this man and woman came up to us. They asked who we were and made us go back up to my room. One of Elisa's dorm mates told the police she was visiting me at Cornell, so they asked police here to tell us about the fire."

Hannah stopped then, but I held myself back from demanding to know what happened next.

Finally she sighed. "I didn't know *what* to do. Elisa was screaming that it wasn't true, that things like that didn't happen to her parents, I thought she was going to start *hitting* the guy. Then she just began to cry and I kept on hugging her. The policewoman wanted to call a doctor, but Elisa wouldn't let her."

"Is she with you now?"

"Yes. She wants to talk to you."

Oh, God. What could I say about the Crosleys? I had to think of something for Elisa's sake. But it was complicated because the Crosleys weren't her biological parents. Hannah was her twin sister. I was her mother.

As soon as I got off the phone with Elisa, I dialed my husband, Colin. Her father. My conversation with her had been perfunctory. I kept telling her how sorry I was; she kept vowing to find out who set the fire and asking me to help her, based on some detective work I had done in the past. I couldn't imagine it but I promised her I would.

Sometimes Colin put his phone on vibrate and I had to leave a message. The surest way to get his attention was to text him, but this was not a subject for badly spelled phrases.

This morning he answered right away. "Hey-lo."

"It's me. Have you seen the news today?"

"I've been *writing*." When Colin was working on a new poem, God Himself would have had to send a text. Although his livelihood was teaching archeology and supervising digs, he had been writing poetry for as long as I'd known him. One of his volumes had actually been nominated for a Pulitzer.

"It's Ethan and Sheila. They *died*. In a fire in Southampton." I found I was gasping out the words. "Ethan and Sheila are dead."

"What are you talking about?"

"Hannah called me. And I saw it on the *Newsday* site. You need to come over. We need to talk."

Chapter Two

By the time Colin arrived, I was back in the farmhouse, making coffee. He came through the kitchen door looking like Santa Claus in the tropics, his Hawaiian shirt and cargo shorts already rumpled. He was a good-sized man and pleased about it, accepting his mound of stomach as evidence of his gravitas. He had also cultivated a generosity of spirit, and his students, rarely glimpsing his steely interior, adored him. I had fallen under his spell for a long time myself.

We sat down at the table and I poured coffee from the fancy glass French press, a Christmas gift from our oldest daughter, Jane. It looked as out of place on the scarred oak wood as disgraced royalty forced to consort with commoners. Our kitchen actually looked like a time warp from the Smithsonian. It had been the beating heart of our family for over twenty years, but nothing had been updated during that time. The harvest gold appliances worked sporadically, the garishly speckled black countertop still made me think of Mardi Gras celebrations, and the 1850s oak plank floor and kitchen table were original.

This was the room where, a year ago last October, Colin had informed me that "a man can't dance with a wife who hides his shoes," and moved out to rejoin the celebration.

"So Ethan and Sheila were incinerated," he said, lightening his coffee with half-and-half. "It couldn't have happened to a nicer couple."

"Colin!" I was shocked to hear him say what I'd only thought. "It's a terrible way to die."

"They were terrible people." But he read reproof in my comment because he added, "*You're* the one who wanted to see them get what they deserved. Speaking objectively, it's not like the world lost Howard Carter or Louis Leakey. Ethan was a good archeologist, but inconsistent. He was always taking leaves of absence to fund private digs, then never telling anybody what he'd found. That's suspicious right there. And speaking personally, he was a terrible friend."

"I know. Do you want a bagel?"

"Cream cheese?"

"I think so." I stood up and went to the refrigerator. "Anyway, Elisa is devastated."

"Of course she is. She grew up thinking they were her parents."

"But once she found out that they weren't, that they had *stolen* her from us . . ."

"C'mon, Del." He tipped back in the ancient wooden chair, a habit that made me fear it wouldn't make it to two hundred. "You thought that once we found Elisa and told her, you'd fall into each other's arms and the past would be magically erased?"

"Of course not!" That's exactly what I'd thought. "I knew there'd be adjustments. I just didn't expect there'd be this barrier between us."

He eyed me like a student who was missing the point. "The 'barrier' was because you were insisting on bringing in the police and seeing the Crosleys punished. She didn't want that."

"Well, that can't happen now." I brought the plastic bag from the freezer to the counter and extracted two poppy seed bagels. "Now it's up to God."

Nineteen years ago a group of young archeology professors and their families had been hosted at a six-week conference in England. I had been a distracted young mother with three little girls and a fourth baby due in two months. Sheila and Ethan Crosley, wealthy with no children, had become secretly enamored of one of our two-year-old twins and decided they had to have her. Not only had they stolen her in a way that made everyone believe she had drowned in the Avon River in Stratford, they had changed our family's life forever. They had destroyed my relationship with Colin and hijacked our future plans. If we couldn't even protect the children we already had . . .

Colin and I didn't talk again until I had toasted the bagels and brought them over to the table, along with the butter and cream cheese. Then we conducted a wake for Ethan and Sheila Crosley. Of sorts.

"I don't understand why you were ever best friends," I said.

He shrugged. "Ethan was different when I met him in grad school. We were interested in the same things and he had a wicked sense of humor. He didn't have time for people who didn't meet his standards, of course." Ethan's parents had inherited a thriving farm machinery company in Pennsylvania, which they then turned into a national concern. Ethan had been an unexpected and adored only child.

"I never thought he was anything special when I met him in

Stratford," I objected. Ethan had been tall and rangy with tight red curls. I was one of the people he hadn't had time for. "So what changed him?"

Colin pursed his mouth. "I don't know. Maybe life. Sheila was always very ambitious. But it was more. Even when I first knew him he was restless, looking for the thing that would make him truly happy."

That sounded like the human condition to me. But Colin stared into his coffee cup as if an analysis of Ethan was written there. "He had his reasons, of course."

"Such as?"

He looked over at me, his eyes as blue as his twin daughters' but set in the weathered lines of a man in his late fifties. "He's dead now, so I guess it doesn't matter. He had testicular cancer as a teenager. He never told me the details, but I know there were certain side effects. Back then they didn't know as much about treatment."

"Yikes."

Colin nodded. "Sterility and impaired function, at least. So he focused on other things."

"Why didn't you *tell* me?"

"He made me promise not to mention it to anyone. I think afterward he was sorry he had told me."

But I was your wife. The old lament. "No wonder they resented us for procreating like rabbits. But didn't Sheila mind about . . ."

Colin smoothed the cream cheese on his bagel with a finger. Since it was just us, I hadn't bothered with plates and silverware. "I guess the money made up for it. Lots of people who *can* have kids don't want them. They could go anywhere, afford anything. "

"And never let us forget it." The Crosleys had not stayed in our barebones academic housing, but in a stylish inn several miles away. They came by only to pick up Colin for dinner several times a week, since we weren't renting a car ourselves. On the pretext that the men would be discussing archeology, I was always excluded.

At first the other wives on the archeology project had tried to include Sheila. But she never stopped flaunting her black-haired beauty and superior way of life. While the rest of us were boasting about shrewd tag sale buys and defending the nutritional value of hot dogs added to mac and cheese, Sheila was traveling to London for concerts and house parties. The tactfulness that the rest of us had developed was lost on Sheila. She said whatever she felt like saying.

I remembered a conversation one late afternoon when she and Ethan had stopped by for Colin. Several of us, friends now, were sitting on lawn chairs on the grass while our children played nearby. Sheila had walked over wearing something lacy and white, something that could have been photographed for *Vogue*. Her dark hair was pulled back with a big bow. After saying hello, she'd stared at my three daughters, at their faded overalls and faces that were grubby and ice cream–stained after a day of hard play.

"What a waste. If they were *my* children, they wouldn't go around looking like they lived in a slum."

A moment of shock, then my new friend Anna said, "If they were your children, you'd be too busy to hang around envying Delhi. If you want kids, have some of your own."

Then I'd added, God help me, "Yeah, Sheila. Money can't buy everything."

"And you know that because?" A flash of dark brown eyes was the only indication I had gotten to her. "You have a lot to learn." Then she noticed Ethan beckoning and left.

As Sheila was leaving, Anna had muttered, "Who died and made her first lady?"

Had that been the catalyst for everything? The moment that Elisa's future was decided? Thinking about it now stopped my breath. It would have had to be Elisa, of course. She had stood out from the band of children like Venus outshining the stars. Not even three, she had been precocious, high-spirited, engaging. *Everybody's darling.*

But I couldn't take credit for fostering Elisa's charm. Growing up I had never pictured myself as anybody's mother. My sister, Patience, had fantasies about being rich, but I had been lost in books, wishing I were in any of the places I was reading about rather than New Jersey. Colin had promised me wonderful experiences and traveling the world, and I'd pictured us as famous adventurers, a husband-and-wife team making wondrous discoveries. But once Jane was born, he'd fantasized a whole tribe of children in our wake, children who needed care and feeding and clean laundry.

If we hadn't lost Elisa, we might have had six or seven.

I wasn't ever sorry that we'd had the ones we did; I was more disbelieving that, still in my forties, I had four young adult children with experiences I didn't know about and different opinions than mine. Sometimes I wondered if I was in the wrong novel.

I brought myself back to the present. "You've actually been in that Southampton house—haven't you?"

Colin's head jerked, then he sighed, as if it pained him to be reminded of his lost friendship with Ethan. "A hundred years ago."

"But you could find it again?"

He looked scornful. "After a fire, it shouldn't be hard."

For a brilliant man, Colin wasn't very practical.

"I'm talking about before the fire."

"Why would I?"

To make sure Ethan and Sheila got the punishment they deserved?

But that was absurd. If killing people was not my style, it was Colin's even less. Though he had once grabbed our son Jason by the shoulders in anger, he had never laid a hand on the girls. His way of punishing Ethan would have been to make trouble for him at Brown or report his theft of antiquities to the Society for American Archaeology. "Do you think Ethan crossed any lines as an archeologist?"

Colin snorted. "I *know* he did. Probably had governments all over the world gunning for him. He used to pass out money like Mars Bars on digs and walk away with whatever he pleased. That was why he never reported finding anything."

"Really? With all the safeguards they have? And he got away with it? How come you never said anything?" Shocked, I machine-gunned him with questions. "He couldn't have been doing it for the money."

"I think it was a game he was playing, to see how far he could go. Not that wealthy people don't always want more. But in the past few years he's come under suspicion and I haven't heard of him going out in the field. Probably he's moved on to some other scheme."

I brought my last bite of bagel to my mouth, then brought it down again. What if some angry investigator had trailed Ethan to the Southampton house and broken in to steal back his country's archeological treasures? I had heard of obsessed investigators keeping people under surveillance for years. Perhaps they had come to the end of their patience, taken their artifacts, then decided to set the fire for revenge. *A tooth for a tooth.* It was more comforting to blame a band of outraged Egyptians or Syrians than to imagine coming under blame ourselves. Not that we would—throughout our search for Elisa, Colin had insisted on complete secrecy—but we did have reasons to exact revenge ourselves.

Especially since the kidnapping had happened in England and I was having trouble getting the American authorities interested. Once, feeling frustrated, I had tried to pressure Colin. "We have to let people know what they've done. Tell Nancy Grace or someone like that. Then the FBI and the police would have no choice but to—"

"*No*, Delhi, we agreed on no publicity! We're not going there. You think Elisa wants everyone knowing her life story? And ours? I'm not going to be known as the guy who was duped by his best friend. Once the media get hold of it, they'll *never* leave us alone. We'll handle this our own way."

Now, sitting there, I had the first frisson of uneasiness about what Colin might have considered solving the problem his "own way."

Chapter Three

As soon as Colin left, I started back out to the barn to call Elisa back. Our conversation had been too perfunctory, too short. There was so much more I needed to say to her. I needed to make sure she was all right. What Colin had said was true; this loss was no different from actually losing your parents, if that's who you believed they were. Passing the pond, I fretted selfishly over what it might do to her just-beginning relationship with us. Would it draw her closer into our family or set her on a path of independence away from everyone, even Hannah?

I tried to imagine what I would have felt at her age, what I would have done. The closest I could come was remembering the time I was nine and my mother had neglected a cut on her foot. She had ended up in the hospital with a bad infection and then sepsis. I didn't know all the details, I was only a child, but I remember the prayer vigils held at my father's church and my black fear of losing her. When my parents had actually died in their seventies, there was deep sorrow and missing them, but some acceptance as well.

Inside the barn I slipped into my office chair and pressed Hannah's number.

She answered right away. "Hi, Mom." She still sounded mournful, not far from tears.

"Hi, sweetheart. How's Elisa? I'd like to talk to her again." It was becoming easier to call her Elisa—the name given to her by the Crosleys. Caitlin, my tiny girl Caitlin, had been left behind in the park all those years ago.

"She's gone back to Boston."

"What? She's already gone? She's driving back by herself?"

"I tried to tell her I'd go with her," Hannah said defensively. "She wouldn't let me."

"She didn't want to stay another day? She shouldn't be driving!"

"*Mom.* If your parents have just burned to death, you don't ride on a *bus.*"

"No, but I'd have come up and driven her back myself. She shouldn't be on the road alone for five hours!" I told myself to calm down, that I was only making Hannah feel guilty. I was sure she had tried to stop her sister, but still . . .

"Was she feeling any better?" As soon as I said it, I then realized how stupid it sounded. Feeling better happened when you had an upset stomach, not when you had suffered the tragedy of your life.

"Well, she'd stopped crying. She's stronger than *I* would be, anyway. If it were you and Daddy, I'd kill myself too."

"No, you wouldn't. It would be hard, but you'd survive. Don't worry about us anyway, we're fine." If Colin and I had died in a fire, Jane would have been the one, pale and determined, making the funeral arrangements. Had we ever told her about being cremated? Jason would be stunned though philosophical, but Hannah would be as lost as she claimed. Her need for our love and approval was boundless. Without us in the world, I didn't know what she'd do.

I prayed for a long life. "I'll call her." But then I worried about distracting her. "Maybe I should wait till she's home."

"She always turns her phone off in the car. That's one thing she's careful about."

"Okay, I'll wait."

"And Mom? I promised her we'd come for her graduation. It's soon, on Friday. Is that okay?"

Graduation? I hadn't even thought about Elisa's graduation, the fact that it would still go on with or without the Crosleys. "Of course. But are you're sure she wants to go through with it?"

"She says it's what they would have wanted."

People always said that, but how could you know? If something happened to me just before Hannah's graduation, would I want the family to carry on with the pretext that they were doing it for me? I didn't think so. *Selfish mom.*

"She doesn't have to be there to get her diploma," I pointed out.

"Mom, it's what she wants!"

"Okay. Of course. Of course we'll be there."

But I knew we would be a poor substitute.

BECAUSE I COULD not think of anything else to do, I Googled "archeologists stealing artifacts." As usual, the Internet did not fail me. I read stories about three German archeologists who had bribed an inspector to escort them to a site after hours and made off with treasures from King Cheops's tomb. A British archeologist served time in jail and was released, only to return to the field and steal more. Ironically, the second time he received a suspended sentence, as if in recognition of his expertise. He was caught when a colleague recognized the two vases he was offering for sale on eBay.

There was another instance, closer to home. An archeology professor had smuggled arrowheads from a New Mexican site not far from where Colin conducted student digs. I wondered if the two knew each other. That archeologist had also received a suspended sentence after he returned the arrowheads, admitted wrongdoing, and pledged to help stop other looters in the area.

As far as I knew, Colin had never purloined anything. Fueled by curiosity and the promise of recognition for his discoveries, he seemed to have no trouble handing his finds over to whatever government owned them. All he wanted was a chance to study and catalog each piece first. Of course, the pottery and small sculpture and tools that he excavated did not have great monetary value. Ethan, I was sure, had gone for bigger prizes than arrowheads.

No, Colin was above temptation. I was the one who would have been tempted to slip a gold bracelet into my backpack if given the chance. Because of my feelings about rare books, I could understand wanting to own something unique, something priceless. Many archeologists handled beautiful objects. Even if they were not collectors themselves, the prices artifacts commanded on the black market had to be a temptation. Ethan had the funds to go after bigger prizes, golden statues from South American temples and rarities from Egyptian tombs.

I wondered why his name was not mentioned in any stories about illegal activity. Not even once. Whatever he had done, they had not been able to prove it. Without evidence there was no story. Colin said that he had handed out bribes, bribes meant to seal the mouths of inspectors as tightly as any tomb. With suspicions but no hard evidence, how could any government succeed in building a case against him? Once again I let my imagination run free and pictured a foreign agent tracking Ethan's whereabouts for years and becoming so frustrated he had decided to end it last Saturday night.

What the Internet was filled with were Ethan's achievements, the lectures he had given, the awards he had received. He had set up scholarships and started several foundations. I kept scrolling and did find one odd story that mentioned him in passing.

Seven years earlier an Egyptian national who was attached to one of Ethan's digs was due to be arrested and charged with antiquities theft. Instead, Youssef Elsar had disappeared. There was no evidence of foul play, only that he had slipped away and was never able to be found.

Ethan had not come under suspicion.

TRYING TO GIVE Elisa time to get to Boston before I called her, I listed some books for the Internet, then walked around the yard. The ground was still muddy from snow melt and the forsythia had recently faded, but everything else was competing like a botanical garden. Walking past the back steps that led to the kitchen, I saw the row of our boots, khaki green rubber with yellow soles. In past years they had been lined up by size and used all the time. Then the children had drifted away and outgrown them,

Yet the boots remained. A rotting wooden sled had stood next to them until recently when I dragged it to the curb for the trash pickup. Passing close now, I saw that the ground around the boots was patted smooth, as if a knife had been run across the top of a cake. Perhaps the runoff from the gutters had evened it. I also noticed that there was an empty space where a pair of men's boots had once stood. Had Jason, when he was last home in March, taken them back to Santa Fe with him?

I walked around to the front of the house. The crocuses beside the porch had finished their purple and white show, and even some tulip petals were beginning to droop. The lawn between the house and the street was thin and brown. Impossible to believe that it would ever turn green and need mowing. I knew if I walked to the road I would see hostas starting to push up, dark anthill shapes.

Back to the barn. If I found Elisa was still on the road, I could always leave a message on her phone for her to call me. As I settled into my desk chair, I thought of the last time I'd seen her in March when all the children had been at the house. Seeing my twins together for the first time in so many years, I had been shocked at how alike they looked, how their dark blond hair sprouted from its part in the same way, how they had the same wry grins. Identical, though Hannah had put on weight at college and Elisa had a curved white scar on her chin created by falling on her ski pole when she was seven.

"My mother wanted me to get plastic surgery," she'd said, referring to Sheila. "But my father said it was part of my history."

"You still could," Jane said.

"She doesn't *want* to. It's who she is," Hannah insisted protectively.

That weekend had been wonderful, a time for my children to get to know each other finally. Yet it had also been bittersweet. It had felt to me like Elisa was a long-lost niece, coming to meet her cousins, not the sister they had never gotten to know. They had spent hours sprawled in the living room before the fireplace, discovering everything they had in common and many things they didn't. Elisa loved skiing and snowboarding and was the only one who adored books and reading—like me. She had met presidents, jumped out of airplanes, and gone on safari.

"You didn't shoot *animals*, did you?" For Hannah, about to enter veterinary school, that could have been a deal breaker.

But Elisa had given her an easy smile. "Of course not. My father taught me how to shoot, but only at targets. I was good at target practice, but I'd never hurt anything living."

Several times I'd noticed her blue eyes watching me speculatively from under tawny lashes. The last time I'd seen her we had disagreed over my need to see the Crosleys punished. Despite the fact that I had shown her photocopies of the Stratford-upon-Avon newspaper that told how she had "drowned" and our terrible grief at losing her, she hadn't believed the drowning had been staged by the Crosleys. I knew she blamed me for their having to flee from Providence and Brown University to the estate they owned in Barbados to avoid prosecution. What she *wanted* to believe was that she had been stolen by criminals and offered to the Crosleys at a price, that they had known nothing of her abduction.

I sat with my elbows on the desk, chin in my hands. Was that the only reason for the barrier between us? Did she feel I was pushing her too hard to be part of the family? By discounting the Crosleys, did she feel like I was invalidating her own life, trying to dismiss the experiences she had had as nothing? Maybe I was no more than an intrusive stranger to her, a seatmate on a plane determined to engage her in my life.

No, it was more complicated than that. That Saturday night at dinner, when Jason and Jane had been teasing me about forcing them to read the books I had loved as a child, I'd suddenly noticed Elisa. Her expression was wistful, that of an onlooker, as if she was seeing the way they had known and loved me all their lives, the in-jokes we shared, and feeling that she could never catch up. Yet in the next minute she was telling a story about rock climbing in Bataan to her admiring brother and sisters.

When the twins left that Monday morning, Elisa had given me a quick hug. "Delhi, thanks so much! It was wonderful to meet the rest of the family. You really put yourself out."

"That's what mothers do."

She'd ignored the comment and I had not heard from her until now. Fortunately Elisa and Hannah started spending every weekend together after that, alternating between Cornell and St. Brennan's College in Boston. Soon they would both be graduating and I wondered what would happen then. I hoped that Elisa wouldn't move on to her next adventure, her next safari, leaving Hannah devastated. To Hannah, everything in life was either magic or tragic.

"DELHI?" ELISA ANSWERED halfway through the song as if surprised to hear from me. It threatened to swamp me. I was her *mother*, damn it. If I had been able to raise her the way I should have, she would have been expecting my call.

"Are you back now?" I asked.

"I got here a few minutes ago."

"I just—I had to see how you were doing. I'm so, so sorry! I can't imagine anything worse."

"I know. I can't believe it. I *don't* believe it. They weren't the kind of people this happens to, they weren't *victims*. I told them not to come back, but my father was determined."

"I would have driven you home if I'd known you wanted to go back so soon."

"There was no point in staying in Ithaca. But it was horrible anyway. I'd get distracted and forget what had happened, then when I remembered it was like being punched. I kept having to pull over. This is the worst thing that has ever happened to me!"

I was shocked at how angry that made me. If the Crosleys hadn't stolen her, disrupted her life, she wouldn't even be suffering this agony.

I pushed my resentment away. *Be here now.* "Hannah said you had an adopted brother?" Hannah had mentioned it several weeks ago, and I'd remembered that Colin had seen him when he was a toddler.

An intake of breath. "Oh, my God—I have to let Will know. I stopped and left him a message on the way home, but he hasn't called back. What if he sees it on the news?"

"He's in school?"

"No. He didn't want to go to college, so he was working for my father. Then a few months ago they had this huge blow-up about something, I don't know what, and Will stormed off. But they never really got along. Will was so beautiful, beautiful to look at and really charming, but he was always in some kind of trouble. In school, everywhere. My parents did everything they could think of, but nothing worked. I think that's why my father gave him a job."

"A job doing what?" Surely not as his research assistant.

"I don't know. My father's always had a lot of people working for him."

Why would an academic need a whole staff? But then I remembered his wealth and his archeological digs, He would need managers and people to do the legwork.

"The last I heard Will was in New York, in Spanish Harlem. He broke my father's heart."

It sounded as if Elisa had come down on the side of the Crosleys. I didn't let myself think about Ethan's heart. "Did Will know about the Southampton house?"

"Of course. Why wouldn't he? We used to spend summers there. But if you're suggesting that Will set the fire—I can't imagine that. How would he even know they were out there so early?"

Would that have been so hard for him to find out? Just because they were estranged didn't mean he wasn't still emotionally involved, especially if they had rejected him. If he had gone looking for the Crosleys in Rhode Island and learned they were not there, wouldn't it be logical to think next of their vacation homes in Barbados and Southampton?

I felt certain, based on nothing, that Will was involved. I imagined a young man banging on the Southampton house door, confronting the Crosleys, and demanding what he thought was financially due him. He could even have still had a key. If they had turned him away or threatened to call the police, he might have waited until later and set the fire in revenge. No, if he was there for money he could have gone back inside and taken what was valuable. Perhaps he had come out to the island with a gang from Spanish Harlem.

"Are you and Will close?"

"I think so. He was two years younger, but we were together a lot, our family was always traveling. But he says he hates them— he'll probably be glad that they're gone!" It was a wail as she was ambushed once more by the reality of what had happened.

I made soothing sounds until she could talk again. "Did your father keep a lot of artifacts around the house? Houses, I mean?"

"You think somebody wanted to break in and steal them? But why burn up my parents and the house afterward?" She was about to cry.

"I know. It doesn't make sense," I agreed quickly.

"Listen, I'm fading. I think I need a nap."

"Of course you do, you're exhausted." I hesitated. "Do you have anything you can take?"

"You mean like sleeping pills? No, I'll be fine." She sounded as if being fine was not a happy prospect. "My friends are here and I have stuff to finish up. I'll be okay."

"What are you going to do after graduation?" It was tactless, but I had to know.

"I'll made plans to stay on in the dorm for a while. They use it for summer session. Where else am I going to go? Unless Hannah wants to do something."

"You could always stay with us."

"Umm."

"Anyway, I'll talk to you tomorrow, Elisa."

"Okay. And thanks for calling me Elisa. That's who I am now."

"I know."

She hung up before I could tell her I loved her.

Chapter Four

THAT NIGHT I could not fall asleep. I was haunted by images of Ethan and Sheila engulfed in fire, the horror they must have felt when they realized there was no escape. I saw the flames eating away the bedclothes as they cowered together and hoped that Elisa was not seeing the same images. But I did not even know where they had died. The newspaper, usually so obliging with details, had not said where their bodies had been found, whether they had collapsed on the stairs from smoke inhalation or been trapped in their bedroom. Why, if you were that wealthy, wouldn't you have had the most sophisticated smoke alarms possible?

Something else was keeping me awake. I had promised Elisa that I would try to find out who set the fire. But lying in the dark my promise felt like what my father called vainglorious—making myself seem more important than I was, promising something I could not deliver. Was I so desperate for her to love me? The other times I had helped the police it was because I had been caught up in what was happening around me, privy to the kind of information that the authorities were not. I had known the people and what I thought they were capable of doing. This time I would be approaching the situation cold.

Just as I was finally drifting off to sleep, a noise from outside my window jerked me back to consciousness. A car door closing. Not slamming, just clicking shut. If my bedroom hadn't been at the front of the house and the window open, the neighborhood silent as a photograph, I would have missed it. I glanced at the small travel clock on my nightstand and saw it was just after 2 a.m. Perhaps my next-door neighbors were returning late from their cabin upstate. Yet in the next moment I heard the unmistakable sound of my driveway gravel being crunched underfoot.

The idea that someone had come to set fire to *my* house grabbed and shook me like a toy in my cat's mouth. Someone with a grudge against archeologists? Someone who had been after Ethan for stealing antiquities and was blaming Colin too? I pushed out of bed at that and raced to the window. The streetlight opposite shed a reassuring light over the still neighborhood. There were no cars in my driveway or parked in front of my house.

Raccoons. It had to be raccoons. Or deer, though they didn't usually arrive in cars and generally came later to feast on the hostas and day lilies. But that didn't mean they weren't searching for food all year round. The car door and driveway noises were probably from somewhere up the street. I stood frozen at the window for several minutes. But when nothing seemed to move and I did not smell smoke, I went back to my bed and lay down.

Not that I could go back to sleep. My cats, Raj and Miss T, sensed my restlessness and kept bumping against me, trolling for attention. Raj, my tiny male Siamese, thrust his damp nose against my cheek, making me jump. During this next bout of wakefulness, I realized that at the least I needed to drive out to Southampton and see the house for myself. I needed to get a visceral feeling of what had happened.

It was probably important to be out there at the same hour as the fire had occurred. I lay there for a moment feeling the weight of both cats sleeping on my back and mourned my lost night's sleep. Then I brought the clock close enough to read and saw that it was not even 4 a.m. No matter. I shook off the cats and pushed myself up.

I decided not to take the time to make coffee myself—I would pick up a large cup at Qwikjava—but I could not get away without feeding the animals. I made sure there was enough dry food in their dish for them to snack on during the day, then opened the back door. It was chilly enough to make me duck back inside for a jacket. The days when it would be mild enough to walk outside in a sweatshirt weren't here yet.

THE BENEFIT OF heading east on Long Island on a Monday morning was that traffic was light and mostly industrial. Contractors were setting up shop at the beautiful estates, trucks were bringing supplies to resorts and restaurants, refrigerated vans stuffed with fish were headed in the other direction, toward the city. The store windows I passed were gray as faded flannel, but the nurseries were alive with deliveries of azaleas in bloom and flats of red and orange impatiens.

I always forget how large Southampton is until I am actually there. Besides the village itself, which formerly had an art museum and still had a multitude of restaurants and galleries on Jobs Lane, there was a large and modern library where I attended book sales. There was the Shinnecock Indian Reservation, the Shinnecock Golf Club where the U.S. Open was sometimes held, and a college campus. It was not the kind of chummy village where everyone knew everyone else. Everyone did know where South Main Street was, though. It arrowed straight from the expensive shops down to the Atlantic Ocean.

In the increasing daylight, I drove slowly past mansions behind hedges, straining to see any that had been destroyed by fire. When I finally arrived, I saw the swaths of yellow caution tape first, stretched inelegantly across the driveway and tied around matching stone urns. I stopped the van and looked up at the house. I told myself that I might be any resident pausing to see what had happened. No one had to know that I was personally involved.

Yet even after seeing the photograph on the *Newsday* Web site, the reality shocked me. Despite the charred foundations, the beams that reached like black bones into the sky, the house was huge, an estate. It must have been beautiful once, a 1920s Southampton mansion that no expense had been spared in building. It was probably beyond repair, yet the center section remained. I wondered how that had happened. Had some kind of Molotov cocktail, some kind of firebomb, been tossed through an upstairs window?

Part of me wanted to just drive away, to let the police investigate in peace. Yet I was already out here . . . I put the van in gear and drove down the street until I came to a house whose windows were still shuttered, then pulled into the driveway far enough so I couldn't be seen from the street. When I slipped out of the van I did not slam the door shut for fear of alerting anyone, and something about that reminded me of the sound I had heard in the night.

I walked back to the yellow caution tape. It was meant to keep gawkers off the property, but I reminded myself that I had a reason for being here. Still I looked up and down the sidewalk. No one was out walking and there were no headlights on the road. I wasn't sure what I wanted to find, only that I needed to be here.

I ducked under the garland of plastic ribbon and started up the driveway, keeping on the grassy verge as much as I could to avoid crunching on pebbles. The smell of burning and cinders began to choke me. I stopped and stared at the shrubs beside the house, dusted in white ash as if from a freak blizzard. Chunks of debris lay on the ground as if a demolition crew had tossed them out of the windows.

I looked up. The windows on the second floor were blackened and as finely cracked as if they had been spiderwebbed for Halloween. I didn't want to be there; Ethan and Sheila were dead, there was no changing that. The acrid odor scalded my throat like frat party whiskey, my sneakers were muddy from the ground where the grass ended. I was too intimidated to go deeper into the yard. I felt a sense of trespass at being at the place where Ethan and Sheila had died. It was as if I had an unfair advantage seeing their vulnerability without their wanting me to.

At the back of the driveway, beyond the house, was a building untouched by the fire, an enchanting miniature cottage. A guesthouse? Perhaps just a giant toolshed. I moved toward it, relieved and charmed, curious as to what was inside.

"You! Stop! Police! Stop right there!"

The voice was rude in the fresh new air, as harsh as if shouting obscenities over a baby's crib.

I froze, my heart spiraling like a shot bird dropping to earth. When it came to rest, I whirled around, blinking at the flashlight beam that had me trapped. Shielding my eyes I could make out a young officer in khaki, with buzz-cut hair. Beyond him, at the end of the driveway, his sedan was flashing red and blue lights. A Southampton Town cop, not Suffolk County police. For some reason that calmed me a little.

Perhaps he was just passing by.

Yet he was staring at me, appalled, as if he had caught me holding a stolen television. "Didn't you see the yellow tape?"

"Yes, but—"

"What are you *doing* here?" It was not a rhetorical question. I had nothing in my hands, no camera that I was taking photos with. It was too early in the morning for casual sightseers.

There was nothing to do but tell the truth. "Their daughter"—I gestured at the house—"is my daughter's best friend. She's up in Boston and I promised I would look around and tell her how bad the fire was. She's already hysterical about losing her parents."

I saw him trying to process that. "But you can't just walk around here. You're disturbing a crime scene!"

"CSI hasn't been here already?"

He squinted at me. "I'll need to see some ID."

Damn. But I pulled out my wallet and showed him my driver's license, then watched as he looked from the photo to my face and back to the photo. He returned it to me without writing anything down. The last thing I wanted was to be associated with the fire in any way. What if the police came to interview me to find out what my interest was? What if . . . "I only wanted to let my daughter's friend know how bad it was," I pleaded. I looked grimly up at the charred ruin. "It's worse than I thought."

"They never had a chance," he pronounced solemnly.

"How did the fire department even know about it? It's so far back from the street and not a lot of people are out for the season yet." It was not information I was entitled to know but I could see he needed to talk about the fire, the way people did after a trauma.

"They think that whoever set the fires threw something through the back porch window when they were leaving to trigger the burglar alarm. Either that or it just went off from the heat. We got here first, then called the fire department. But it was too late."

"The paper said there was another fire around here recently?"

He moved closer to me, as if telling me a secret. "We think we know who's responsible. It's just a matter of proving it." Then he straightened up formally. "You need to leave. Now."

"Okay. Sure."

He walked me back to the sidewalk. I turned in the opposite direction, toward town, as the whirling lights of his squad car splashed over me. Once he had driven away, I turned back to retrieve my van. Though I had planned to park on the street and watch for activity in the other houses, I knew I couldn't do that now.

STARTING THE ENGINE, I made a U-turn, and drove slowly back up to Montauk Highway. I remembered seeing a convenience store and found it easily. Time for breakfast. It was still not even 6 a.m. but I was feeling weak from lack of sleep.

I was at the counter paying for my coffee and corn muffin when I realized something I should have thought of immediately. "Are you open all night?" I asked the young black clerk in the red-and-white smock. She was pretty, with small, neat braids sprouting from her head.

"Uh-huh." She twisted around to look at the clock behind her. "Just one more hour for me."

"Are you busy, say around three or four?"

"In the morning? Naw. That's when I get my work done." She jerked a shoulder at the textbooks on a stool behind her. "Nothing happens before five. It's always the same guys anyway, fishermen heading out, delivery guys starting up."

"Were you here last night? Saturday night, I mean. Around one or two, say?"

"Ye-ss." She stared at me, less sleepy now.

"Did anyone come in you didn't know? Some young guys?"

This was beyond casual conversation. With my tangled hair and navy jacket, my face innocent of makeup, I did not look like anyone official. Unless I was some kind of undercover cop.

"No kids. A couple with two little girls who should have been in bed. Two older guys came in for coffee. No," she corrected herself, "one large coffee, one beer."

"Did they look like they were staying out here?"

She shrugged. "Could have been. One was dark, really good-looking, you know? Like that old-time movie star."

Old-time? Douglas Fairbanks? Clark Gable?

"Omar Sharif I think his name is? I bet he used to be a knock-out."

Used to be? "What was the other one like?"

"Younger. Geeky." She gave a laugh. "They weren't a *couple* or anything."

Three men in fishermen's vests, not yet shaved, came in and looked us over. "Hey, Steph," one called. "Wanna bait my hook?"

She rolled her eyes at him, then laughed. "What passes for humor out here. Are you looking for someone special?"

"Not really." I couldn't think of any excuse to give her, so I didn't. "Enjoy your morning off."

There was no reason why Will Crosley would have stopped at the 7–Eleven, especially if he did not want to be seen. She had described the handsome man as dark, but also referred to him as older. Will couldn't be any more than nineteen or twenty. Besides, if the fire was the work of a local arsonist, there was no reason to suspect him of being out here at all.

Chapter Five

WHEN I GOT home from Southampton, I crashed on the living room couch for several hours. The couch was not that comfortable, a stiff olive-and-gold striped wood-framed antique that had been passed down from Colin's parents, but it seemed decadent to crawl back into bed. I woke up about eleven, had more coffee, then headed out to the Book Barn.

No matter what else I was preoccupied with, I could not abandon my business. Seasonal sales would begin in earnest after Memorial Day and I would be back on the hunt for treasures. It wasn't that I didn't have cartons of books waiting to be listed on AbeBooks.com and the other sites. They stood on the dusty Oriental rugs, waiting patiently for their turn, as humble and undemanding as soup kitchen recipients.

There was nothing *wrong* with the books in these boxes; they were mostly history, biography, and vintage novels, a few esoteric craft guides on weaving and glass-blowing, and some nautical sagas. But there were no wildcards left, nothing that collectors would fight over. No one would bid competitively on eBay for *these* books or pay a premium price on viaLibri. There were no *Tarzans* in dust jackets, no early John Steinbecks, no signed Patrick O'Brians. I had skimmed the cream from last summer and sold off those prizes long ago.

Nevertheless I should have dragged a carton of these books over to my worktable and started describing them to sell. But I was too restless from what had happened that morning. Shirking my duty for a few hours longer, I went back out to my van and drove down into the village to the bookshop I was being paid to oversee.

Before a shocking murder last July, Port Lewis Books had been known as The Old Frigate. But once death invaded our Long Island seacoast village, the shop had stayed vacant, tributes crowding the doorway—handwritten messages, cone-wrapped flowers, and literary toys like Paddington Bear and Madeleine. Another bookseller, Marty Campagna, finally bought the property. He'd had it cleaned and fumigated and tried to hire me to sell his expensive stock.

Unfortunately he'd acted as if Secondhand Prose was my little hobby, something I could give up as easily as knitting sweaters for soldiers. I'd refused and persuaded Marty to hire a younger bookseller, Susie Pevney. To do so I'd agreed that I would supervise her.

As soon as I came into the shop that Monday morning I sensed trouble. Susie's eyes were swollen, her normal optimism vanquished. Marty was sitting in one of the leather wing chairs, scowling down at the phone in his palm. Dressed as he was in a red Goodfella's Bar T-shirt with a white line drawing of a pair of handcuffs, he looked as out-of-place as a mechanic who had wandered into the Harvard Club expecting to be served.

He could at least replace his black-framed glasses, which were duct-taped at the bridge, I thought, but appearance had never been Marty's thing. He spent the money he had inherited from his grandfather's cesspool cleaning business on books and books alone. He bought books constantly, as if he would not be satisfied until every single volume ever published had passed through his hands. I had seen him vault sofas and push aside old ladies at estate sales to get to the good stuff. Yet as soon as he owned a book, he seemed to lose interest in it. His goal became to sell the book for as much as he could.

Marty, Susie, and the bookshop. This was my everyday world.

I moved toward Susie first, inclining my head questioningly toward Marty. If he had been bullying her . . .

She shook her head quickly.

"What's the matter?" I said, my back to Marty so that he could not hear our conversation.

"Nothing!" She gave me a quick, insincere smile, then looked back down at what she had been doing. Whatever was troubling her, she was not ready to share it.

I turned back around to Marty. "What are *you* frowning about?"

He looked up at me and shook his head, then growled, "Never trust little old lady librarians!"

"What happened?"

Marty leaned back against the leather chair, pressing his muscular arms into the armrests. "You know those books I picked up last month in Boston?"

"You mean the Mary Shelley and the Lincoln?"

"Yeah. Those were the best of the lot. This old bat, very genteel, said she was selling off her dead husband's collection. The books were all embossed on the title page to the Melrose Library

and some had 'Discard' stamped in red over the blind-stamp. So
I thought—"

"You thought they'd be discarding a first of *Frankenstein*? That
they'd deface it that way? C'mon, Marty!"

"Well, I could hope. Maybe they had too many first editions.
And what she was asking for them wasn't crazy."

Meaning he probably thought he had slipped into the bank
and found the vault unlocked. "So you didn't check."

Of course he hadn't. *I* would have, which was probably why
I was still getting excited over twenty-five-dollar sales. I tend to
forget that everyone hasn't been raised in a Methodist parsonage, hasn't been taught at a young age, "If it's doubtful, it's *dirty.*"
When I was twelve and had shoplifted a red lipstick and a Baby
Ruth bar, my father had asked me how much I was willing to "sell
my soul for."

It was a question I still pondered. Would I sell my soul for a
Shakespearean folio? A signed *Gone with the Wind*?

I knew I wouldn't, though in Marty's defense, seeing books
stamped as discards made it easier to turn a blind eye.

"So how did the old lady trick you?"

He shook his head at the ugliness of humanity. "She told me
her husband had been this high-rolling Boston lawyer and book
collector. The house was full of antiques. But it was small. Very
small." Marty frowned. "That should have told me something."

"She could have moved to someplace more manageable after
she was widowed."

"Right. So I buy the books and I sell a Harriet Beecher Stowe—
signed—and the Lincoln to two of my collectors. Then the Lincoln
guy actually contacts the Melrose Library to find out the book's
provenance—what an idiot—and next thing I hear, the library is

claiming that the book was *stolen* from them. They have a whole list and they want them back." Marty looked so outraged that I almost forgot he was not the true victim.

"Really? After they stamped them as discards?"

"Turns out there was no 'husband.' She was a clerk at the library for forty years and smuggled them out in her 'corset.' She had plenty of access to the official 'Discard' stamp. So she was all set to finance her retirement."

"So you have to give the books back?"

"No! How can I? I bought them in good faith. My collector returned the Lincoln to that library, now he wants his money back from me. I have to give it to him. He's a good customer, but I'm the one who's out. I can't take a hit on the other books she sold me. I bought around thirty."

"Thirty! Can't you get your money back from the librarian?"

"Naw. Turns out she has a little gambling problem too."

I leaned on the top of the other wing chair. "Well . . ."

"Anyway, I was thinking. I'll deny I have any other of their books, but they'll be watching everything I do. But *you* could list them, just say they're ex libris without giving any details. If you do one or two at a time, they won't make the connection with you."

"You want me to sell stolen library books." I tried to keep my voice neutral. Didn't he know me well enough to realize it was never going to happen? How was it any different than selling electronic goods that had "fallen off the truck" on eBay? Or offering purloined artifacts to secret collectors?

"I'll make it worth your while."

"That's hardly the point."

Our eyes locked. Marty was used to getting what he wanted, but I had a code of ethics I could not violate.

He leaned forward in the chair with a disarming humility. "You know I can't take a hit on this, blondie, I don't *have* it." He gestured at the bookstore. "This goddamn money pit would be the first thing to go."

"I'll do it," Susie called out from behind the counter.

We both turned to stare at her, then Marty scowled. "Do what?"

"Sell those library books on eBay." Her wholesome face was flushed, her large brown eyes bright behind her glasses.

"Susie, they were stolen from a library in Massachusetts," I objected.

"Marty didn't know that when he bought them."

"He does now."

Marty pushed up from the wing chair, apparently too restless to stay still any longer. "It wouldn't work," he told us, as if I were part of Susie's scheme. "As soon as the title came up, they'd be notified by e-mail. Everybody monitors eBay. Besides, you have to put photos on eBay, right? They'd be able to tell."

"I wouldn't show the library stamp," Susie said stubbornly.

"Naw. I'll think of something else."

Then he was out the door.

"Were you really going to do it?" I asked her.

"Oh, probably not. I didn't think he'd go for it. But it gives me street cred with him."

I wasn't sure I believed her. I knew she could not afford to have the bookstore close.

On the other hand, neither could I.

Chapter Six

By the time I finished at the bookstore it was early afternoon and I was starving. I thought about stopping at the deli for egg salad on a roll, then decided that the bread and peanut butter I had at home would be fine. Skippy's Smooth with a light overlay of mustard was my sandwich of choice, had been since childhood.

When I turned onto my street, I saw a dark blue sedan parked in front of my house. Frank Marselli's unmarked police car. But what was he doing here now?

I turned the van slowly into the driveway and killed the motor, but didn't climb out. I should have stopped for lunch. My stomach felt scooped-out and something told me I would need the strength food would have given me. I watched the navy car—a Taurus?—and waited for its door to open. Finally it did, but instead of Frank, a woman pushed herself out. Skinny legs in beige slacks. A man, rotund in a dark green windbreaker, opened the passenger side door and climbed out too.

I got out of the van then and stood by the open door, waiting until they could reach me.

The policewoman—what else could she be?—had light red hair secured in an odd arrangement on the back of her head, loose pieces dangling everywhere. When she came closer I saw that she had large green eyes in a narrow face. White shirt, a waffle-textured tan pantsuit that hung from her shoulders. A circular grease stain on one lapel appeared as permanent as a decoration.

Neither of us smiled. I was too apprehensive and she seemed to be all business.

"Mrs. Fitzhugh?"

"Yes, but that's not what I call myself. I'm Delhi Laine."

She sighed as if I had given her a name from a nursery rhyme. "Are you Colin Fitzhugh's wife or not?"

"Yes. And you are?"

"Ruth Carew. Suffolk County Police." She pulled a leather holder out of her pocket as if she were used to doing it, and flipped it open to show me a badge.

"Has something happened to Colin?" Were they here to tell me that he was dead, the victim of an automobile accident or a campus shooting? In police procedurals they always sent two with bad news.

"Isn't he here?" she demanded.

"Now? I don't think so. His car isn't here." At this time of day he was always at the university.

"Can you check?"

"Sure." I turned toward the front porch and they followed me.

Walking up the path, I tried to remember if the kitchen was presentable, if I had washed last night's dishes. I didn't think so. I settled us in the living room, which had books everywhere, but only my morning coffee cup. The pair sat down tentatively on the striped couch, facing me like job applicants. I made myself comfortable in Colin's brown suede wing chair.

I wasn't comfortable, of course. I was frantically running down reasons why they wanted to talk to Colin. When we'd stepped inside I'd called out his name but there had been no answer.

The plump man held out a perfunctory hand, as if belatedly remembering his manners. He didn't expect me to get up and shake it. Evidently just waving it in the air satisfied the bonds of civility. "Arlen Olson, Arson Squad."

Say that fast five times.

I forced myself to look calm and disinterested. *The Arson Squad?*

I watched the policewoman take out the requisite black notebook from her suit jacket. "How well did you know Ethan Crosley?"

She might as well have punched me in the stomach. It lurched as if she had. How could she have found us so fast? "Ethan? I haven't seen Ethan for nearly twenty years. He was my husband's friend, not mine. But I don't think Colin has seen him in years either. I read about the fire online."

She peered down at her notebook as if to confirm something. "And Sheila Crosley?"

That was harder. I stared through the window at the front porch, at the green rocker that should have been taken in for the winter. "I saw her in January," I admitted finally. "But it was only for a few minutes. Colin didn't see her. I was alone."

Detective Carew tilted her head. "What was your business with her?"

It was a curious way to put it. Not asking, "How did you happen to run into her?" Or "What did you talk about?"

"You really want to know? It's a long story."

Agent Olson sighed and looked over at the photos of my great-grandparents under rounded glass. It seemed evident that long stories bored him.

"Of course we do, Ms.—" But she couldn't remember the name I had given her and gave up.

There was a disturbance in the doorway from the kitchen and Raj and Miss T strode in to look us over.

"Oh, *cats*," Detective Carew said as if they were just one more annoyance in a trying day.

"Are you allergic?"

"No. It's just—" She didn't finish.

"They won't bother you." I stared back at their sweet faces, upset on their behalf. This was *their* house, not hers. "Would you like coffee or anything?"

"No. Thanks."

I leaned forward in the wing chair that was too big for me. "Nineteen years ago we spent the summer in England, in Stratford-upon-Avon. Shakespeare's birthplace? Colin was in an archeological program that visited different sites, and Ethan Crosley was in the program too." Should I tell her they had been best friends since graduate school? I decided not to. "We were staying at a residence with the other visiting families, everyone except the Crosleys. They had more money than the rest of us so they stayed at an inn.

"I had three daughters, a four-year-old and two-year-old twins. I took them to the same park every day by the Avon River. This one day I was taking photographs, and the girls were playing. I—should have been watching them more closely. Suddenly Jane, my oldest, came running up and said that Caitlin had fallen in the river. I jumped into the water, everyone did, but we couldn't find her. They never found her body." I couldn't believe it; my eyes were starting to water, my voice sounded choked. Hadn't the story had a happy ending?

I put it down to too little sleep and the fact that they were here at all. I brushed a hand across one eye.

The policewoman was looking at me thoughtfully. I felt forced to go on.

"All these years we thought she was dead. Then last November I got a handprinted note from England that said, 'Your daughter did not drown.' I had no idea what it meant! But my daughter Jane and I went over to England to try and track it down. Long story short: The note was from the son of a woman who had been paid by the Crosleys to kidnap Caitlin from the park when Jane wasn't looking, then tell me she had fallen in the water. Nice, right? The Crosleys called her Elisa and raised her as their own daughter. It was a miracle we ever found her again."

Agent Olson was staring at me now, not the photos. He looked skeptical.

Sorry it's not a better story. "You think I'd make something like this up? She and my other daughter Hannah are twins and look identical. You can do a DNA test if you don't believe me. Or call DCI Sampson in Stratford. He knows all about it."

Belatedly I looked at Detective Carew. There was something in her green eyes close to sympathy. "And you never suspected they took her?"

"We never suspected anything. Everyone assumed Elisa had drowned, especially the British police. We never saw Ethan and Sheila again. Ethan kept in touch occasionally with Colin by e-mail, but they always taught at different universities. We didn't start looking for Elisa until we got that note."

I wasn't going to tell her that over the years I'd fantasized other scenarios. Sometimes I'd imagined that Elisa—Caitlin then—had floated downstream—she was a resourceful little girl—and been picked up by someone in a boat. Why they had kept her instead of returning her to her family was something I didn't spend much time thinking about. The story and her photo had been in the area papers.

Over the years there had been a few sightings here at home, people on vacation who claimed they had seen Hannah on the ski slope or on a neighboring sailboat and were shocked when I told them we hadn't been anywhere near there. I had always tried to learn more, but never could.

"When did you suspect the Crosleys?"

Never. "Not until the trail led to an Elisa Crosley. Even then, at first I thought the last name was just a coincidence."

"You must have been devastated. *I* would have wanted to kill them."

Did she think that would make me confess? "What I wanted was to see them punished. Disgraced, and sent to jail. It was a little complicated because it happened in England and American authorities didn't want to jump in. But no, I didn't want to see them dead. I wanted them to *pay*." I sighed. "The thing was, Elisa didn't agree."

"She's the one in Boston?" Agent Olson rejoined the conversation.

How did he know anything about her? "Yes. We're going up for her graduation Friday."

Detective Carew shifted on the striped couch, pushed up a sleeve, then looked at her watch. "Let's go back to Saturday night: Was your husband here with you? Did he leave the house at all?"

The uneasiness in my stomach, which I had assumed to be

hunger, flared into four-alarm flames. Why were they so focused on Colin? My first instinct was to lie, to assure them we had been here together all night. After what we had been through at the hands of the Crosleys, we deserved a pass. Except that I couldn't lie about that. Oh, sometimes I pretended to be someone other than I was in the interest of getting at the truth. But this was different.

"Colin has his own place," I said. "His own condo where he lives most of the time. I don't know where he was Saturday night."

They jumped to attention like recruits faced with their commanding officer. "He doesn't live here?" Agent Olson demanded. "This is the address the university gave us."

"He's been subletting a condo for the past year."

"So who was here with you Saturday night?" Detective Carew broke in.

"Just me. But I was home all night. I wasn't out in the Hamptons setting fires, if that's what you're asking. I told you, I wanted to see them arrested and made to pay. I wanted people to know that no matter how much money you have, you can't go around stealing other people's children!"

I stopped, aware that I was losing control.

"Did your husband feel like killing the Crosleys when he found out?" Detective Carew was like a search dog who never lost focus. "Did he ever threaten Ethan Crosley?"

That was a dangerous question. I thought back to the night I told Colin that it had been Ethan and Sheila who took Caitlin. I had come back from Boston after confronting Sheila and met him in a Port Lewis seafood bar, the Whaler's Arms. At first he had refused to consider that someone who had been a close friend could have stolen his child. I'd seen his face gradually harden into stone as he realized it was true.

"What should we do?" I'd asked.

"You mean besides tracking him down and killing him?"

I supposed you could call that a threat. But it had been said in the heat of angry disbelief, and to me, not Ethan. So I told them, "No. He wants to move past it too. I don't know why you're connecting us with the fire."

"Your daughter corroborated your kidnapping story to the Boston police." Carew's glance flickered to Olson, who seemed surprised that she had not shared this with him. "She showed them a letter Dr. Crosley had sent her, mailed express mail Saturday, that she got this morning. He sent her a check for a graduation present. He also warned her in case anything happened to him." She flipped back several pages in her small notebook, then read aloud, " 'If anything happens to me, blame Colin Fitzhugh.' "

I nearly jerked out of the chair. "What? He said that? He wrote that to Elisa? That's crazy!" If she had pulled out her service revolver and pointed it, I could not have been more shocked. "How could he even know that something was going to happen to him?"

"He could if he had had threats before."

"But anyone could have threatened him; he had enemies all over the world. He antagonized a lot of people in his profession, archeology, and he stole artifacts from other countries." Pure conjecture, but I hardly cared.

"You know that for a fact? Had he been convicted?"

"Not that I know of. But it was an open secret. He was known to cross a lot of lines and someone probably caught up with him. Well, boo-hoo."

Shut up, Delhi. It was not what you were supposed to say to the police about someone who had just been burned alive. I was exaggerating anyway, something I tended to do when I felt pushed against the wall. "I don't mean I'm happy about the fire," I apologized. "It's been terrible for Elisa. But we didn't set it."

When Colin had driven up to Brown University to confront Ethan a few days after I told him about Elisa, Ethan and Sheila had already fled to Barbados. At least that's what Colin had told me. He'd said the archeology department at Brown, people he had known professionally for years, had told him that Ethan had taken a sudden leave of absence for health reasons. The Crosleys' next-door neighbor confirmed that they had left for their estate outside Bridgetown.

But what if that wasn't true? I saw a different scenario, the former best friends, now bitter enemies, standing outside a Providence mansion screaming at each other. Colin could have threatened Ethan then. Maybe it was whatever Colin had said that night that made Ethan and Sheila leave the country.

The police did not seem to know about that trip, though. And I was not going to tell them.

I was suddenly restless, wanting to be by myself. "Why are you asking *me* questions about Colin? Why aren't you asking him?"

"We thought we'd find him here," Detective Carew said evenly. "Would you like to tell us where he lives?"

I gave her the address, then said, "You can always find him at the university."

"He was not at the university."

Of course. That was why they were here. But where else would he be on a Monday afternoon?

Chapter Seven

NOW THAT THEY knew where to find Colin, I nearly pushed them out the door. I stood up, signaling that our conversation was over, and after a moment they got up from the couch. There was that awkwardness when a warm good-bye isn't appropriate but something needs to be said. Suddenly they seemed too large for the room, Agent Olson bumping his knee against the antique trunk we used as a coffee table. As she moved toward the door, Carew turned and gave me a studiedly casual look. "We saw your collection of rubber boots out back. Could we take a look?"

Out back? Why had they been walking around outside the house? They probably didn't need a search warrant for that, but it seemed like an invasion.

"Nobody uses those boots," I said. "They're left over from when the kids were small."

I hadn't said yes, but they were on the front porch at once, then down the steps and moving briskly around the house as if they were afraid that I would stop them.

But could I? And why were they focused on the boots anyway?

When we reached the overhang where the boots were stored, I saw the house through their eyes. I noticed how splintery the wood was, how in need the white farmhouse was of fresh paint. The forest green trim hadn't been touched up since we moved in. As far as I knew, the university had done nothing but collect our rent and pay the property taxes. But *we* had done nothing either. I'd assumed that upkeep was the college's responsibility, but perhaps because the rent was so reasonable we had not pressed them. What did it say about us that we hadn't had enough pride to keep our home looking trim? Did it make it more likely that we would burn down someone else's?

Not that Ruth Carew looked like she lived in anything from *House Beautiful*. She was not wearing a wedding ring, and I imagined her in an untidy apartment where she did little more than sleep. In her early thirties, I judged. But she did not seem to be noticing my house anyway. She and Agent Olson were staring at the boots that were lined up by size as if in a drawing from *The Three Bears*. I had never liked the rubbery cloth feeling of the inside and had rarely used mine. They looked nearly new.

Olson extended his hand and gave me a questioning look.

I shrugged.

The agent leaned over and picked up the pair that had been mine, then held them aloft as if he were examining a kitten by the scruff of its neck. The mustard-yellow tread of the soles still shone and the bottoms were clean and dry. A few bands of dirt were held in the ridges, but they looked ancient. One even had a stalk of grass sticking halfway out.

He turned to me. "Yours?"

I nodded, though it was possible they were Jane's last pair. Hannah had her boots at Cornell, explaining that they came in handy for examining barnyard animals.

Agent Olson reached for the largest pair and held them up in the same way. These treads were different from mine. They were clogged with fresh mud.

I must have gasped.

"Mind if we take these?" he asked. I noticed that his round cheeks were slightly flushed, but that could have been from the cooler outside air.

What could I say? What I *should* have said was that they weren't mine and I had no right to give permission, that they should either ask Colin or get a warrant. They might actually be Jason's last pair from high school, though that hardly mattered. He was in New Mexico and hadn't worn them lately.

Yet even if I had been smart enough to refuse, they had *seen* the boots, seen the new dirt for themselves. It would only be putting off the inevitable. I had a whirlwind image of myself refusing and when they were gone washing and cleaning the boots with a toothbrush, replacing the mud with dirt from around the property. But even as the thought flitted across my mind, I knew I wouldn't do it. With all their high-tech equipment, they probably would be able to tell and I would fall under suspicion myself.

Detective Carew produced a plastic square from her tan leather bag. She shook it out until it became magically larger and larger and turned into a sack large enough to hold a pair of green rubber boots.

"But what about the firebug?" I asked. "The paper said there was another fire in the neighborhood last month."

"There was," Olson said quickly. He had let Carew handle most of the interview, but arson was his area. "We believe it was set for the insurance. The owner is swimming in debt."

"Oh." In my mind, the door to *my* fire escape route clanged shut. "But wouldn't it have been easier just to sell the house?"

Olson shook his head. "The contents were insured for three million. Except that he removed them first."

"We have a choice," Detective Carew interrupted, back in charge again. Her voice was tense. "I can leave Agent Olson here while I try and find your husband, to make certain the interview isn't tainted. Or we can leave you in peace if you tell us you won't contact him yourself."

"You don't want me to warn him."

"Actually, I have a better idea. Why don't you call him and see where he is? Then we'll go talk to him."

Wasn't that entrapment? Once more I had the choice of cooperating with the inevitable or doing something that would create suspicion. "My phone's inside."

The detective reached into her pocket. "Use mine."

I started to say that Colin wouldn't recognize the number and answer, but that was not true. When he was available, Colin always picked up. He was a man used to expecting good news, even with his poetic star in abeyance. I remembered the excitement when *Voices We Don't Want to Hear* had been shortlisted for the Pulitzer—that had been how many years ago?

I took her BlackBerry and punched in the number I knew by heart.

"Colin Fitzhugh." He sounded more formal than usual.

"Where are you?"

"Home. Delhi? Where are *you*? Why did this strange number come up?"

I was surprised at how relieved I was to hear his voice. Not dead in a car crash, not on the lam, just a little impatient for me to get to the point. He was still Colin, still my husband of twenty-five years, the man who wooed a nineteen-year-old away from her education and into his life. For all his faults—and I could enumerate them easily if anyone was interested—I knew he was not capable of setting a fatal fire.

"You're at the condo?"

"I've been home all day. I have an important article due at the end of the week. You didn't answer my question. Are you stuck somewhere?"

"No, the police are here. They have questions about Ethan and Sheila, how they died. They went to the university but you weren't there."

"Ethan and Sheila? Did you tell them what they did to us?"

"It's what they think we did to *them*. They're here at the house collecting evidence. Rubber boots and things."

Carew's head jerked up and she reached for the phone, as if to take it from a child who was making prank calls.

"I gave them your address so they can talk to you."

"If they have to."

I handed the phone back without saying good-bye.

The detective was looking at me as if a bobcat she had been assured was a house pet had suddenly bared its teeth at her.

I was beyond caring. "How can you think he'd be stupid enough to commit a crime wearing those boots, then put them back where they could be found?"

She cocked her head. "I'm sure he'll have time to think of a reason."

Chapter Eight

I STOOD BY the window, arms wrapped around myself, and watched the dark blue car pull away from the curb. I was so terrified I could hear myself breathing. I had been in frightening situations before, fearful for my children, being attacked physically. But it didn't compare with Colin or me been suspected of murder. Mistakes could be made; I could not stop my frightened mind from racing ahead to arrest, a biased trial, incarceration, or worse.

When there was nothing more to see I moved toward the wing chair dizzily, as if I were seeing the couch, the fireplace, the photographs through wavy glass. Was this what a heart attack felt like? I sank into the chair and made myself breathe slowly. But now I couldn't stop playing what had happened over and over in my mind, excoriating myself for not handling it differently. I had thrown our legal rights to the wind.

If I called Colin right now, he would have time to leave the condo. I could meet him and we could go anywhere—anywhere away from here. I imagined us frantically removing money from roadside ATMs and driving straight through to Mexico. We could sort out everything—my books, his job—later on. The crucial thing was to get away before we were caught and chewed up in the dangerous gears of Justice.

I closed my eyes and let the scenario unspool. Thank God the children were grown. Or almost grown. We would make it right for them, of course we would, but right now we had to save ourselves. Yet I didn't reach for my phone. Was it all my fault? What if the fire were Colin's way of handling the situation to keep me from going to the media in desperation? Colin navigated through life with the ease of someone who presumed himself to be on the side of the angels, someone who met challenges with a raised hand and sweet reason. But perhaps he had a buried ruthlessness that, if aroused, was capable of anything.

What if he *had* gone to the house in Southampton Saturday night to confront Ethan? They had argued and Colin had gotten no satisfaction. I thought of Ethan's superciliousness, remembered how his cold eyes had discounted me all the way back in Stratford. "Bimbo" was hardly the word you would use to describe your best friend's heavily pregnant wife, but it was what I had read in Ethan's face.

Remembering him, I could imagine him treating Colin scornfully in Southampton, perhaps even laughing at him. Suppose Colin had stormed out in frustration—then waited until Ethan and Sheila had gone to bed and torched the house? Could I imagine him spewing gasoline against the foundations and tossing in a match, knowing the Crosleys might die?

I couldn't. And that was *after* Ethan had sent the letter accusing him. I tried an alternative. Maybe Colin had first driven out to see him Saturday morning, demanding—what? An apology? Some show of remorse? Same outcome and Colin had left. But perhaps it had eaten at him all day until he returned that night to take his revenge. Ethan meanwhile had been concerned enough to write to Elisa warning her about Colin.

Imagining it that way, Colin would have had time to pick up the boots. But why would he have gone out of his way to do so, wear them in Southampton to commit arson, then go out of his way one more time to put them somewhere they could easily be found? I thought of a book I had sold last year, *Cruelly Murdered*, the story of Constance Kent, accused of murdering her four-year-old half brother because one of her nightgowns could not be located. It was decided that it must have been bloody and she had burned it.

Surely no one would have examined the boots and decided that Colin's were missing—would they?

And now it was too late to call Colin. Pressing deeper into the chair, ignoring my great-grandmother's reproachful gaze from under glass, I tortured myself with images of Olson and Carew arriving at Colin's condo and asking tricky, intimidating questions. What if he admitted it and tried to justify what he had done to Ethan? I saw him being dragged off to jail in handcuffs, his archeological career, his life—all our lives—ruined.

But he can still write poetry, a little voice chirped, making me laugh at my own idiocy. Poetry was not his life. His position was as an eminent academic authority in archeology. I reminded myself that judges, doctors, politicians, financiers had all been tried, convicted, and sent to jail. Then I thought about the children and their futures.

Stop! Nothing has happened yet!

In my experience, thinking of the worst possible outcome nearly guaranteed that it wouldn't happen. It was like imagining that your plane would crash or obsessing that you had a brain tumor. Since you were not able to predict the future, it would not happen. Life liked to sneak up on you. An example: I had never worried about one of my children being kidnapped.

Elisa. I had promised I would call her, but I didn't feel strong enough to do it right now. What made her show Ethan's letter to the Boston police? Did she think Colin had set the fire? It had come to a choice between the Crosleys and us, and she had not chosen us.

Didn't it mean anything to her that Colin was her real father, that she had spent a weekend starting to get to know him? But a weekend was hardly enough set against a lifetime of adventure with Ethan. I closed my eyes again.

Then, like finding a check you'd forgotten to cash, I thought of someone else who might want the Crosleys dead.

Nearly twenty years ago, Ethan and Sheila had hired an actress, Priscilla Waters, to impersonate a nanny, distract Jane, and smuggle Caitlin into an empty stroller. Priscilla had been told it was a "prank" to teach me a lesson. When she realized she had taken part in a kidnapping scheme, instead of going to the police to report it, she had demanded more money from Ethan and Sheila. She had been lured to a country road by their promise that they would give it to her, and ended up as a hit-and-run victim. Priscilla had left behind two teenage sons, Nick and Micah Clancy. It was Micah, now with a small daughter of his own, whose conscience had bothered him enough to send me the anonymous note that set everything into motion.

Nick was the one who had vowed revenge on his mother's killers, but I had called Micah, exultant, as soon as I found Elisa. No doubt he had told Nick as well. Had one of them come over from England and murdered the Crosleys?

I stared out at the fading daylight. I didn't want it to be Micah, but I knew I had to call DCI Sampson and find out if either brother had been out of the county last week.

I couldn't call today, of course. It was already late evening in England. Instead, it was time to make the call I was dreading.

As I LISTENED to her ringtone, I wondered what Elisa's mood would be. Would Ethan's letter have changed everything?

"Delhi?" She sounded shocked to hear from me.

"Yes. Hi."

She didn't say anything for a moment. "I have to tell you. My father sent me a letter this morning. I mean, he mailed it Saturday."

"I know. The police were here."

"Already? I shouldn't even be talking to you!"

"Elisa, Colin didn't hurt the Crosleys."

"Oh, no?"

"No. He was home with me the whole time." The lie slipped out before I had a chance to even think about it. All I knew was I couldn't lose her now.

"Really?"

"Really." What I should have said to Carew and Olson. Now it was too late.

"But why would my father warn me about him?"

"I don't know. Except that he was very angry with us. He thought we'd disrupted his life."

"Well, you did. If you hadn't come looking for me, none of this would have happened! They'd still be here, living in Providence, and planning my graduation party. They were going to have a big party at the yacht club, on the dock, with lights and everything."

What could I say to that? "But he sent you a graduation present?"

"He did. A check for sixty thousand dollars."

I caught my breath.

"You still don't get it. I don't *want* the money, I'd live on the street if it would bring them back." Her voice ended in a wail.

"I know. It's a terrible thing." But I fought to push back the bitterness that was rising in my throat, burning as fiercely as the residue from the fire when I had gone to the house. The Crosleys had ruined our lives by kidnapping our daughter. But in her eyes she had thought we were the criminals. "I wish I could make you feel better," I added.

"Well, you can't."

I had a flash of Elisa as a toddler when we hadn't had time to stop for the ice cream she was demanding. She had turned her head away from my explanations, refusing to be placated, and nursed her anger the whole way home. And that was when she was *two*.

"And the police there are no help. They said they have to autopsy them to find out how they died and confirm their identities. Like they can't tell? I can't even plan a funeral!"

"I know the police. I can try and find out more." As I said it my mind was running through the five stages of grief. Disbelief first, but anger came soon after. It was hard to believe Elisa would ever reach acceptance.

"I went out to the house. It's—bad.Was there a caretaker or anything, someone who stopped by to get things ready when your parents were going to be there?"

"What—why do you want to know about her? Do you think she was careless and left something flammable around?"

"No. But anything she saw might help. Maybe she saw someone lurking around who shouldn't have been there."

"Huh."

Just thinking about a caretaker made me realize again how different Elisa's upbringing had been compared to the one she would have had with us. We had traveled to digs and guest lectureships at universities as well, but strictly on the no-frills track. She had already seen our house.

Rather grudgingly Elisa looked up the caretaker's direct number and gave it to me.

"Hannah told me about graduation," I said. "We'd like to come."

Silence. "I definitely want *Hannah* there."

"I'd like to come too."

"Well, I can't stop you."

No, you can't. I'm your mother for God's sake and I have every right to be there! It's not my fault that our lives were interrupted.

"But not *him*. I don't want him there."

She broke the connection.

IF YOU HADN'T come looking for me, none of this would have happened.

I sat in the living room as the evening darkened around me, nursing a glass of Yellow Tail Chardonnay. That was true enough. If I had never gone looking for Elisa and found her, she would've been having a triumphant graduation Friday and a wonderful party afterward. I could see the lights shimmering across Narragansett Bay, hear the laughter and congratulations. The live musicians assembled on the dock. Rejoicing and many gifts.

While we, her real parents, struggled on without her, doing our best, our lives forever marked by the tragedy of her death. But *she* would have been happy. Was that what Colin had been thinking when he'd advised me not to look for her?

I took an angry sip of wine, glad of its burn. We were not birth parents who had given Elisa up and regretted it later, though things could not have turned out worse if we had. My daughter, far from being grateful for being found, hated me. My husband was being threatened by the police.

I can't stop you from coming.

Would she really be upset if I came to her graduation? Despite how I felt, I would not force myself on her. How would she feel about Jane being there? They had gotten along well enough that weekend at the house. In some ways Jane and Elisa were more alike than Elisa and Hannah in their direct approach to the world. Jane had been the only one not surprised when she had scored perfectly on the math portion of the SAT and been accepted by NYU, then gotten an important finance job.

No matter what happened, Jane would be okay. Even if Colin . . .

Why hadn't he called me yet? Surely Carew and Olson had finished interviewing him. Had they taken him in for questioning? *Arrested* him? Out of nowhere I was haunted by the memory of the peeling paint on our back stoop. Did we really have anything to give Elisa that she hadn't gotten better from Ethan and Sheila? Surely not money or exotic adventures, parties on yachts. Just a twin sister. *And the truth.*

Pulling my iPhone out of my bag, I pressed Colin's number. It would be a short call, just to tell him I was on my way over.

But he did not pick up. Where *was* he? All my fears came rushing back, my terror stronger than before. Had he been taken away as a "person of interest"? Perhaps he had broken down and confessed, asserting it had been his right to retaliate. He was just arrogant enough to do that, just out of touch enough not to know the consequences. Why wouldn't he know that you should never ever confess to anything? What would that do to the rest of us, left to flutter helplessly like cloth rags on the tail of his kite?

After my lie to Elisa, our relationship would be gone for good.

My voice hoarse, I left a message that I was coming and found my keys.

Chapter Nine

COLIN WAS STAYING in a condo that belonged to a friend, another professor, who was teaching in Japan for two years. I did not know what financial arrangements they had made, but Colin had left the interior exactly as it had been when he moved in. The condo was part of an upscale complex, though not gated, three miles from the farmhouse.

Driving over, it was dark enough for headlights—but light enough at the complex to see that the two allotted parking spaces in front of number 47 were vacant. Colin's dark green BMW convertible was nowhere to be seen. I prayed he had just gone out for food. I had the key and knew he wouldn't mind if I waited inside.

I knocked on the door anyway. To my surprise, Colin pulled it back, looking scruffy in jeans and a red Seawolves sweatshirt. The mythical animal seemed to snarl at me as I stepped inside. Why had the university picked such an ugly animal as its mascot?

"I didn't see your car," I stammered.

"They took it. And my laptop. *And* my phone."

"Really? *Why?*" No wonder he hadn't called me or picked up when I called. Thank God I hadn't said anything about fleeing the country!

Colin closed the door behind me and sighed. "Just looking for evidence. Making sure I wasn't doing Internet searches on how to burn my enemies alive. If the phone comes up clean—and it will—they promised to return it tomorrow. I'm lost without it."

I stared into the room at the Asian decor. A full-sized kimono with a beautifully embroidered stork, wings unfurled, hung over a dark red couch. There were a lot of low ebony tables and brass pieces. A flat-screen TV hung between some framed calligraphy.

I felt too shaky to stand any longer and sank onto the brocaded couch. "What did they *ask* you?"

Colin pulled up a black lacquered chair across from me. "They wanted to know where I was Saturday night."

I held my breath. "Where were you?"

"At a dinner at the Three Village Inn. Cliff Mallow, the head of the anthropology department, is retiring. He was here when I began. We didn't always see eye to eye, but we go way back."

I didn't want him to start reminiscing. "What about after that?"

"I went home. I read for a while, then went to bed."

"So you didn't drive out to Southampton." A terrible thing to say, but I had to know.

"Delhi." It was a look he would give a student who had made a rude comment in class.

"I know you didn't, I'm just trying to think like the police. They were taking Ethan's note so seriously."

"What note?"

"The note he sent Elisa. They didn't tell you?" I felt as if I were on the carnival ride where the floor drops away pinning you against the wall. Any moment gravity would fail and I would crumple to the floor.

"What note?" he repeated.

I realized my fists were clenched and made myself relax my fingers. "Ethan sent Elisa a letter that she got this morning. Express mail because there was a check inside. He said that if anything happened to him to blame *you*."

"What? That doesn't make sense. Blame me for what? How could he know he was about to die?"

"I don't know."

"He mentioned me by name?"

"I don't know why they didn't tell you." That was terrifying, though I wasn't sure why. Were they holding the note back to spring on him in a courtroom setting? But no, that only happened in Perry Mason novels. Now there was some kind of disclosure law where both sides had to know the evidence before the trial.

"Because they're just looking for a fall guy."

Yes, that's what they do. "Did they ask you about the mud on the boots?"

"They showed me the boots, they practically shook them in my face! They're going to check out the mud to see if it's from the Southampton house when I wore them out there Saturday night. The problem is, I was never there." He eyed me resentfully. "For that matter, it could just as easily have been you. The boots were at the house where you are."

I jerked up on the sofa. "What—you're ready to throw me under the bus? You think I'd try to frame you? Or be dumb enough to put them back outside if I'd worn them?"

"You think *I* would?"

We glared at each other for a moment, then I said, "Of course not. I told them that. How stupid do they think we are?"

"You're sure you didn't put them on when it was muddy just to walk around the yard?"

"Of course not. You know I hate those boots."

"Maybe when the kids were home for the weekend they used them."

"But that was back in March."

"True. If they damage my car . . ." Colin's vintage BMW was his baby.

"Your car's the least of it. Thank God they didn't arrest you!"

"How could they do that? On what evidence? Besides, I'm—"

"Yes, I know, you're a very important person. You're Colin Fitzhugh." A joke, but I needed to step back from the abyss. "Elisa thinks—" I stopped then.

"What? She's rushing to judgment too?"

"After that letter, she doesn't know what to think."

"I'll talk to her. You have her number?"

I hesitated. I knew she wouldn't want to talk to him. But he *was* her father. I pulled out my phone, found it, and gave it to him. "I told her you were at the house with me all Saturday night."

"You—what?" He did not seem accusing, just as if he was trying to understand.

"Because she was sure, after Ethan's comment, that you had set the fire. I couldn't let her think that!"

He nodded.

"When they were on the way to your condo I thought about calling you so we could run off and just leave. Hide out somewhere."

He actually smiled. "That doesn't look guilty?"

"It doesn't matter. Just until they found out who really did it. We could still go, we still have the van. Or we could just fly somewhere."

"We wouldn't get very far."

I blinked at this roadblock. "Why not?"

"They have my passport."

"Oh, God." The net had already dropped over us.

Chapter Ten

I SLEPT WORSE than ever that night, if I slept at all. When I'm upset it goes first to my stomach, then sends my mind racing like a gerbil banging against its wire cage. A caged creature who knows there is no escape but can't stop trying. I twisted back and forth under the quilt and blanket that were much too hot and finally set my arm free into the chilly night.

Why couldn't I have Colin's confidence that justice would prevail? He knew he hadn't killed Ethan and Sheila would never take any life. He was appalled by the death penalty and lectured me about it when I wavered over some horrible serial killer, But though I knew he was innocent, the part of me that wanted to run and hide had no faith that it would all work out. If someone had planted the boots to make Colin look guilty, why would they stop there? What if they had tampered with the red plastic gas can he kept in his trunk, to make it seem as if it had been recently filled and emptied? I had no idea who "they" were except that they were the real murderers of the Crosleys.

I suddenly remembered the noises I had heard early Monday

morning, a car door clicking shut, the sound of footsteps on the gravel driveway. Could it have been someone returning the boots? The house had been dark and they would have assumed I was sleeping. It was only chance and anxiety that I had not been.

If the police arrested Colin, what would it do to our already fragile family? Hannah would suffer the most. It would have been better for her if we'd never found her sister. She would drop out of veterinary school, start collecting abandoned animals, and live like a hermit in a shack somewhere in upstate New York. She wouldn't find it such a bad life perhaps, but I would mourn what she had lost.

The world tilted dangerously. My exposed arm was suddenly icy cold, its chill threatening to freeze the rest of my body with it. I jerked the arm back under the covers as if out of danger and rubbed it back to life.

Things couldn't get any worse.

Don't ever tell yourself that.

AT 4 A.M. I was awake, as alert as if someone had pulled me out of bed and slammed me against the wall. The mud! One thing they were checking Colin's car and the boots for was the Southampton dirt. If they found nothing in the BMW, my van was where they would look next. And what would they find? Mud from when I walked around the Crosley house Monday morning and climbed back into the driver's seat. I could protest that that had been the only time I had been there, but why would they believe me?

I had watched enough television procedurals to know that they did not need a large sample. CSI was so good that a few grains could be identified as coming from a specific locale. Put Jeffrey Deaver's Lincoln Rhyme on the case and you would barely need that. If they couldn't prove Colin had driven his car out there, they would make a case for his using my van. Or my using the van.

Panicked, I pushed out of bed and pulled on the jeans and sweatshirt that were draped over the rocking chair. It was still dark outside, which I found reassuring until I realized I would have to turn on some lights. My small portable vacuum that I used to remove dust from cartons and the edges of books was out in the barn.

I crept down the stairs into the kitchen, crept as stealthily as if someone was watching, with a trail of cats behind me whining for food. I ignored them and felt around for the flashlight magnetized to the side of the refrigerator. Without turning it on, I stumbled down the back porch steps and moved toward the barn. Slowly my eyes adjusted to the early morning. The waning moon was full, though the blackness of the pond made me think of pits of damnation.

I unlocked the barn and closed the door firmly before deciding I was being ridiculous and switched on the flashlight. I could be out in my Book Barn in the early hours for any reason. Still, the black corners beyond the small beam were menacing, filled with ghostly police detectives. If one of them had suddenly stepped forward to accuse me, I would have screamed, but not been totally surprised.

The shop vac was on the edge of the worktable, a large silver egg laid by an electric hen. I switched it on experimentally to check the batteries, and the drone was much too loud. Hastily I flipped it off. What was I doing? Tampering with—no, *removing* misleading evidence.

Carrying the vacuum handle in one hand, the flashlight in the other, I slipped out of the barn without locking it. Daylight was now edging the sky just enough to make the way to the house visible. I thought I was moving silently until the German shepherd next door gave a yapping bark, freezing me on the path. I imagined the neighborhood waking and coming to life like actors at the beginning of a play. The retired cop across the street, everybody's friend, would hurry over to see if I needed help with my van.

"Shh, Mamie," I said as loud as I dared. "It's okay. It's just me."

Either that calmed her down or I stopped hearing her. I was as alert for other sounds as Miss T stalking a mouse. I stayed in the shadow of the house until I reached the van, then pressed the handle down gently. When I opened the door the light inside flashed a brief greeting before I reached in and switched it off.

I trained the flashlight on the floor beside the gas pedal and brake. As I had imagined, there was a dried tan residue, sprinkled across other grit that had accumulated over time. Rather than work with the door open, I closed it softly, then went around to the passenger side and climbed in. Bending over, I switched on the vacuum and sucked up everything I could see. I had just finished when I realized it would look suspicious to have only that area vacuumed, and went on a cleaning rampage, scouring all the floors and the seats. To do so entailed moving jackets and umbrellas, even a carton of books, but I did not stop until the van was as clean as when I bought it six years ago. And it had been used then.

I moved around to the back door, carrying the vacuum carefully. Then I went into the bathroom off the kitchen, opened the bottom, and shook it over the toilet. Fortunately the little cloth bag had already been half full, so I did not have to worry about Southampton residue left at the bottom. I flushed the toilet twice, then went upstairs, and flung myself on the double bed. I had read somewhere that resting was almost as good as sleeping. Surprisingly, I dozed off.

Chapter Eleven

Two HOURS LATER, acting under a territorial imperative of my own, I drove out to Southampton. At 8:30 a.m. I called the Crosleys' caretaker, Mairee Jontra. As I pressed in her number, I wondered what kind of name Mairee was. Made-up, of course. On the other hand, what kind of a name was Delhi? I didn't bother to explain it unless people asked, and most people didn't. My parents' dream had been to go to India as Christian missionaries. My father had accepted the call to the church in Princeton with the caveat that as soon as the mission field details were worked out, the Methodists would have to find themselves a new pastor.

Only it had never happened. Once partitioning was a reality and India had rid itself of the British pestilence, the government was reluctant to allow other white faces in. They were no doubt sick of being told how to live. By then the idea of foreigners coming to convert the "natives" was losing traction all over the world. If my father had had a specific skill, medicine or engineering, he might have had an entree. But he had been a scholar, and a religious scholar at that.

All I know is that it did not work out. My sister and I were born when they were still actively trying to get to India. They named me Delhi, and my twin Patience, as if to remind themselves where they wanted to go and the attitude they needed to cultivate.

Mairee Jontra answered her phone brightly. "Mairee here!"

"Hi. My name is Delhi Laine. I was wondering if I could talk to you."

"If it's about engaging me, I'm afraid you'll have to speak to the agency directly. You can ask them for me, I'll be pleased if you do, but they do all the hiring. I can give—"

"No, I need to ask you about some people you worked for."

I could feel her wariness crackling across the line. "I really can't discuss our clientele. I'm sure you understand."

"I'm asking on behalf of Elisa Crosley."

"Elisa? Oh, my God, what a terrible thing to happen! *Unbelievable.* I can't get my head around it, Ethan was one of my favorite people. How is poor Elisa doing?"

I sighed. "She's holding up. But she has some questions she wanted me to ask you. And since I live out here . . ." I let my voice trail away.

"You were a friend of the family?"

"Not exactly. But Elisa is my daughter's best friend. She was with her when she heard the news."

"Oh, my God. What do you need to know?"

"It would be better if I could see you for a few minutes."

"Oh, Lord, today is crazy. So's tomorrow for that matter. And probably the rest of my life."

"Just five minutes?"

"Okay." She seemed to be thinking. "I'm due out on Meadow Lane to let some painters in. They aren't coming until nine, so if you could get there immediately . . ."

"Just tell me where."

MEADOW LANE RUNS parallel to the Atlantic Ocean, which can be glimpsed if you are driving only in snatches between mansions, guesthouses, garages, and greenhouses. My twin sister Patience's vacation home is in the opposite direction, east on Dune Road, and more modest—if you can consider a house that has seven bedrooms and multiple bathrooms a cozy hideaway.

This house I braked at did not look like the typical gray-shingled homes that Southampton was known for. It was more recent, no doubt the work of a well-known architect, and had round ends like fat silos with a recessed middle section. The windows in the center part of the house were very large and lined up with those on the beach side to give a view of the ocean.

The slender figure standing on the slate steps waved.

I waved back, surprised. The title "caretaker" had evoked the image of an old family retainer coming to the house in advance to make sure everything was in order, and stocking the refrigerator with provisions from *Barefoot Contessa*. In my fantasy she would leave a plate of homemade muffins and jam, perhaps even have dinner in the refrigerator for whenever the family arrived.

Mairee upended my fantasy. She was my age, with a mop of dark red curls and an expressive mouth. She managed to look elegant in a peacoat and jeans—elegant and harassed at the same time, her iPhone an extension of her arm.

"Hey there! You're a book dealer?"

I glanced back at my dented white van with its blue logo, "Got Books?" on the doors. "Right."

"Great! Give me your card. People are always looking to downsize and they never know what to do with the books."

Perfect. I was always looking to upsize my collection. Quickly I reached into my bag and extracted one. My sister's husband, Ben, was always urging me to get a more professional-looking business card but I was too attached to mine to do so. It showed Raj sniffing at a stack of leather-bound books with my "Got Books?" slogan. My information was on the other side.

Mairee unlocked the door and brought me into a living room that overlooked the ocean. We sat side by side on a pale cream leather sofa. The furniture was understated, neutrals and glass tables, a stone fireplace built into a wall to work from both sides. I saw from the plastered walls and some of the woodwork that the house was older than I'd first thought.

"We haven't had a fatal fire out here in *years*," Mairee announced. "An artist died recently in a house fire in Sagaponack, but that's miles away. You think Elisa will rebuild?"

"I never thought about it. It's hard to imagine she'd want to be out here by herself."

"It's a great location."

"The house may need to come down."

Mairee nodded, but she seemed to be listening for the crunch of vehicles arriving on gravel at the same time. "That house was in the family forever."

"When did the Crosleys let you know they were coming?"

"They didn't! That's what's so weird." She put her head back on the leather and closed her eyes as if she had already put in a long day. "The first I knew they were even out here was when I heard about the fire."

"Was it unusual that you wouldn't get things ready for them?"

"Unheard of." She considered, straightening up. "At least, let's say it never happened before. But they've never come out this early before either."

I hesitated. Did she have scruples about talking about dead clients? I decided to find out. "You got along with them okay?"

Mairee sprawled back against the sofa and closed her eyes again, red curls against cream. "I thought so. Ethan was a doll. Sheila was . . . difficult. I never saw where she got off being so fussy, wanting everything up to these impossible magazine standards. It was an older house and had the problems you'd expect. Unless you ripped out the bathrooms, which Ethan refused to do, you're going to have off-color grout. It's a fact of life. But she blamed the cleaning service for not getting it snow white."

I thought of Lady Macbeth, obsessively trying to whiten her hands, haunted by bloodstains no one else could see. "Out, out, damn spot," I murmured.

"Exactly! She was hipped on everything looking perfect. Here her father was a construction worker. Ethan was the one with the background." She clapped her hand over her mouth. "I've said too much."

"What kind of marriage did they have?"

"Not my kind. I mean, he was away a lot, totally focused on his career. When he was home they were never alone, the guys who worked for him stayed here too. Craig, he was a few years older than Elisa, and I forget the other one's name. But Sheila was the one who kept the home fires burning. *Oof.* My bad."

She looked at me and I laughed. "How long were they your clients?"

"Probably ten years?"

"What did you think of Will?"

Mairee was off and running again, a colt that refused to be confined in the paddock. "That poor kid? He tried, he really did. But it was tough to be a Crosley. Ethan was disappointed that he wasn't a better student and Sheila was always comparing him to their friends' kids. And not in a good way. *Elisa* was the one they thought was perfect. Yet even with her—Sheila wasn't exactly the affectionate type. All she cared about was how things looked to other people."

"Do you think Will was into drugs?"

"I wouldn't be surprised. What else was there for him? He was good at making things, but nobody cared about that."

We heard the rumble of the truck at the same time. Mairee jumped up. "Speaking of perfect, we have until Memorial Day to get everything in shape here. We still have to install the scent diffusers."

"The what?"

She laughed at my expression. "It's the latest thing. The air goes through the house's ductwork and gives off a different scent in every room. Sandalwood in here, Fresh Linen in the bedrooms."

"Pumpkin Pie in the kitchen?"

"Exactly."

I thought of my own house. Book Dust in the barn, Cat Box when I wasn't paying attention.

Outside, pushing through the sand to my van, I saw workmen sliding the ladders out of a large truck. They didn't have a clever business name or a cartoon character printed on the side of their van, just heavy-duty tools and no-nonsense faces. These guys were the real deal. I hoped I was too.

As LONG AS I was out east, I decided to visit my favorite Hamptons booksellers—the WOOFF (Welfare of Our Furry Friends) thrift shop, the old Bridgehampton Fire Department that now housed rooms of books, and the Ladies Village Improvement Society in Easthampton. They accepted donations from the community and over the years I had picked up some prizes. The prices weren't the most reasonable—nothing beats an estate sale where every book is fifty cents—but like most dealers, I was mindful that it would take only one treasure to change my life.

My hopes had just been refueled by the story of a scrap metal dealer who nearly melted down a Fabergé egg for the gold, then decided it was too pretty to destroy. For his good taste he went on to collect millions. That's what I fantasized happening to me. Nothing on such a grand scale, but perhaps a short story hand-written by Edgar Allan Poe or a missing Massachusetts Bay hymnal inscribed by Cotton Mather.

That day I found no Russian eggs, no trillion-dollar manuscripts, but I turned up some vintage art catalogs. Three were inscribed by the artists, which alone made the trip worthwhile.

I WAS WRAPPING books to mail in the early afternoon when there was a quick knock at the barn door. People rarely came here looking for books, but when they did I invited them in to browse. I kept the books that were already cataloged on the downstairs shelves.

When I opened the door it was not a bibliophile but Ruth Carew. She was by herself today and wearing a pantsuit the pale yellow of Long Island corn. This jacket seemed a little grimy around the cuffs, but at least there were no food stains on the lapels.

"We're interested in examining your van and your computers," she told me bluntly.

I didn't say anything.

"We can get a warrant, of course."

Why don't you do that?

"This just seems easier."

"You can look at my van in the driveway," I said. "It's unlocked. But I need my laptop for my book business."

"Is that your only computer?"

"Yes."

She eyed me as if dubious that I could conduct a business with just one laptop. "Do you have a smartphone?"

Did a phone keep a record of Internet searches? Or was she looking for calls to the Crosleys? "Yes, but I need that too."

"We can get a warrant," she repeated.

"Do whatever you have to." With no evidence of any criminal activity on my part, I doubted a judge would give her one.

I didn't slam the door in her face. I waited until she had turned and was walking down the gravel path before closing it.

Chapter Twelve

"MOM, ELISA'S NOT answering my texts!" Hannah's voice on my phone sounded frantic.

It was Thursday morning, the day before graduation at St. Brennan's College. Jane was scheduled to take the train out from Manhattan tonight and we would be on the ferry to Connecticut early tomorrow morning. The plan was for Hannah to drive over from Ithaca and meet us at there.

"She has a lot on her mind," I reassured Hannah, as I poured extra dried food into the dish for the cats. Yet even this small twist ramped up the tension I was already feeling. One more thing to worry about.

"She's just going to be staying on in the dorm, they told her she could. And her classes are over. Why isn't she answering my texts? She doesn't want us to come." My daughter was veering into tragic mode.

"Don't be silly. She definitely wants you there. She probably just forgot to charge the battery on her phone. Are you all set for tomorrow?"

"I put gas in the car over the weekend."

"Are you sure it will get you there?" That *would* be tragic, if her car broke down and she missed everything. "Maybe you should take the bus."

"*Mom.* It's fine. I always use it to go to Boston."

"Okay. I figure we'll get to the parking garage about ten so we can get good seats in the stadium. Where should we meet?"

"By the big eagle?"

"Fine." I remembered the large bronze statue from the day I found Elisa, when I'd gone to the college in late January.

"Is—Dad coming?"

Something about the way she asked, the question mark in her voice, made me wonder if Elisa had told her about Ethan's letter,

"No. He can't get away." The old family pattern of trying to shield the children from bad news. Most famously, we had repressed all mention of Elisa and her drowning when they were growing up, believing that they had been too young to remember and that they were better off not being raised in the shadow of death. Now I wondered if it had been more Colin's and my attempt to bury the pain rather than anything to do with the children.

"And Mom? They still haven't released her parents' bodies! How can she plan a funeral without her parents being there? I mean—"

"I know what you mean. I know one of the detectives in the department and I'll talk to him."

After I hung up with Elisa, the next call I made was to England, to the Stratford-upon-Avon police constabulary about Nick and Micah Clancy. I had forgotten to do it yesterday until it was too late. As I dialed, I imagined DCI Sampson with his precise salt-and-pepper mustache, his military posture, seated in his office surrounded by his antique prints of fish and birds, and his tea-brewing paraphernalia. He had been the policeman involved both in Elisa's initial disappearance when he was a young constable, and when I had returned to Stratford last December. He hadn't believed my story initially, though after interviewing Nick Clancy he became more convinced.

I asked for his extension and listened to the pulsing tone. Had it been only five months since I had walked into the constabulary in Shakespeare's hometown? Perhaps it was because it had been winter—snow icing the stucco half timbers and curling wrought-iron signs—that it felt like something from a storybook.

"Sampson here."

"Good afternoon!" I said, surprised at how happy I was to hear his calm voice. Somewhere in the world there was sanity and orderly procedure rather than grasping at any debris floating by. "This is Delhi Laine." *Your American pen pal.*

"Ms. Laine."

"Things have been happening here. The Crosleys—my daughter's kidnappers and Priscilla Waters's killers—died here in a house fire over the weekend."

"Really. No news of it here."

"So it means you don't have to pursue extradition. If you were going to. The police here think it was arson, that the fire was deliberately set."

Silence as he waited for me to go on.

"When they were trying to figure out a motive, I remembered Nick Clancy. I did tell Micah about the Crosleys and he asked me where they lived. I know Nick was vowing to get revenge on them for killing his mother . . ." I trailed off, waiting for him to pick up what I was suggesting.

Finally he did. "And you're thinking that one of them hopped a plane, set the fire, and came home again?"

Would that it were that easy. "They may still find out it was a local arsonist. But is there any way to find out whether either of them left the country last week?"

"You mean check remotely without their knowledge? Yes, I can do that. All travel itineraries in and out of the UK are computerized now. Since 2009, and held for ten years."

"Can you let me know?"

"Hadn't I best be talking to my American counterpart?"

"Yes, of course." He still seemed to find my version of the drowning and kidnapping as insubstantial as a paper chain glued together by a clumsy child. He had agreed that certain events had occurred but they were open to interpretation. No doubt he wanted to check with his "American counterparts" as to whether the arson story was even true.

"Wait." I looked up the number of the Suffolk Homicide Bureau and gave it to him. "The detective in charge is Ruth Carew."

"I'll speak with her forthwith."

"Thank you." It was not really appropriate to thank him for doing his job, but it came out automatically and I left it between us.

Chapter Thirteen

My last call was to Detective Frank Marselli. I told myself I had every right to talk to Frank. I had met him when he was investigating the deaths at what was now Port Lewis Books. The second time, after another murder in an artist's home where I was working, I had insisted on calling Frank. Our relationship was a one-way street, of course. He never phoned me for *my* insights.

My call went to his voice mail and I pressed the extension to talk to someone else. The young officer who answered told me Frank was out on a homicide. I persuaded him to tell me where by saying I had some important information on an arson case that I could only give him in person, information he needed to have as soon as possible. I can't lie directly, but I can expand the truth when it's necessary.

According to the officer, there had been a drive-by shooting in the Pace Park area of Bellport. Bellport was on the opposite side of Long Island from Port Lewis, located on the Great South Bay instead of the sound. The village is a community of large colonial homes and has the advantage of being closer to Manhattan than

the Hamptons. Its charm has attracted residents like Isabella Ros-
sellini and Charlie Rose. Main Street has trendy shops and a pier
you can park on.

The charming village was not where the shooting had been.

The other area of Bellport, Pace Park—farther from the water
and truly on the wrong side of the tracks—is a downtrodden area
of wooden tract homes built in the 1950s to provide housing for
workers in the defense weapons plants. When the defense indus-
try on Long Island collapsed a few years later, many of the unexpectedly unemployed lost their homes to foreclosure. Decades
later Suffolk County's poorest residents are placed here in rentals
by social services.

As I crossed Sunrise Highway and drove down Station Road, I
remembered that the picturesque waterfront village had originally
been an African-American resort in the 1880s, complete with its
own orphanage and retirement home. Unlike the Sag Harbor community that has remained a wealthy African-American enclave, a
malignant hand seemed to have reached down and shoved the first
residents' descendants back into the run-down area of Pace Park.

Pace Park was as depressed as I remembered it. I soon saw
flashing red and blue lights and other signs of police activity in
front of Chubby Charlie's Bar-B-Q Chicken. A large tin sign of a
well-fed, rosy-cheeked chef in a white cap and apron dominated
the front of what might have once been a KFC. I pulled my van up
next to a wooded lot across the road and got out.

I found Frank Marselli gesturing to a patrolman and looking
as if his last shred of patience had just disintegrated.

"Frustrating case?" I asked sympathetically.

"Ms. Laine." His flat hazel eyes gave me a wary look. "Tell me
you just happened to be driving by."

"Well, no. I need to talk to you." As I said it, I noticed that he was still keeping his colorless hair clipped close to his head as befitted the least vain man I had ever known. He was good-looking enough, but his mouth too often had the set of someone who did not trust the world to do the right thing. His default expression seemed to be "Why *me*, God?" His clothes, clean and pressed, looked more like government-issue than if he had gone to a shop.

Frank turned his palm over, a gesture that I took as a signal to begin.

"You know about the fire in Southampton?" I asked.

"You know I can't discuss that with you."

"But it's so unfair! That detective is blaming Colin with no good evidence."

"Even if I agreed with you, it's Ruth Carew's case. I'm only part of the team."

Did that mean he didn't agree with her? I hoped so, tucking it away like a ten-dollar bill I might need unexpectedly. "Okay, but at least tell me this. When will the bodies be released? My daughter—Elisa—is upset because she can't plan a service and get any closure." Like half the population, I hated that word, but here it seemed the only one that fit.

He studied me as if holding a debate with himself about what he could tell me.

I pulled my jacket more tightly around me and stared back at him. Despite the sunshine, it was a chilly day on the South Shore.

"This is not a simple case," he began. "Before the main fire, accelerant was poured over the bodies and they were badly burned. That makes identification challenging."

"You mean they were burned before the fire outside was started?" Then I realized the significance. Someone setting the

Crosleys on fire first ended any thought of casual arson. No wonder Detective Carew had her sights trained on us. "But that's horrible! Do you think they knew what was happening?"

"They were probably unconscious. They'd been drinking heavily. It's only a formality, but we haven't been able to locate the Crosleys' dental records. So the ME can't sign off yet. No dentist in the Providence area has identified them as patients. We've widened our search for them by name, but so far nothing. Not that I'm surprised: The ME says the woman's teeth were badly neglected and the man's teeth were perfect. No work at all."

Had Sheila been afraid of dentists? "But Ethan might have gone for checkups anyway. Doesn't Elisa know who their dentist was? Didn't they use the same one?"

"She still saw her pediatric dentist. Her teeth are very good too."

"What about DNA?"

"You want my job? I'm only telling you this much so you can let your daughter know why things are delayed. DNA is hard. We'd have to get a warrant to get into their home in Rhode Island to check hairbrushes or toothbrushes, then send the samples to the FBI lab. The warrant's easy, same day, but analyzing the DNA can take a couple of weeks. No one's questioning their identity anyway. It's just a formality."

"Why would you need a warrant if they're dead?"

He gave me a calm look. "You can't just break into people's houses and collect evidence."

"Can't Elisa give you permission?"

"Family members can. But you told Detective Carew she wasn't related to the Crosleys. That she's your biological daughter and there was no formal adoption."

I nodded.

"We're allowed to check on their credit cards or bank accounts, their cell phones, and there's been no further activity." He remembered something else. "Dr. Crosley was wearing one of those expensive watches, a Patek Philip, and they had on their wedding rings."

"Patek Philippe. That's odd." Why hadn't whoever incinerated them removed jewelry worth thousands?

"Also—" He stopped and pressed his lips in a narrow seal as if to keep more words from leaking out. We both knew he shouldn't have said as much as he had.

"Did you know the Crosleys had a son?" I asked.

"I'm not sure, but he's not in college. He's younger than Elisa and I think he was adopted legally from Nicaragua. But he was estranged from the Crosleys."

Frank watched me. He seemed to be expecting more.

"His name's Will, William Crosley, I guess, he's around eighteen or nineteen. Elisa thought he was living in Spanish Harlem."

Frank began writing in his notebook.

"Can you find him?" I asked.

"We have no choice. We have to interview any next of kin. Did you mention this to Carew?" His mouth drew in, annoyed that they had not had this piece of information earlier. My fault, of course.

"She didn't ask. All she's interested in is framing Colin!"

Frank gave me a reproachful look. But he said, "As you probably know, his car came up clean. So did his apartment. Nothing on his computers."

"So he's not a suspect?" *Please God, make it so.*

"You'll need to speak to Detective Carew about that."

"I don't think she likes me."

"It's not her job to like you or dislike you. She's a professional and that's all that matters."

"She hates my cats." I said it to make him smile and he did.

Chapter Fourteen

WHEN JANE AND I arrived at St. Brennan's College Friday morning, the stadium parking garage was jammed with excited families, each escorting a graduate in a baby blue robe.

"You'd think they were giving away souvenir bats," Jane grumbled as we circled the tiers to the rooftop.

"I guess we should have come earlier."

"To do what? We're fine."

I felt lucky to find a space on the top level, even though it was far from the exit stairs.

Hannah was waiting under the eagle clutching a handful of silver and red "Happy Graduation!" balloons. Instead of her usual sweats, she was wearing dark jeans and a green and white poplin jacket, her hair down around her face. Peering through the balloons, her face lit by excitement, she reminded me of the little girl she had once been, and my heart squeezed. A little girl caught up in her own dramas who would never have imagined being at the graduation of a twin sister.

Yet here we all were.

"Have you heard from Elisa?" I asked immediately after hugging her.

"No." The excitement in her eyes faded, and I cursed myself for making it the first thing I asked her.

"You brought those all the way from Ithaca?" asked Jane, eyeing the garish balloons. She was carrying a tasteful sheaf of long-stemmed red roses. It was obvious that she was not thrilled to be here.

"I kept them in the trunk so they wouldn't block my view. I was afraid they'd lose their helium or something, but they're fine." She gave an experimental tug downward and they bounced back immediately.

"Oh, goody," said Jane.

"You know what? You're such a spoilsport. I'll bet she likes the balloons more!"

It was hard to believe sometimes that there was only a nineteen-month age difference between them. Jane, with her lucrative job in finance, had settled quickly into a Manhattan lifestyle. Her short blond hair and perfect features made her the prettiest of the girls.

My gift to Elisa, if it was that, was lunch at the Purple Pig, a boutique restaurant that Hannah claimed was her favorite. It would not be the graduation party the Crosleys had planned, but it was the best we could do. Elisa would be with people who loved her.

But why hadn't we heard anything from her?

The crowd entering the stadium was so thick that we were funneled to the gate slowly, like theatergoers to a ticket taker. I tried to ignore the din of excited voices and my own sadness. These people carrying balloons and flowers had every right to be here. They had seen their graduates at every permutation of life, watched them weep over dead goldfish and smile into the camera for their senior prom photos. There was so much about Elisa's life locked away. Had St. Brennan's been her first choice? Had the Crosleys insisted she attend a college close by?

And the overhanging question: Would she ever let me get to know her well enough to find out?

We had to settle for bleacher seats halfway up the stadium, far from the dais. This was the large general graduation, the one everyone attended. The individual programs had separate ceremonies later on where the graduates would be handed their diplomas and presented with awards.

"I don't see her," Hannah worried a few minutes later when the graduates marched in and took their places on folding chairs below us. "I should have brought binoculars or something!"

"Here." Jane opened her Coach bag and pulled out a small pair of pearl-toned opera glasses, handing them across me to her sister.

Hannah blinked at her, awed. "How did you know to bring those?" It was the same expression she'd had when they were much younger, and Jane claimed to have made something happen by magic.

Jane laughed. "A no-brainer. I always keep them in my bag for plays and museums."

"Wow." Hannah fitted the round metal circles to her eyes and scanned the rows of blue caps and gowns. But after several minutes her hands, still holding the glasses, dropped into her lap. "She's not *there*."

"Of course she is," I said. I held out my hand until she handed me the delicate binoculars. Still trying to improve life for my children, though I doubted I could see anything Hannah hadn't. The dark black balloon of fear I'd felt was growing inside me, threatening to crowd out everything else. *She had to be here.*

I scanned the graduates slowly, row by row, but it was not easy trying to identify individual faces under identical caps. I did not know my own daughter well enough to recognize her body language, though there was plenty of motion. Although I was sure they had been ordered to sit quietly on their folding chairs and face forward, few of them did. The robes dipped and swayed like clusters of bluebirds' wings. Using the opera glasses I could read the messages spelled out in colored tape on some of the caps: "$165,000"; "HIRE ME"; and the usual "HI, MOM!" When I did not pick out Elisa, I went back to the front of the section, trying to focus on blond hair this time. I found one girl who looked like her, but had a long braid down her back.

"Well, this isn't her real graduation," I said finally, handing Jane's opera glasses back to Hannah. "I'm sure we can find her at the arts and sciences diploma ceremony."

"No, she said to come to this one first!"

"Maybe she put her hair up under her cap or something," Jane suggested.

"She *never* wears her hair that way."

The music began a formal march, and a procession of dignitaries climbed onto the platform. One of the men wore the colorful regalia of a Roman Catholic bishop, and I remembered the college's roots. Had Elisa been raised Catholic? When she was a few weeks old she had been baptized Methodist in my father's church. I would have to tell her that.

The ceremony dragged in a way it wouldn't have if I had been able to look down and watch Elisa's reactions. I recognized the name of the commencement speaker, a congressman who was no longer in office, and agreed with what he said about fighting climate change, eradicating disease in foreign countries, and stamping out extremism. As if handing out a classroom assignment, he reminded the graduates that it was now *their* responsibility.

Jane had her eyes closed as if asleep, and Hannah kept pulling out her battered maroon phone to look for a message from Elisa, then frowning and snapping it shut. A woman sitting in front of us whipped around to glare at her, but Hannah didn't notice. Colin had promised her an iPhone for a graduation gift, but Hannah seemed lukewarm about the upgrade.

"Let's go," I said as soon as the last notes of the recessional faded and the aisles were less crowded. Below us happy parents were already swarming the field. "We should wait outside the gym for the next ceremony so we can see everyone who goes in."

"She hates us," Hannah moaned, brushing away a strand of hair that had been released from its ponytail for the occasion. "She's never going to talk to me again!"

"*Stop*," Jane said sharply. "It's not just about you. Why don't you try putting yourself in her place for a change? Maybe at the last minute she couldn't face going through the ceremony without her parents here. Mom told me how upset she was."

I jumped in to agree. "There's so much hype about graduation, it was probably too much to face. They've only been gone a week, Hani. Less."

My daughter turned her fury on us. "Will you two stop! I *get* it. But she said she was going to meet us here. If she'd changed her mind, she would have texted me. But she didn't. That's what I'm talking about!" Her face was turning red, her eyes growing wild.

I grasped her shoulders. "It's okay! Maybe her car broke down. She got a flat tire where there was no one around to help. Anything could have happened." Considering that it was less than a mile that seemed unlikely, but I needed to calm her.

"But she would have—"

"No, Hannah. You can't make guesses about her phone."

"We could check her room," Jane said. "Drive back along the way she would have come. Just to see."

We had just reached the path outside the stadium. It was a beautiful spring day, the sun splashing the leafy campus, red and white azaleas blooming, the dogwood trees making lace curtains over the dark leaves. But I didn't want to be there a moment longer. "That's a good idea. The next ceremony's not for two hours."

"I have the keys," Hannah said.

"You have the keys to her room?" Jane turned, surprised.

"Of course I do. She gave me both keys in case she wasn't back from class yet when I came for a weekend. She has my keys too."

But at the parking garage elevator I realized the implications of going back to Elisa's room. If she was there—and wanted to see us—she would have let Hannah know. If she was not there, it would only raise more questions. Worst of all, if she hadn't been able to handle the Crosleys' deaths and had done something to herself . . . but I wouldn't let that thought take hold.

Chapter Fifteen

GIN FACTORY STREET was half a mile from the campus in a working-class neighborhood that did not seem interested in becoming gentrified. Rossi's Italian Butcher and I Am Your New Cleaners! appeared to have been facing off on the corners for decades. I had been here once before, the late January morning I had learned that Elisa was a student at St. Brennan's and rushed up to Massachusetts. After catching a glimpse of her on campus, I had driven to this street and sat for over an hour waiting for her to return to her dorm.

Today I had no trouble parking in front of the residence hall, sliding in behind Hannah's creaky blue Honda. A sign warned us that there was an hour maximum for nonpermit parking, but I doubted we would be here that long. My best guess was that we would not find Elisa here, an idea that shattered like a dropped glass when Hannah cried, "Look, Mom, there's her car!" She was pointing to a black VW Passat farther up the street.

"Are you sure it's hers?"

"It has her Rhode Island license plates."

Jane, seeing Hannah holding the balloons, moved back to the van and extracted the roses. Even if Elisa had not been able to let us know she would not be at graduation, she would be glad to see Hannah. I thought for a moment about letting her go up alone to not overwhelm Elisa. But then the darkest thought intruded. Sending Hannah up to find her sister's body would be a terrible mistake.

The residence hall had probably been built in the 1920. It had a door with decorative black iron bars and a brass plaque that read "Montfort House." I was sure it had first been a hotel, then purchased by the college to use as a dorm. We crowded into the tiny black-and-white tiled foyer and clustered around the buzzer system. Hannah had her keys out, but I said, "We should ring the room first."

"Well, *duh*."

Behind her, Jane gave me an amused glance.

Hannah jabbed at the button twice.

The lobby stayed silent except for our breathing. We waited another minute, but there was no confirming buzz.

"Try again," I said. "Maybe she was in the bathroom."

When there was no answer a second time, Hannah said, "Let's go up. She's on the fourth floor."

The inner lobby was a collection of faded floral couches, porcelain lamps with tarnished brass bases, coffee tables with magazines that looked decades-old. The room could have passed as the set for a Tennessee Williams play.

Hannah moved quickly to the elevator and pressed the button. The doors opened immediately as if it had been waiting for us.

"Why did she want to live here instead of in her own apartment?" I asked as we reached the fourth floor and followed the frayed maroon runner.

"She wanted to be like everyone else. All her friends live here."

The closer we got to her room, the more frightened I felt. Had I overestimated Elisa's strength? Just because she had sounded calmer the last time I talked to her didn't mean she had accepted the deaths. As a tiny girl she had been resilient, able to deal with setbacks. Though she would campaign tirelessly for what she wanted, disappointment never crushed her for very long. But being denied a trip to the playground was far different from losing both parents at the same time. They had been her world, Ethan especially.

Her comments about guns and shooting that weekend at the house chilled me. What if we unlocked the door and found . . .

"I don't know what we're going to learn if she's not here," Jane complained from behind me. "We should have tried harder to find her on campus."

"This was *your* idea," Hannah reminded her.

"Why don't you let me go in first," I said.

Both my daughters stared at me.

"What are you talking about?" Hannah said. "She's probably left a note for *me*. She knew I was coming."

A note. A cheerful clue at the end of a treasure hunt, explaining everything. But that was Hannah. *Magic or tragic.*

Elisa's room was at the very end of the hallway, on the left.

"Knock first," I warned.

"You think I don't know anything?" Hannah gave me a furious look and banged on the door. We were all at the edge of the precipice.

Hannah waited just a moment, then inserted the key and pushed the door back. But none of us stepped inside.

"Liss?" Hannah called into the silence.

When there was no answer, we did move inside. It was a typical college dorm room, though the layout with one window at the end made me think of a hotel again. There was also an unsettled feeling, as if someone had packed in a hurry. The closet door was ajar, showing gaps and bare hangers, but plenty of clothes were still hung inside. The desk chair was pushed askew as if someone had gotten up quickly to answer the door and never righted it. Yet the desk itself had been wiped clean of books, computer equipment, and photographs.

No, that wasn't completely true. As I moved closer to it, I saw that one photo in a tortoiseshell frame stood alone—the picture taken at our reunion weekend. Colin and I were in the center, with Jane, Jason, Hannah, and Elisa all crowded around us, laughing as we waited for the delayed timer to go off. The fact that Elisa had framed the photograph and displayed it on the desk as her family meant something, didn't it? And yet she had left it behind.

I studied the rest of the room, turning to the single bed that was neatly made. Moving closer, I caught my breath. Sitting as desolately as if he had been abandoned at a bus depot was Sheepie, Elisa's pet lamb since babyhood. It was the stuffed animal I had pressed into her hands at our reunion.

"I don't get it," Hannah cried. "She didn't leave a note or anything!"

I turned away from Elisa's rejection of us. Evidently she believed what she had said on the phone. Because we had insisted on finding her, she had lost her family. We had taken away their lives. Perhaps their deaths had brought her to her senses and had poisoned the brief happy interlude with us, even with Hannah.

Hannah discovered something else. "She left her phone," she gasped, pointing to the top of the dresser. "She didn't take her phone!" In the next moment she was holding the smartphone and scanning it, then punching in keys. She looked over at me, stricken. "All my messages are here, unread. She didn't even get my messages!"

I turned back to the closet and had a vision of Elisa selecting enough clothes for a week or two in Barbados with the Crosleys. But that was impossible. I had talked to her here after they had died. Yet the image would not go away. I had to make myself remember that

Ethan and Sheila were lying in refrigerated boxes in the mortuary.

"Did she ever talk about any relatives from the Crosleys?" I asked Hannah. I knew that Ethan had no siblings, but Sheila might have had brothers and sisters.

"Why would she leave her phone behind?" Jane demanded at the same time.

Hannah's eyes were filling, her fist to her mouth. "I don't know! She would never leave her phone behind. And why is her car still here? Something terrible's happened to her!"

I'd forgotten the car. Besides the phone, that was the most frightening thing of all. I couldn't shake my terror that something catastrophic had happened to her. It might not even be related. She could have been struck down and injured just crossing the street. "What about a purse? Did she use a purse?"

"Yes, it was leather with a lot of little compartments. She got it somewhere in South America."

Then we were opening drawers, sweeping our hands over the closet floor, kneeling to look under the bed. I found a semester's worth of dust, a balled-up white athletic sock. A copy of *Swamplandia!* that might have been bedtime reading.

We could not find the purse anywhere.

That was the worst news yet.

If she was planning to end her life somewhere else, she would have taken her purse to get where she was going or for identification purposes afterward. Still, it didn't explain her missing clothes or photographs. "Was her computer a desk model or a laptop?" I asked Hannah.

"Laptop. But her printer's gone too. And a lot of books. I'm taking her phone!"

"You can't." Jane reached out a hand to stop her. "What if she comes back for it and it's not here? She'd never get your messages then."

Hannah's tears were tracking down her face now. "What's the point? She doesn't *want* to get my messages. She doesn't want to see us again, any of us. She thinks Dad killed her parents and—"

"But that's *crazy*." Jane looked appalled. "Why would she think that?"

I was not surprised that Hannah knew, only that she had not mentioned it immediately or called me when she found out. "Did Elisa tell you that?"

She stared at me as if I were the enemy. "She got a letter from her father saying that if anything happened to him, to blame Dad. And by the time she read it, something *had* happened."

"Hani, listen to me. Your father hasn't done anything to the Crosleys. That was just spite to try and spoil our relationship with Elisa. His dying so soon after was a coincidence. Besides, I talked to Elisa after she got that letter and she certainly wasn't blaming *you*. She didn't want Dad here today, that's true, but she specifically told me she wanted you to come. She wasn't sure about me though." The way I said it, it could have been a joke, but no one smiled. "Do you think her friends know where she is?"

"They're probably at graduation," Hannah said. "Or gone home for the summer."

Had she given away books, clothes, or computer equipment to them before they'd left? I didn't know if that was something she often did or if she had had a darker purpose. If only I'd realized how desperate she was still feeling. If only I had been astute enough to know she should not be left alone. It would have been hard to come up here with everything that had been going on with Colin, and she had acted as if she didn't want me here, but still—I was the parent. *I should have known*. If I had failed her a second time by my carelessness, the assumption that things usually worked out fine. I would never forgive myself. Never.

Hannah laid the phone back on the dresser where she found it, handling it as gently as if it were a rare porcelain teacup.

All I wanted to do was check with the police and local hospitals. Yet I couldn't do that while Hannah was here.

Jane laid the roses on the end of the bed. "No sense in carrying these around."

"Right." Hannah released the balloons she had been clutching for hours. They shot to the ceiling, where they bobbed gently. "Happy Graduation! Congratulations, Graduate!"

I hated the way the roses looked lying in their green florist's paper, too much like highway memorials left where a death had taken place.

"What about Sheepie?" Jane asked suddenly.

I sighed. After we thought that Elisa had drowned in Stratford-upon-Avon so long ago, I had wrapped him up carefully in tissue paper and placed him in a carton with her tiny dresses, toys, and photograph albums. We had unpacked the box last November, and the first time I saw Elisa I had hoped the little stuffed animal would stir some long-buried memory. Obviously Sheepie meant something if she had kept him in the center of her bed.

Still, if she was just going away for a few days, she wouldn't have taken him. She was not a toddler anymore.

I moved to the bed and picked up Sheepie, thrusting him into my bag. "If she doesn't come back for her stuff, he could get tossed out and be lost forever."

"I don't know," Hannah said slowly. "If she comes back and finds he's not here . . ."

"*If* she comes back," said Jane darkly.

That was the question I didn't want to face.

Lost forever.

Chapter Sixteen

A TEARFUL HANNAH wanted to get back on the road to Ithaca, but I insisted that she have something to eat first. None of us wanted to go to the Purple Pig, though I had a brief, hopeful flash of us sitting at a table and Elisa bursting in, full of smiles. But I knew that would not happen now. In the end we stopped at an IHOP. Food not for celebration, but for comfort, for fuel. Food to get us through the next few hours. We ordered pecan pancakes drenched in syrup, sausage patties, and sweet juices instead of coffee.

It was already early afternoon, but the restaurant was crowded. We sat at the table not talking.

Adding more syrup, cutting the sausage with the edge of my fork, I forced myself to eat and tried to get a read on Elisa's room. If she had taken the time to pick out particular clothes to bring and pack up her laptop and printer, it meant she had left of her own accord. Unless she had given those away. But who would want her memorabilia? I could understand her leaving the photo of us behind, but why her smartphone? Sitting in the buzzing restaurant, I realized I should have searched her room more closely.

I hadn't even looked in the wastebasket! Why hadn't I looked at what she was throwing away?

Should I suggest going back? I glanced at my daughters. Jane was picking moodily at her pancake stack, her head bent. Hannah was chasing the last bit of syrup with a sausage bite. Her mouth drooped with desolation and her eyes were sad. I knew I couldn't put them through visiting the room again. Besides, I had to get to the police.

Out in the parking lot I questioned Hannah, making sure she was not too upset to drive back to Ithaca by herself. I had not wanted Elisa to drive back to Boston alone, but once she had gotten here safely I had abandoned her. How long would it take me to learn to do the right thing?

"I guess I'll see you guys at graduation," said Hannah. "*My* graduation. When are you getting there?"

I looked at Jane. She had said she was planning to get to the house Friday night. She and Colin and I would drive up the next morning. "I thought we'd be there around lunchtime Saturday. Is that good? Is there anything going on Saturday night?"

"Just a concert and a dinner for people whose parents can't come."

"We'll go out to dinner somewhere nice," I said, though I was too worried about Elisa to get my pleasure from the idea of food.

Hannah shook her head. "We can't. Everything's already booked."

"There must be a Taco Bell," Jane teased. "We like Southwestern food."

"We'll find something," I said quickly, grasping Hannah in a tight hug.

"It doesn't matter," she said dolefully when I finally released her. "Elisa won't be there."

"You don't know that. It's still a week away."

She didn't bother to answer, just moved toward her car.

"Oh, for God's sake," Jane said when she and I were alone in the van. "Six months ago she didn't even *know* Elisa. Now it's all that matters."

"Well . . ." I wondered if Jane was feeling displaced. "She's really worried by all this. And feeling rejected."

Jane nodded, then demanded, "What's all this about Dad?"

Starting the engine, I told her about the letter Ethan had written Elisa, telling her to blame Colin if anything happened to him.

Jane raised her chin stubbornly. "But how could he know something was going to happen to him? Had Dad threatened him or anything?"

"He says not."

"What do the police think?"

I turned into traffic. "They're still investigating." I didn't have the energy to explain about the boots.

"That's ridiculous! Can you see him splashing gasoline around and setting a fire to kill anyone?"

The trouble was, I could. Oh, not Colin specifically, that was hard to imagine. But after a lifetime of reading novels, taking my worldview from fiction, I believed that most people, when pushed against the wall, were capable of anything. Growing up I had been reminded scornfully by my sister, Patience, more gently by my father, that books were not "real life." Yet one look at the headlines on the CNN Web site—"Parents Turn Daughter in for Sexting" or "Suspect Escapes Through Dog Door"—blurred the line more and more.

IN THE END, Jane took the train from Boston directly to New York City. I pointed out that it was faster than going back to Port Lewis

Haldimand County Public Library
CALEDONIA BRANCH

and taking the train from there, and she quickly agreed. "That way I can at least get some work done," she pointed out.

I drove her to the nearest terminal, on Station Street, hugged her hard, and watched her go safely inside. Then I double-parked in the next block and took out my phone. "Siri, find me the nearest police station."

"Checking . . ."

Not only did she locate one, she guided me expertly to Schroeder Plaza.

The multistory building, all gray stone and glass, was large enough to make me wonder about the crime rate in Boston. Feeling intimidated, I went inside and tried to explain to the woman behind the desk what I wanted. She frowned and directed me elsewhere. After feeling like a package that no one knew where to deliver, I was settled into an interview room. It felt calming, though there were no windows or posters on the plain yellow walls.

I stared at the golden area in front of me, my eyes blurring out of focus, and lost myself in a world of sunshine. Beach days, damp sand from my bathing suit under the towel I was lying on. I was twelve again, lost in *Miracle at Carville*, the story of a young Southern woman engaged to be married who discovers she has leprosy. I was so thoroughly back at the beach that I jumped when the door clicked open. I couldn't remember for a quick moment what I was doing there.

Still escaping into books. . .

Then a man about my age was turning the chair across from me backward and sitting down to face me. He was not in a uniform but a white shirt and a navy striped tie. He smiled. "How can I help you?"

The story ran out of me: Elisa's sudden silence, the missed

Haldimand County Public Library
CALEDONIA BRANCH

graduation, the unsettled state of her dorm room. Her upheaval over the recent deaths of people she was close to. He jotted down a physical description, then went to make the calls I hoped he would. But my beachlike calm had vanished, replaced by a nervous terror that made me sit upright with my hands pressed painfully together. What if he came back bringing terrible news? I could see it clearly, his face a sympathetic mask, a policewoman in tow to offer comfort.

It was 3:25 p.m. when he returned. By himself.

He sat down backward in the chair, the same as before. "Nothing from the hospitals. One unidentified young woman found dead in Castle Island Park but the description is different."

My heart began a terrible tattoo. People looked different in death. It couldn't be Elisa. Not now. Not after what we had been through. "How different?"

"About twenty, but African American. I don't think it's her."

"*Oh*. No." Thank God, thank God! I felt sad for the young woman whose life had been cut short, but all I could think was that it was not my daughter.

"You've checked with her friends?"

"Not yet, no. We just found out and I wanted to check with you . . . first."

He nodded. "No news is good news in this case. Good luck with finding her. It sounds like she's maybe gone off on a whim."

Did he really believe that? I gave him a watery smile. Still, I insisted he take my phone number and let me know if anything happened.

Chapter Seventeen

THE IDEA OF a quantum leap has always intrigued me, the process of a jump from Point A to Point B without having to go through the steps in between. You were in some usual place, then suddenly somewhere else completely without knowing quite how you arrived there. As I crept down Route 95, reaching Connecticut as everyone was leaving work for home, I experienced my own quantum leap. Landing on Point B, I wouldn't believe it at first.

That's crazy.

But if it isn't?

No, it's impossible.

But around Hartford I began to believe it.

By the time I boarded the ferry at Bridgeport and settled into the dark red vinyl booth, I was sure.

I called Frank Marselli immediately.

As soon as he heard my voice, he said, "Ms. Laine, you're putting me in an awkward spot."

"But aren't you part of the investigation?"

"That doesn't mean I can discuss it with you. Especially since—"

My heart began pounding the way it had in Boston. "Since what?"

"Your husband was brought in for questioning. There's an arraignment Monday morning."

The ferry tilted suddenly to the right and I felt as if I would be pitched into the dark gray water. "But *why*?"

"You know that dinner he was attending?"

"Yes?" The retirement dinner for Clifford Mallow. A time of bonhomie, reminiscences, and gift certificates for golf clubs and local restaurants.

"Dr. Fitzhugh was there, but he left early. He told the people he was sitting with that he felt a cold coming on."

"How early?"

"Before ten."

I held on to my phone to keep it from sliding out of my hand. "But how does that prove anything? You said the fire was set in the early hours. Early in the morning."

"It was. But the time of death for the bodies was before midnight. Detective Carew's theory is that he went out there to talk to them and things got out of hand. Then he set the second fire to cover it up."

"But why would he wait several hours?"

"Less chance of someone passing by and reporting the fire too soon? She didn't explain why."

I was going to be sick. I swallowed the pecan pancakes and orange juice that were threatening to erupt, and made myself speak calmly. "Do you have a positive identification?"

"No, but we're getting a warrant in Rhode Island to check the DNA. We have no grounds to search the house otherwise."

"But what about the bad teeth? Can't you ask Elisa if Sheila was dental-phobic?"

Then I remembered. "That's another thing! Elisa's disappeared. She was supposed to graduate from college today and we went up to Boston. But she wasn't at the ceremony. *Or* in her room. Some of her clothes and her laptop and printer were missing, as if she'd started to pack, but . . ." I couldn't think of why she had been interrupted, Except—

He didn't say anything.

"There's only one reason that I can think of she would do that. And that's if the Crosleys came up to get her."

"What are you talking about?"

"Suppose the bodies were badly burned on purpose, so they couldn't be identified and the police assumed it was the Crosleys. What if they staged their own deaths so they wouldn't be arrested for kidnapping and murder?"

How's that for a quantum leap, Frank?

Now that I'd said it aloud it was easy to see the Crosleys arriving in Boston Wednesday and confronting an amazed Elisa. Alive! Her parents alive! The eerie vision I'd had of her selecting clothes from her closet might be true. Of *course* they wouldn't let her bring the photo of us or Sheepie. Perhaps not even her smartphone if they were on the run and did not want to be traced in any way.

"And where did these substitutes come from?" Frank was asking. "The bodies that were burned instead?"

"I don't know. Have you checked for missing people in the area?"

"As a matter of fact, we have an extra body to account for, a man who was beaten and left in Mecox Woods. Let me tell you something, Ms. Laine—Delhi—even when a body is as badly burned as theirs are, the ME can still check out their skull structure, the distance between the eyes, and so on. The person's approximate height."

"You mean like *Gorky Park*."

"*Gorky Park*," he agreed, though I was snobbishly sure he was referring to the movie. "In this case, since we know who the victims were, we can use photographs and physical descriptions. We were able to find their doctor, the doctor who operated and placed two stents in Dr. Crosley's chest three years ago. Everything matches up."

I was stunned. There was no way to fake the results of heart surgery. We were back to the Crosleys lying in the morgue and Colin under suspicion.

"Even if your theory were true, it doesn't let your husband off the hook. He could have set the fire when he thought they were the ones inside."

"Wait! You said that they had been badly burned before the fire outside was set. He wouldn't go inside and incinerate two strangers."

"Which is why it was probably the Crosleys."

My head was spinning like the metal radar bar on deck. This was hopeless. "But in my theory it makes sense for Ethan to write a letter accusing Colin. He was deliberately setting him up to be blamed. They probably planted the boots!" I remembered the sound of a car door, someone walking on the driveway in the middle of the night. Someone returning the mud-caked boots to the back of the house.

"They'd have to know we'd find out eventually."

"By then it wouldn't matter. They'd be far away. With Elisa. You don't understand how much money these people have."

"We're aware of their financial assets," he said dryly. "Even so, why would they leave expensive wedding rings and a priceless watch behind? If they'd staged it, they would have at least taken the watch. Wouldn't you?"

The ferry rocked rhythmically, hypnotically. Something about the Patek Philippe watch bothered me. "Are you sure the watch is genuine? Not a fake?"

That amused him. "You're making a simple situation complicated."

"That's what I'd do. Get a fake watch in Times Square and save the real one." I thought of something then that chilled me through my light cotton blazer. "They aren't *holding* Colin, are they?"

"No. He's no flight risk. They know he'll show for the arraignment."

"You're making a terrible mistake!"

"That's up to the judge."

The world seemed to go dark. I mumbled good-bye, then dialed Colin's phone immediately.

"Hello?" His voice was tired, cautious, even though caller ID undoubtedly told him that it was me.

"Colin, something terrible happened! Elisa wasn't at graduation. We went to the stadium, but she wasn't there. She wasn't in her room either." I described what we'd found and told him about my trip to the police station.

"She wouldn't do anything to hurt herself, she's much too feisty. Did I tell you how she attacked me when I tried to call her? How's Hannah holding up? She's the one you should be worried about."

"Really? She's upset, she's sure Elisa hates us and never wants to see us again."

Colin made a soft noise that I couldn't identify. "Elisa probably went off to visit some friends. She wouldn't think she owes *us* an explanation."

"But we're her parents!"

"Delhi . . ."

"Anyway, I'm worried about you too. There's an arraignment scheduled? Do you have a lawyer?"

"Of course I have a lawyer. Stanton Miles. He thinks the whole thing is ridiculous."

"I hope he's right. Oh, God, Colin, how can this be happening to us? We've always been so careful to keep out of trouble. My father was a *minister*. We don't even cheat on our income tax!"

"Easy, Del. It's just a misunderstanding."

"A *misunderstanding*?" All the shock and terror of the day, Elisa's unexplainable absence, my guilt at failing her yet again, the stress of waiting in a police station to hear the worst, was converging into a whirlpool threatening to pull me under. "Why is everything I do the wrong thing? If I hadn't gone looking for Elisa in the first place—"

"Delhi, stop. Stop that. That ship sailed a long time ago. It's better to know the truth. We'll get through this. I promise."

Even though our relationship felt more like slogging through the dunes than frolicking on the beach, I loved Colin then. He was the only person on earth who loved our children the way I did. More than ever, I had to find out the truth of what had happened.

Chapter Eighteen

EARLY THE NEXT morning, I drove back to Southampton. If there was any answer, it had to be there. I was not sure what I was looking for, but I knew I would recognize it when I found it. It was too early to knock on any doors, so I sat on Dune Road with a large cup of 7–Eleven coffee, watching the Atlantic Ocean. The sun on the water collected diamonds, then gambled them away. The surf smacking the sand left white leis of foam. The water was still too cold for swimming but a few recreational fishermen were standing in the surf casting out lines.

I rolled down my window to breathe in the fresh salt air and tried to create a scenario from the ragged pile of facts in front of me. My theory was right, I *knew* it was right, but I kept coming up against things I could not explain. Like two implanted stents. If what Frank had said was true about facial structure, it was another black mark.

At 8 a.m. I called Mairee Jontra, the Crosleys' caretaker.

"Mairee here!"

"Hey Mairee, this is Delhi Laine. I talked to you about the Crosleys last week? Now I have a different kind of question," I added before we could head back down that path.

"Fire away."

"Are there agencies out here who specifically bring in people from other countries to work? You know, like waitstaff and summer help?"

"There'd have to be, wouldn't there? Especially since so many come from Eastern Europe now. Some restaurants still hire local college kids for waitstaff, but mostly foreigners—pardon my French—for housekeeping and yard work. Are you looking for household help?"

In my next incarnation. "No, I'm not hiring this month."

"It's so hard," she agreed. "I had to let the butler go last week because he was sneaking Oreos."

I laughed. "I have some general questions to ask an agency."

"About the Crosleys?"

"No, this is something else."

"I'll tell you who the main ones are. Have a pen?"

"Sure. Are they out here?"

"Most are based in Manhattan, but they have local representatives who do the hands-on stuff. There is one guy who's local."

"Give me him."

Mairee gave me his name and address, then added, "I doubt he's there yet. How's Elisa doing?"

"Holding up. It's very hard." I thought about telling her that Elisa had disappeared, then decided I wouldn't.

"Poor kid." She sounded as if she meant it.

I DROVE UP South Main Street very slowly. This time I noticed that as the houses got closer to town they were nearer to the road.

The dense hedges and large front yards gave way to sparser cover. Though still large enough to house several dozen people, they had less privacy.

I parked opposite the Crosley house but farther down the street in case the same town cop was on patrol. Being at the house again would be too hard to explain. The yellow tape was drooping, as if the party hadn't been that much fun after all. I wondered if the town would decide the house was a hazard and tear it down.

I wasn't sure what to do next. I could wait and see if anyone came out of the nearby houses or I could begin knocking on doors. This was the weekend, a better chance to find people out here. Yet I hesitated. What would I ask them other than whether they knew the Crosleys and had seen them last week? Had the Crosleys wanted to be seen? No, if they were afraid of being arrested, yes if they wanted people to know they had been here and died.

One decision was made for me when the door to a Tudor mansion across from the Crosley house opened and a miniature woman emerged. She was at least sixty with cropped gray hair, and rounded shoulders in a light blue windbreaker. She was being tugged along by a dancing white poodle.

I leaped out of the van. By the time she reached the sidewalk and turned toward town, I was there too. "Nice morning, isn't it?" I said.

She looked up at me, her beaklike nose and squinting gray-green eyes reminding me of every teacher who had been sorry to have me in her class.

"I was wondering if I could ask you something."

"No." She turned away, adding, "You are not permitted to accost residents on the street!"

Well, damn. I had taken care to dress in a black turtleneck, embroidered denim jacket, and nearly new jeans. My hair was neatly brushed. At least the dog was sniffing, fascinated, at my leg, keeping her owner from moving ahead to the village.

She sighed. "What are you selling?"

"Nothing. I was a friend of the Crosleys. I'm trying to find out some information for their daughter."

She looked beyond me as if I had not spoken.

"The people who lived across from you? Where the fire was?"

Now she finally turned. "I was not acquainted with them." She gave each word its full value. *And I don't want to be acquainted with you.*

Well, we don't have to exchange friendship rings. "Did you see them here before the fire?"

"The police already asked me that. I did not."

"Did you see anyone else around the house? People just loitering?"

"The only unusual thing—" She cut herself off.

I waited. Absently I reached down and stroked the dog's eager head. It had a warm, matted feel like lambs in a petting zoo. I knew she was dying to tell me.

"The only unusual thing . . ." I prompted.

"I don't know why I should tell *you*." She was petulant now. "Where are you from, anyway?"

"Port Lewis." It wasn't the Hamptons, but it had a nice reputation.

"I saw a yellow Ryder truck backed into the driveway late Friday night. Two men were sneaking out items wrapped in quilting as if they didn't want anyone to see. They didn't even have their headlights on! I only saw them because Mimi has to go out one more time before bed."

If it had been one of my neighbors' homes, I would have crossed the road to make sure they were not thieves with a moving van stripping the house of valuables.

"Did they see you?" I reminded myself that confronting them would not have been the best idea.

"No, I don't think so. They were busy with what they were doing."

I realized we were whispering. "Could you see what they looked like?"

"It was too dark. At first, after the fire, I thought it was fortunate that they had removed the valuables the day before. Then I realized it was part of an insurance scam." Her eyes held mine, indicating that people were no better than she imagined them to be.

Mimi had abandoned my leg and was now tugging her leash in the original direction of town.

"But you didn't mention it to the police?"

She looked affronted. "I answered the questions I was asked."

Then she and Mimi were gone.

AT NINE I drove to At Your Service. If Mairee were any example, year-rounders started their days early. The agency was located in a clapboard house, gray boards with white trim. The only decoration was on a sign in the yard, the silhouette of a butler bowing.

I thought of how Poodle Lady had been scornful of my attire and wondered if I should have phoned instead.

Too late. I had already knocked on the white wooden door. Maybe they would think I was looking for a job in service.

The man who opened the door would never have been mistaken for the butler. He was about fifty and had the confidence of someone who, though not wealthy himself, would be comfortable around the likes of Ralph Lauren or Donald Trump. More than comfortable, because he understood them a lot better than they did him.

I liked his smile and his perfectly woven fair hair. He looked relaxed in a kelly green Izod polo shirt and khaki chinos.

"How can I help you? You're a reporter from *Dan's Papers*?"

He was good. "No, but I did come for some information. Can you tell my age too?"

He laughed. "I didn't figure you for someone needing a pool man. But I've been wrong before."

He introduced himself as Patrick Leahy, brought me into a dollhouse-sized living room, and gestured me onto an apricot-striped settee. Then he took a down-filled chair across the way and looked interested. This was not a man needing customers. Instead he seemed to welcome my visit as a break from his routine.

"How did you find me?" he asked.

Were you lost? "Mairee Jontra gave me your information."

"Mairee. What a pet. Really. How can I help you?"

"Do you place a lot of foreign students in summer jobs?"

He shook his head. "Not really. They can only get a three-month visa so they don't get here until Memorial Day and leave before Labor Day."

"But there must be people who are here for a longer time," I said.

"Of course. Permanent workers have green cards. Life doesn't shut down out here in September."

"How would I find out if any of them had stopped showing up at work?"

He laughed then, a short bark like a seal who has seen a woman in a funny hat. "Seriously? You'd have to canvass a thousand restaurants, nurseries, and motels. Even then you wouldn't know the real story, whether they'd gone back home or just gotten fed up. They aren't known for giving two weeks' notice. Are you looking for someone in particular?"

"No. Just . . ." Suddenly it seemed hopeless. I'd thought the Crosleys might have picked someone transient, someone who would not be easily missed. If the people were here illegally, their disappearance might not even be reported to the police. Even if I came across two people who had gone missing around the time of the Crosley fire, that did not mean they had been used as sacrificial lambs. "Do workers live in special areas?"

He looked at me thoughtfully and I realized it was a touchy question. Rents on Long Island were high and wages tiny. It was a pretty thought that each did his or her fair share, rich and poor living together as cozily as an Amish community. A pretty thought and a pretty fiction.

"Some places like Gurney's Inn provide their own housing, dormitory style. And people can always rent places together in Springs or Riverhead. Converted summer bungalows or motels that went belly-up."

"Do the people who work here really live an hour away? Isn't there anywhere around Southampton?"

He sighed. "There's some Section 8 housing off Route 27." I knew he was referring to program that provided rent subsidies for low-income families. "It's just a few blocks where landlords have agreed to the program and a place where other workers rent rooms in houses." He described where it was. "It would help if I knew what you wanted."

"It would help if *I* knew what I wanted. Businesses who hired workers from you wouldn't contact you if any of them went missing?"

"Not after the first week or two. We're basically an employment agency." He reconsidered. "We might hear from private individuals where we placed a nanny or cook. They'd be upset and blaming us." He pressed the back of his hand to his forehead dramatically. "I detest nannies! Give me an illegal gardener any time."

Something stirred at his comment. "Any nanny problems recently?"

"No. Not since last Christmas."

False alarm.

Chapter Nineteen

BACK IN THE van, I settled my phone on the seat beside me. If you needed spare bodies, where else would you look? Funeral homes, of course, where people were already dead. But surely someone would notice if a body went missing. The media loved stories like that. A few years ago there had been a scandal when a nearby pet cemetery collected money for individual burial plots, then stashed the animals in a mass grave.

Certainly a funeral home employee would check before trundling a casket to the crematorium or releasing it to a church. Yet employees could be bribed to keep quiet or even paid to help in the transport.

I watched an open truck loaded with a riding mower and other landscaping equipment go past, several dark-skinned workers balancing among the machines. Surely a medical examiner would be able to tell how long a person had been dead, especially if they were filled with embalming fluid. But in that case, why use them at all?

The alternative, that a man and woman had been burned alive, would make the Crosleys killers again. Would they go to those lengths to protect themselves from being tracked down and prosecuted, exposed for what they were? Not unless they could also make Colin appear guilty and send him to jail. That would ruin our lives a second time and permanently estrange Elisa from our family.

I liked that theory, though it had far too many problems. Yet what else did I have?

I started the van and drove farther up Main Street to Route 27. I had long passed the charming clothing shops, the galleries filled with beautiful art, the upscale real estate agencies whose properties were too expensive to list their prices in the window photographs. The houses out my window were becoming increasingly modest.

If I had not been told where to find the Section 8 housing, I doubt I would have stumbled on it on my own. The homes did not look any different from those in other parts of Long Island. Many of them were well-tended with just a few hints that too many people lived there. In one scruffy yard there was a clutch of rusting cars missing tires. In front of another house there was a dirty white couch, several chairs, and a coffee table, as if its residents didn't understand the difference between indoor and outdoor furniture.

I knew that I needed to knock on doors and find out if anyone was missing, an activity that seemed time-consuming and probably futile. People would be suspicious of me. I would have to keep reminding them that I was not selling anything or collecting for a charity. At least I wasn't dressed like anyone official, a social worker or immigration agent.

I remembered the word for "missing" in Spanish, *perdu*, but wasn't sure I could piece together a coherent conversation. Once again it all seemed too much. Then I made myself remember Colin and the arraignment hearing Monday. I thought of all the things I had read about innocent people being railroaded for crimes they hadn't committed. Even if Colin were acquitted, Elisa would never believe he had not been responsible. Our family would never be the same.

Sitting on Flanders Road, thinking about the best way to approach people, I thought about the police officers I knew. Frank Marselli had great integrity and was devoted to his work. He would scorn any attempts at bribery or someone trying to coerce him into an arrest he did not believe in. But if a suspect seemed to fit a crime, if there was any evidence at all, he would look no further. Was Ruth Carew even worse?

The question was enough to make me pick up my bag, climb out of the van, and lock the door. If I had to spend every minute until Monday morning knocking on doors in the Hamptons, then I would do it.

The Section 8 neighborhood consisted of two long parallel streets, Flanders and Madison, connected at the far end by a horseshoe curve. At the first two houses, there was no answer when I knocked. The next five brought me puzzled expressions and denials that anyone who lived there was missing. Nobody invited me in for coffee or told me to have a nice day. I pushed on, walking up every path, knocking on every door, knowing how I must look to anyone watching. I was tempted to skip the houses with mowed lawns and yard ornaments, houses with only one late-model car in the driveway, but I persisted. Just because they appeared to be single-family homes, not immigrant housing, did not make them exempt.

Finally at the end of Flanders Road where it curved into Madison, I saw a large white house even more in need of paint than mine. Several front porch floorboards were broken off at the ends and two small boys were building a tiny fortress in the dirt where there should have been grass. I glanced at the porch, expecting to find their caretaker, but I could see no one. So I smiled at them and approached the door.

The young woman who answered me in Spanish was wearing a yellow sweatshirt with a Corona logo, and expecting a baby very soon.

"*Hola. Como estas hoy?*" I ventured.

"Okay." But she did not sound sure. "Are you the teacher?" she asked in Spanish, looking around me at the boys.

"No. I'm looking for someone who is lost. A missing person."

"A missing person?"

"Someone who did not come home when they should have. Someone who has disappeared."

"You mean—like Kathleen?"

Was it possible? I pressed down my tremor of excitement, reminding myself that this was a transient population. "When did she leave you?" My Spanish was not very good.

"Only on the weekend. She went with a man."

"A man? Do you know him?"

She frowned as if trying to figure out what I had said. "The man—I did not see the man."

"Did she meet him somewhere? Like a restaurant?"

She nodded. But I could tell she was already afraid she had said too much.

The boys, about five and seven, had decided they needed her attention. They clumped up the porch stairs, slipped around me, then pushed at her, demanding cupcakes, chips, Coca-Cola. I don't dislike children, but I wished they'd go away.

"And she never came home?" I prodded.

A sudden torrent of Spanish. She seemed to be telling me that Kathleen's roommate, Moira, had thought she was staying with the man and laughed about it. But then on Monday someone from the hotel where Kathleen worked called to find out where she was. "She did not come back for her clothes."

"Can I see her room?"

"But—Moira is there."

Even better.

"She is not a friendly person. Not like Kathleen."

"That's okay. I just want to talk to her. What's your name?"

She cradled her bulge of stomach before deciding to trust me. "Valentina."

I followed Valentina deeper into the house, through an institutional-style kitchen to a narrow wooden staircase that appeared to have once been the servants' stairs. The kitchen counters seemed sectioned off with individual collections of canned goods in stacks. I imagined the refrigerator was similarly divided, the food carefully labeled.

We climbed the stairs and came out in a hall with a tattered brown carpet and closed doors, each with a different style padlock. There was an odor I couldn't identify, the chaotic present at war with the stale past.

Halfway down the hall, Valentina knocked on a door.

An exasperated "Yes?" from inside the room.

"Yes, hello," I called. "Are you Moira?"

Perhaps because I was speaking English, she opened the door quickly.

Moira was my height and seemed close to my age but very thin, her blackbird-wing hair chopped unevenly around a pretty face. She reminded me of WPA photographs of exhausted Okies in the 1930s. Not just exhausted, but with the resignation that nothing good would ever happen again.

"Hi, I'm Delhi Laine. I'm looking for Kathleen."

"She's not here." She said it matter-of-factly, as if that closed any interrogation.

"Has she been home since last Saturday night?"

She peered at me more closely. She had light blue eyes framed by black lashes that most women could only dream of having. "Do you know where she is?"

"Can I come in?"

She pulled the door wider. I looked behind me as I stepped inside, but Valentina had vanished.

The room was not tiny, but small for two adults, with just one uncurtained window at the end. Two single beds, two dressers, an overstuffed boudoir chair of faded roses. Moira motioned me to the chair and sat on the edge of a bed opposite. Unlike the hall, this room had the fresh scent of coconuts. I breathed more deeply.

"You know where Kay is?" she said, searching my face for the answer.

"I'm not sure. Have you lived here long?"

"Too long. Can I smoke? Do you mind, I mean? They don't like it here, but I'm careful."

Her voice had a pleasant Irish lilt despite her dour expression. "We had jobs at home, *good* jobs. I was in tech, she was an estate agent. We were set for life. But the Internet moved on and nobody could buy a house anymore. Kay's husband wanted a divorce—after twenty years! So we came here to find a better life." She gave a laugh as if the joke had been on them. She seemed desperate to make me understand that she did not belong in this house, with these people.

"What kind of work do you do?" I asked.

"Kay is a hotel receptionist. I do the books for a nursery. A grower. It's not bad, except for the money. In Dublin I had my own flat!"

"What's your rent here?"

"Eight hundred dollars. Each."

"Yikes." Sixteen hundred dollars a month for *this* room, shared kitchen and bath, shared everything else.

"You don't know of somewhere else do you?" She was pleading with me now. "This is no way for two middle-aged women to live!"

I wanted to save her. "I'll ask around. There has to be something better."

"The thing is, if Kay doesn't come back before the first, they'll stick somebody else in here. She was frantic to meet a good man, I hope to sweet Jesus she has, but it puts *me* in the crapper."

"Do you think that's what happened?"

"Nah. That's not Kay. She has my mobile, she'd let me know if something good had happened." Her intent, blue-eyed stare. "You know something about her. Don't you?"

Where to begin? There was nowhere to begin. "Do you have a photo I could see?"

Moira pushed off the bed and went to a dresser, then came back and handed me a five-by-seven framed photograph. Two smiling younger women, probably taken when they were still in Ireland. Moira just as thin but happier. And a dark-haired, brown-eyed woman who could have been Sheila Crosley's sister.

Chapter Twenty

I HAD TO let the police know, both about the Crosleys moving valuables out of the house and about Kathleen. It was too much of a coincidence that she would disappear the same night as the fire and not be heard from since. But which police? I couldn't keep using Frank Marselli as a conduit. Even if I'd wanted to, he wouldn't let me. No, I had to call Ruth Carew. I asked Siri to get me the number for Homicide.

I hoped that I could just leave a long message at her extension—it was Saturday, after all—but she answered the phone.

"Carew." She sounded impatient, as if I was interrupting something important.

"Hi, this is Delhi Laine. Colin Fitzhugh's wife?"

"Oh. Good. I need to ask you some things. I was planning to stop by your house."

"Okay."

"Why did you vacuum your van?"

A jolt. How could they tell it had been done so recently? "I always vacuum my van *and* my work space. I'm a rare book dealer. I can't have dust around." It was a lie but I didn't care.

"Did your husband use your van the night of the fire?"

"No."

"Without your knowledge?"

"I have the only key."

"No one has just one key."

"My son, Jason, lost the other one."

She sighed. "Did you research accelerants on your laptop?"

"This is ridiculous, you know?"

"Just answer the question please."

As if I would admit it to you if I had. "No. I didn't. I called to give you some information you missed."

"Wait, I'm not done. What can you tell me about a Micah Clancy?"

"Micah?" So DCI Sampson had followed through. "Well—Micah was the son of the woman who kidnapped my daughter from the park in Stratford. There's another son, Nick."

"Has Micah Clancy been in touch with you since he's been in New York?"

"Micah's in New York?" I couldn't have been more surprised if she had said he was taking the first flight into space.

"He's here to film a TV series set in Queens. You knew he was an actor?"

"No." Yet why should I be surprised? His mother had been a member of the Royal Shakespeare Company. Micah had been tall and black-haired with eyes as deep blue as the Irish Sea, as crisply attractive as a young Paul Newman. Hearing he was an actor made me wonder now if he had been wearing tinted lenses.

"Mr. Clancy says he never heard of the Crosleys."

A stab of surprise. "I called him in February to tell him who they were. What about his brother, Nick? Is he here?"

"Mr. Clancy negotiated a small part for him on the show."

"Wonderful." Nick Clancy was a thug. He drank too much, dressed up as William Shakespeare to extort money from tourists, and had a chip on his shoulder the size of a small child. He was also handicapped by a high-pitched voice, an unpleasant whine. "I doubt if they gave him a speaking part."

"What?"

"Nothing. Nick's the one you should be looking at." I hesitated then. Did this invalidate my new information? I decided it did not. "I was talking to the woman who lives across the street from the Crosleys, in the Tudor house? She told me that two men in a moving van took a lot of stuff out of the house the night before the fire. She made it sound like they were removing valuables." Okay, that was my interpretation. But why else would you sneak things out in the dark of night?

"What did she say?"

I repeated it.

"But why would she tell *you* this instead of the police?"

"She said you didn't ask. She's—"

"No, why was she talking to you at all? Were you out at the crime scene?" She sounded as if I had been shoplifting at Tiffany's.

"What do you expect me to do when you're threatening my family? I have a right to find out anything I can. Anyway, there's something else. Now I'm wondering if it was actually the Crosleys who died in that fire. Too many things don't add up." She didn't break in to object, so I listed them for her. "Ethan's accusing my husband *before* the fact and then moving their valuables out. That's what you would do if you were going to burn your own house down."

"*Ms. Laine—*"

I didn't let her stop me. "I went to the neighborhood where foreign workers live and asked around. I found a woman from Ireland who looked exactly like Sheila Crosley. She disappeared the night of the fire and hasn't been heard from since."

"And you think she was burned in the fire in the Crosley home."

"I know it's a long shot. But I think they found a man to substitute for Ethan too."

An audible sigh. "Ms. Laine, there are so many things wrong with that theory that I don't know where to begin. So I won't. But you've got to stop this! You're interfering with police business. You can't conduct your own investigation. You *cannot* go around interrogating witnesses as if you're the police."

"I'm not saying I'm from the police. If I were a private investigator or a newspaper reporter you couldn't stop me from asking questions. You're going after my husband and it's the wrong thing to do!" They hadn't even gotten important information from the neighbors.

"If I hear about you questioning anyone else, I'll have you cited. Stay out of Southampton!"

I knew she had no legal grounds. But I had to have her investigate what I was telling her. "Will you at least think about the Irish woman? I have all her information."

An exaggerated sigh. "Frank Marselli told me that you like to play detective. But I'm in charge of this investigation and I don't need any help."

Play detective? Frank said that I liked to *play detective*? When I wasn't baking cookies, I dabbled in crime? I broke the connection, ready to kill them both.

Chapter Twenty-One

NEVERTHELESS, I LEFT Southampton. I hadn't found the missing man, but I told myself that finding him was probably impossible anyway—like going to a book sale and trying to find a specific novel published in the 1950s. In the unlikely event that I located a man who looked like Ethan Crosley and had disappeared that night, I would not be able to convince the police anyway. Or maybe I was just tired of knocking on doors.

When I came into Port Lewis Books, Susie glanced up from behind the counter and smiled at me weakly. She did not look any happier than she had a week earlier.

"Hey," I said. "Are you okay?"

She shook her head and plucked at a large argyle sweater, probably her husband, Paul's. I realized it was meant to hide her dawning pregnancy.

That thought took me somewhere unexpected. The weekend in March that all the children were home, the family finally complete, had felt like going up in the attic and finding a Shakespearean folio. With a full house, Colin and I, the happy parents, were forced into the matrimonial bed. It had been me, I admitted to myself, who had been caught up in the fantasy that now the family was miraculously repaired we could go back and recapture the lives we had been meant to live. It was not impossible to have another baby at forty-five, a symbol of a fruitful beginning.

By the time my period came three weeks later I already understood that a baby would only complicate life. It would be the answer to nothing. Yet for several days after I still felt times of sadness for what might have been.

"What happened?" I asked Susie. Had she miscarried?

No, her round face still shone with new life.

Probably her husband, Paul, was insisting that she quit working at the bookstore now that she was expecting. He had been opposed to her working in the shop from the moment I mentioned it. His plan was for her to continue staying home, chained to the computer, selling worthless books on eBay. He had been forced to take a job at Home Depot last fall to keep from losing their cottage to foreclosure, but he had vowed to stop as soon as their book business "took off."

Which would never happen. Susie and Paul Pevney were as low as you can get on the bookseller tree, so far down that the other Long Island dealers called them the Hoovers. The name reflected their practice of coming in at the end of a book sale and vacuuming up the dregs that the organizers were worried about having to dispose of: movie star biographies, fad diets, the James Patterson novel that everyone had already read. The sale organizers were practically ready to pay the Pevneys to cart them away.

And Paul expected Susie to fritter her life away trying to sell those books. One reason I had campaigned for her to work in the bookstore and earn a regular salary was because she was so anxious to move ahead and start a family. She had pointed out to me more than once that a gerbil on a wheel was having more fun out of life than she did.

"Does Paul want you to quit working here?"

"Well, he'd always be happy with that. But—it's even worse." Susie's voice caught and her glasses glinted as she checked the door to make sure no new customers were coming in. Those already here were settled in, browsing as contentedly as a herd of Guernseys. "I thought he'd be excited about the baby, you know? We're already in our thirties! But he's saying I should put it off a few years." She pulled off her glasses to see me better, and her large brown eyes locked onto mine.

"Wait. Putting it off is what you do when you're still making a decision, not . . . He knows you're pregnant, right?"

She nodded, her face as stricken as a little girl's who's had her birthday party postponed.

"You mean he wants you to have an abortion." The words sounded ugly in that traditional room.

"He says we can try again in three or four years. As soon as our *business* is established."

I pressed my lips together as if applying ChapStick, to keep myself from saying something I would regret later. Paul Pevney was even crazier than I thought. Maybe not crazy in the way of shooting up a Home Depot, but it was hardly normal to think of your own child as disposable as an old shirt, one that could be replaced when you wanted a new one.

Susie's full lower lip trembled. "He says we should have talked about it first."

"You must have talked about it."

"Well, we did when we got married, we both said we wanted

kids. But then he'd get mad when I'd bring it up. So I didn't. But this is what women do. Have babies!"

Maybe in 1940s romantic comedies where Cary Grant comes home from his steady job and is surprised and delighted to hear Mrs. Grant's news.

"He thought I was still on the pill. But it was time." Her chin jerked and I remembered how stubborn she could be.

It must have struck Paul like a sack of wet cement. "He probably just needs time to get used to the idea."

"I don't know, Delhi. He really wants me to—put it off."

"Can't you go back home till the baby comes?" Surely returning to South Dakota, back to the pioneer stock that had created her, would give her what she needed. I had an image of her family coming together for Saturday night suppers and rodeos, observing the rituals of birth and death.

Susie's hand, still holding the receipt pen, jerked. "Home? You mean to Huron? Why would I do *that*?"

I felt my footing on the polished oak floor slip a little. "I thought you missed your family. You were so happy when you came back from seeing them at Thanksgiving."

"Of course. I love them. But I hated growing up there. Anyway, Paul is my husband and I understand him. We've been married eleven years!"

I put my hand out, but didn't quite touch her. "Okay, but you still have time. You don't have to do anything yet."

She nodded. "I don't have a doctor's appointment for two weeks."

"Good. Do you want me to go with you? Sometimes it helps to have someone else there."

"No. I was going to ask you to mind the store."

"Of course. Whatever you want."

I turned away from the counter just as my iPhone rang. Groping around, I pulled it out of my bag. Hannah's number flashed up at me.

"Hi, honey."

"Mom? I just heard from Elisa. She's okay!"

"Oh, thank God!" I stumbled over to a leather wing chair and sank into it. "Thank *God*. Thank God. What did she say?"

"Nothing. She just sent me a text saying she was okay."

"She didn't say what happened to her at graduation? What did she say exactly?"

Hannah sighed. "She said, 'I'm okay. Be careful.'"

"That's it? She told *you* to be careful? Be careful about what?"

"She didn't say."

Be careful. What did that mean? If Elisa was in danger, was she afraid Hannah would be next? No, she had said she was okay. But did "okay" mean safe or just alive?

"Did you text her back?"

"How could I? She left her phone behind, remember?"

It was suddenly chilly in the bookstore. "She could have gone back for it."

"Well, she didn't. She was using another number. It flashed and then disappeared. I don't have one of those fancy phones like you and Jane."

"You will. But what happened when you tried to retrieve it?"

"How do you do that?"

I sighed. I didn't know what to tell her. I barely understood my own new phone. "How did the number start?"

"Nine-something."

"Could it be 917?" The area code flashed in my mind though it wasn't by magic. Most New York City cell phone numbers seemed to start with 917 including my sister, Patience's.

"Yes! That was it. I noticed it especially because I didn't know who'd be texting me from a strange area code. But I can't remember the rest."

"She signed her name, though."

"No . . ."

I stared at my phone, my Christmas present from Colin that I was still learning how to use, and debated what to say next. An anonymous text from a strange phone had to be a misdial. But Hannah was so easily crushed, so excited that Elisa had contacted her, that I couldn't point that out. Sometimes I felt as if I'd spent my life popping her fantasy balloons.

She read my silence as disagreement anyway. "I know what you're thinking, but it *was* her. Who else would text me to say she was okay? I'm her *twin*. I know when she's trying to reach me."

Perhaps that was true. "Okay then, but you should pay attention to what she said about being careful. Don't go off by yourself anywhere deserted. Look out for cars when you're crossing the road. Just—be careful."

"I will. But why is she being so mysterious?"

"I don't know." But I could think of several possibilities, none of which I wanted to share.

Chapter Twenty-Two

THE TIME BETWEEN that Saturday afternoon and Colin's arraignment Monday morning was slow torture. I was as jumpy as a frightened cat, unable to concentrate on what I was doing for more than a minute or two. I tried listing the art catalogs I had bought earlier in the week, and wrapping sold books to mail, but my mind kept slipping into lurid scenarios: visiting Colin in jail when I wasn't fighting for his conviction to be overturned. I saw myself latching on to every encouraging wisp, trying to keep his hope alive. But it wouldn't work. I saw him behind the glass, hulking and unkempt, mumbling into one of those phones. Hannah would have dropped out of vet school and a successful life and we would never see Elisa again.

Colin, meanwhile, was away for the weekend at an archeological conference in New Haven. I knew that he had to go, he was part of a panel discussion, but it left me to obsess on my own. I didn't begrudge him the distraction the conference would be or the comfort of being with friends and colleagues, though I knew Ethan's death would be a lively topic. But no one yet knew that Colin was being linked to the fire. After Monday that would change.

On Monday morning, Colin and I drove silently to Central Islip in my van. We were taking my van so that if bail was denied, his precious car would not be stranded in the parking lot. Although he would not admit it, he did not trust me to drive the BMW home. I realized how upset he was when he didn't even complain about the condition of my van. Because it was my mini office, there were loose books, umbrellas, and thermal cups I never remembered to take back inside to refill. Although he hated artificial scents like the vanilla given off by the tree that dangled from my rearview mirror, he had not even mentioned it.

Yet Colin did not look as frantic as I felt. His trim white beard and tiny rimless glasses made him look, as always, like Santa Claus out of costume. Today he was wearing a lightweight tan suit and a yellow tie with brown dots. I tried to assess what a judge would think of that tie. Too frivolous? As if he didn't take going to court seriously enough? Yet Colin appeared sober and learned, a responsible citizen, so maybe the tie would be okay. I planned to fade into the background. I was dressed in black slacks, a cotton blazer, and a white shirt Jane had left behind. My wild hair was pulled into a sober twist.

The Cohalan Court Complex had been built in 1991 on the outskirts of the struggling town of Central Islip. The anonymous beige buildings rose out of a neighborhood of tract houses, check-cashing storefronts, and bodegas. The town was a haven for newly arrived immigrants. Neon palm trees and smiling yellow suns glowed from grocery store windows, but nothing else made you think of days at the beach.

Even though we were early—I had been awake and ready to go since 4 a.m.—the lobby of the Criminal Court building was jammed. It was easy to identify the lawyers, the only people wearing suits and carrying briefcases. Next to them, Colin and I were the most respectable-looking people in the lobby. I glanced around critically. Why would someone show up for a court appearance in a T-shirt that read "Beer Gut" with an arrow pointing at the overhang? Why hadn't anyone told that clutch of teenage boys in matching silk jackets with skulls on the back that judges weren't impressed by gang solidarity?

I also frowned at the number of small children running wild, darting in and out of the lines of people and stopping to stare up at security guards. Their mothers were on cell phones or deep in conversations with other neglectful mothers.

No, I was not in a good frame of mind.

Colin and I were midway through the line that snaked to the metal detectors when Colin's lawyer, Stanton Miles, hurried in. He planted himself in front of Colin and glanced around, disgusted. "The low end of the gene pool. Come on, we can go right in. We're in Part 17."

I hadn't seen Stanton since a Christmas party five years ago, but he had not changed very much. The adjective that came to my mind was smooth: smooth even features, smooth dark gray suit. I felt that if I put out a hand and touched his cheek it would feel like silk.

After shaking Colin's hand, Stanton turned to me. "Delhi! I didn't know that you'd be here today. Not much will be happening."

"Really?" I was lifted on the wings of hope so quickly that I only then understood the depth of my fears. "I thought they might— you know . . ."

"No, no, they won't hold him. He'll be ROR'ed for now. It's all ridiculous. Every year it gets more ridiculous."

I was desperate to believe Stanton. I had done some research of my own and knew he was talking about "released on own recognizance." I had also read that granting bail, much less ROR, was rare in premeditated murder cases.

Stanton sprang us from the line and escorted us to a guard

with a metal detector. Then we headed down a corridor. Given the size of the four-story building, the courtroom was smaller than I could have imagined. Its pale wooden benches were barely filled and Stanton settled us halfway down on the aisle. As we waited, groups of two and three people began straggling in.

"I think we'll be first," Stanton leaned over to tell us. "They have to bring some of the defendants from the holding cells, and that won't be before eleven."

I shuddered.

At 10 a.m., after we had waited for a restless hour, we were instructed to rise, and Judge Cooperman took the bench. I hadn't known what to expect. He looked to be in his sixties, with gray hair that had thinned even at the temples. His glasses were invisible unless he turned his head to one side. A black robe can look stagy on some people—professors in an academic procession, for instance. This judge's robe seemed as natural to him as an old cardigan. He gave a brief nod, a smile that reached no one, and settled himself to face us.

Two men and a woman, obviously lawyers, took their places at a table to the right. I decided they were from the district attorney's office. *The enemy.*

Perhaps because I had never been in a courtroom before—I'd been excused from jury duty twice because we were out of the country—I sat with my hands jammed in my lap to try to calm myself. I lived in fear of being sued, shuddering at stories of innocent people getting tangled in nightmare situations and spending thousands of dollars trying to extricate themselves. Even glimpsing an official seal on an envelope made my heart race. I got very few complaints about the books I sold, but when I did I offered a refund right away.

Yet despite all my precautions, I was trapped in a web that I could not have imagined.

As Stanton had predicted, our case was called first, and he and Colin rose and walked to the front. The woman lawyer stood up as well, but did not leave her place at the table. I disliked everything about her, from her short, slicked-back hair to her frumpy navy suit. I condemned her for not wearing makeup though I rarely did myself.

For a minute the judge looked down, reading a sheet of paper that his clerk had handed him. Then he looked up. "Counsel, has your client read the criminal complaint?"

"Yes, he has, Judge."

The judge turned to Colin. "You have been accused of one of the most serious crimes known to mankind, premeditated murder. The State asserts that you cold-bloodedly dowsed two people with an accelerant, people you have known for many years, watched them burn, then went outside and"—he scowled at the paper—"several hours later set fire to their home. This was allegedly in revenge for your daughter's kidnapping nineteen years ago. How do you plead?"

"Not guilty." Colin's voice was calm. Too calm? Maybe the judge would think he was a sociopath without emotion.

I imagined myself up there instead. *Listen, Judge, whatever that paper says, I didn't do it I would never set anyone on fire, much less stand there and watch them burn! This is all a terrible mistake.* I would continue babbling until they led me away.

Judge Cooperman turned to the prosecutor and regarded her. His gold-rimmed glasses were visible now.

"Good morning, Ms. Turnelli. Let me say first that I find the State's case remarkably thin. I notice that the principals were in possession of crystal balls. Dr. Crosley gazed into his and saw that he would suffer grievous injury at the hands of Dr. Fitzhugh—despite the fact that he had not seen him for nearly twenty years. Dr. Fitzhugh gazed into his and saw that Ethan and Sheila Crosley were not at home in Rhode Island or in Barbados, but staying at a vacation house in Southampton.

"How else could he have known after all these years except by magic, even the address where to find them? The Internet perhaps, but there is no evidence from the State that a search for that information was found on Dr. Fitzhugh's computers. Tell me, Ms. Turnelli, what did the police find from the forensic examination of Dr. Fitzhugh's automobile and place of residence? I assume such a search was conducted."

I could see only the prosecutor's profile, but I was happy that her cheeks seemed to redden. *Tell him the truth, you idiot!* "Nothing substantial, Your Honor. But—"

He peered at her. "No trace evidence at all?"

"No sir. But the boots—"

I winced, but the judge interrupted her.

"Ah, the boots. A pair of common rubber boots left outside a home where Dr. Fitzhugh no longer lives. That suggests to me that someone not knowing that fact could have planted them there. Has that not occurred to anyone else?"

Me, me! It occurred to me, I wanted to shout.

Ms. Turnelli looked down sullenly but did not answer.

He leaned back in his leather swivel chair and sighed. "If this weren't such a serious case, I'd be tempted to dismiss this complaint. I doubt that a grand jury would return a true bill based on what's here." He slapped the paper with the back of his hand, startling the room.

"Your Honor, we are pursuing other avenues, such as Colin

Fitzhugh's trip to Rhode Island in April to confront Dr. Crosley. I believe that by the time the case gets to a grand jury, the evidence will be considerable. We are asking for no bail as befits a capital offense."

I pressed my hands together, shocked. How did they know about Colin's attempt to confront Ethan? Would the people he spoke to in Rhode Island have to come down and testify? What if they were Ethan's friends, and wanted to avenge his death? What if they *lied*?

The judge sighed. "Ms. Turnelli, my duty is to make an assessment based on the evidence in your complaint, not some pie-in-the-sky you hope to feed us at a later date."

Someone in the front snickered.

Stanton Miles finally stepped forward. "Judge, we move that you dismiss the bill of criminal complaint based on insufficient evidence."

"Motion denied, Counsel."

I slumped back against the bench. From the way the judge had been attacking the prosecution's case, I'd thought he was on our side. Maybe he had been playing a game with her that had nothing to do with us, a game that he let her win at the end. So much for my hope of Colin walking out of here free.

"Your Honor, Dr. Fitzhugh is a tenured member of the Stony Brook University faculty and has never been charged with a felony or misdemeanor, not even a speeding summons. He is a noted archeologist whose behavior has always been exemplary. He owns property and he has four children. The police are holding his passport, so he could not leave the country even if he wanted to."

"Hitler had a pet kitten," the judge mused.

Stanton was undeterred. "Dr. Fitzhugh is no flight risk. Furthermore, there is simply no physical evidence to place him at the scene of the fire, nothing incriminating on his computer or in his home or car as Your Honor has pointed out. He did not drive to Southampton the night of the crime. Based on this fairy tale, I'm requesting that Dr. Fitzhugh be released on his own recognizance."

"Granted." Judge Cooperman lifted his gavel but Ms. Turnelli was lifting an arm too.

"Objection! We are in the process of gathering more information that will lead to a stronger indictment."

"Overruled. Next case."

I COULDN'T BELIEVE that we were walking up the aisle and out of the courtroom, that Colin was walking next to me and on his way home. My legs seemed weightless as we pushed through the swinging doors. A man and a woman close to my age jumped up and followed us.

"Dr. Fitzhugh, Dr. Fitzhugh," the man cried.

Colin turned, startled. A former student?

"Is it true that you hadn't seen the deceased in years? Or was there more recent contact? How *did* you know he was out in Southampton?"

There was a sudden flash, a tiny supernova, and I saw that the woman was pointing a camera at Colin.

Stanton grabbed Colin's arm. "Damn newspaper ghouls. Even when there's no case, they'll try to make one." He hurried us down the hall toward the lobby, turning back only once. "We have no comment. If you listened to the judge, you'd know they have no case."

"Why are they doing this?" I gasped as we entered the nearly empty waiting room.

"Because nothing exciting ever happens on Long Island and

this is the kind of gruesome news they love. Don't be surprised at what they concoct for *Newsday* tomorrow morning."

"*Newsday*!" Colin and I were both dismayed.

"They're going to put his picture in the paper based on nothing?" That bothered me almost as much as Ms. Turnelli's threat to find better evidence.

The reporter and photographer had circled around and were waiting for us by the outside doors. They had been joined by a freckled, sandy-haired man. He was the one who asked the next question. "Dr. Fitzhugh, what did the judge mean about the Crosleys kidnapping your daughter nineteen years ago? Did you ever get her back?"

"Don't say anything," Stanton hissed, and we didn't. The woman with the camera ran around in front and photographed all three of us. There was something aggressive about her action, a slap at us for being uncooperative.

"How did they know we were going to be here?" I asked Stanton.

He blinked at me. "They didn't. They're in the Arraignments Part every day. Today they just got more than they were expecting. Be thankful News 12 has bigger fish to fry."

As we crossed the parking lot, I held tight to Judge Cooperman's assessment of the weakness of the case, as weak, I hoped, as the elderly man tottering across the parking lot supported by two attendants.

"Let's get some coffee and we can talk about what's next," Stanton said.

Next? Could there be something worse? A black cloud showercapped the sky. I knew the prosecutor had threatened to strengthen the case, but what more was there to find?

"There's a diner, the Starlight, nearly in the village," Stanton told us. "Just turn left when you pull out and keep going till you see it."

"But what else could *happen*?" I demanded.

"We'll talk."

Back in the van, I collapsed against the driver's seat. *Safe.* We were safe. We could still leave Long Island, drive and drive until no one could ever find us. "Thank God they let you go," I gasped.

"For now."

"But what else can they find? Except . . ."

"Except?" His head whipped around.

"You know." I cranked the ignition too fast; it made a squawking protest. "Nobody knows that you've been to that house before. On vacation with Ethan."

"What are you talking about? That was almost thirty years ago! I told you, I couldn't even find it again. What the judge said was true. I had no idea that they were out there last week."

I sighed, holding the steering wheel. There was nobody left to tell them about those long-ago vacations. Whoever might have known—Ethan, Sheila, the elder Crosleys—were dead now. "But how did they know you went to Rhode Island in April?"

"That's easy enough. Someone from Brown probably told them. Or his neighbor from across the street who I talked to afterward."

"But the neighbor was the one who told you Ethan and Sheila had already left for Barbados. So that's good—isn't it?"

"Go on. Stanton's waiting."

I backed the van slowly out of the space. "I was hoping the judge would dismiss the case due to lack of evidence." Praying, even. "If only he had!"

"Yeah, but there's always the boots."

Those damn boots.

Chapter Twenty-Three

As soon as I dropped Colin off at the university and got back to the house, I called Hannah and Jane to let them know that things were still fine, that we would be heading up for Hannah's graduation on Saturday as planned. Neither girl answered her phone so I left voice mails.

Stanton hadn't had anything earth-shattering to say. He was more interested in recapping what had happened, in accepting our praise for how well he had done for Colin—even though I felt privately that the credit belonged to the judge. On the other hand, it hadn't hurt to have someone of Stanton's stature representing us. He explained that the case would now go to a grand jury, which could take several weeks.

Jane called back that night. Talking to her heartened me enough to call Jason in Santa Fe and tell him the whole story. I didn't expect much sympathy from him, given his estrangement from Colin. But Jason was outraged. "They can't do that to Dad," he protested. "The whole thing's nuts!"

"I know."

"What planet are they operating from? How can they think anyone like him could kill people?"

"I don't know, but I wish you were here." I hadn't meant to say that. I wanted the children to be free to pursue whatever they wanted in life without making them feel guilty. "I miss you."

A pause. "But I *like* it out here, Ma. I have friends. There's even a gallery that thinks my art is interesting."

"You're so far away."

"I'll come back if anything happens. I was just home in March. Two months ago!"

"I know."

Jason had not been an easy child to raise, dyslexic and uninterested in academics. He had fixated on computer games and horror movies, creating artwork showing aliens attacking each other in clashing colors that made Colin wince. But my life felt emptier without Jason close by. My instinct was to huddle the wagons together for safety. What if something happened to *him* so far away? I needed everyone in one place so I could protect them.

Why hadn't Hannah called me back?

I still hadn't heard from her next morning. I knew I had to look at *Newsday*, but I made coffee and ate a bowl of granola with blueberries first. Then I moved into the living room and turned on my laptop. I didn't even have to scroll down the page before I encountered myself, looking older with my hair pulled back. Stanton, Colin, and I all looked serious, as if in the middle of a mission. At least the paper hadn't unearthed an earlier unrelated photo of us grinning like idiots.

The story was slanted to create as much drama as possible, and did not even mention Judge Cooperman's scathing assessment of the evidence. Most of the account focused on what had happened to Ethan and Sheila and showed a small picture of them at a gala New England event. They *were* smiling, and their smiles only added to the poignancy of their deaths.

Then the reporter told me something that the police hadn't. Earlier on the evening that they died, Ethan and Sheila had eaten at the John Dory Inn in Southampton. That dinner was the last charge they made on their American Express card.

I stared at the screen. How had *Newsday* had gotten a copy of their credit card activity? From what I knew of Carew, she would never have released that information. I reminded myself that in our electronic age, newspapers had their own ways of getting information, their own "experts." *Newsday* no doubt knew other things I needed to know. What time the Crosleys had left the restaurant, for instance, and whether they had met anyone there. How they had spent their final hours. Did the paper have a way of hacking into police files?

I made a note of the reporter's name—was he the one with the tortoiseshell glasses, or the sandy-haired man with freckles?—and pushed the "Contact Us" link, writing down the phone number as well.

I stopped myself right there. It was too crazy, the wife of a murder suspect talking to a reporter. But I only had to ask him one question, though he was in a position to know other things as well. I was sure the answer was something he already knew from researching the story.

Contacting a *Newsday* reporter was not as difficult as calling the mayor. Louis Benat was on the phone right away.

"Lou Benat." He sounded rested, ready to spend the day upsetting other people's lives.

"Hi, this is Delhi Laine. Colin Fitzhugh's wife? I think I saw you in court yesterday." Was this the stupidest thing I had ever done?

"Yes, right! What can I do for you?" He sounded as if a sack of winning lottery tickets had just been dumped on his desk.

"I read your story this morning about the Crosleys' dinner at the John Dory Inn. I was wondering how much the bill came to."

"You mean how much they paid for dinner?" He did not sound as if that was the question he was expecting. "I could find out. For a consideration."

Here we go. "What kind of consideration?"

"Well, we could start with an interview. How it feels to have your husband kill someone. The details about the Crosleys kidnapping your daughter. I could find zilch on that. Where did it happen?" He talked fast, as if he feared being hung up on before he could finish what he had to say.

For good reason. My rush of outrage was disproportionate to the mild spring day outside. I muttered, "Sorry I bothered you," and pressed end call.

The phone rang immediately and I picked it up, ready to tell him he was offensive beyond belief. "Do you always—"

"Yeah, I know. I come on too strong. But I really want to talk to you." He turned it into a pickup line.

"I'm not interested. I only wanted some simple information that I can get from the restaurant anyway." I couldn't imagine how.

"Why would you want to know that? I think you had a deeper reason for calling me. You want the world to know the truth."

Did I? What if I told him my theory that someone other than the Crosleys had died in the fire and he was able to help me find out what had really happened? How could I have thought he would give me any information without quid pro quo? No one did anything without payback. But if it meant Colin would not have to go to trial or be convicted . . .

"What's important about what they ate for dinner?" he wheedled.

"I'm not sure."

"You think it will help your husband's defense? Did he eat dinner with them before he set the fire?"

Reporters, like booksellers, were not *all* insufferable, but this one was close to the top. "My husband was never *in* Southampton. If you'd listened to the judge you'd know they have no case."

"So why are you pursuing it?"

Fair question. "Because I want to know what really happened." It occurred to me then that I knew something important he didn't. It had not been reported anywhere that the bodies had been burned to disfigurement before the house fire was even set. The police had not released that information to the media and none of them had thought to ask about it.

The judge had referred to the time lapse between the Crosleys' death and the fire, but it had not been in the newspaper story.

"I bet I know lots of things you don't," Louis Benat teased.

"I'll bet you do."

"I'll trade."

"This isn't a junior high sleepover." *I let Shaun Daniels feel me up under my sweater.* "I'll tell you what: If I find out anything earth-shattering, you'll be the first to know. That's all I have to trade." I was ready to end the call when he said, "It came to $523 with tip. Are you surprised?"

"Yes."

"Your husband didn't tell you?"

"For the record. My husband was at a retirement dinner in Stony Brook with over two hundred witnesses. Confirmed by the police."

"Okay, but what does that kind of money tell you?"

"That they were eating with other people and picked up the check."

"Yeah." He sounded thoughtful. "Why didn't I think of that? I just figured they were drinking expensive wine or something."

You need to get out more. Even wealthy people don't run up that kind of bill for a casual night out.

"If they were eating with other people, why didn't those people come forward after the fire?" he asked. "Why didn't they go to the police?"

"You don't know that they didn't. But maybe they didn't think the dinner had anything to do with what happened later." *Maybe they're dead.*

"Rich people think they're above the law," he pronounced.

Oversimplify much? How could I have ever been tempted to sign him on?

"So you're going to keep me posted." He sounded as if he didn't believe me.

"I said I would."

"Okay, but tell me this: How come the police aren't blaming *you*?"

I broke the connection.

Chapter Twenty-Four

IT WAS TOO early to go to the John Dory Inn. I called Hannah and left a message reminding her that we would get to the house where she was living on Saturday around lunchtime, then made myself go over and open the carton of sale books I had bought last week. The train into summer was pulling out of the station, and I had not yet jumped on board. Estate and book sales were increasing just as Internet sales slowed down for the summer. I should already be researching the ads and checking with Marty about the best upcoming sales. I promised myself that after the weekend at Cornell I would settle down.

As if . . .

But I had no choice. The small salary I received from Marty for managing Port Lewis Books would hardly be enough if the worst happened: if Colin's court costs wiped out our savings and he lost his position at the university.

We wouldn't even have a place to live. Once Colin was no longer on the faculty, we would not be eligible to rent this university-owned farmhouse. It would be the end of having the barn to store my books and work out of. Thank God that Jane and Hannah were finished with college. I could even be grateful that Jason was insisting he would never go back.

I pulled open the carton flaps. Inside were more signed art catalogs from the Hamptons. I had been saving them up to savor the way you would an unopened box of chocolates. I carefully removed several and brought them back to my worktable. The first one I looked at was a Robert Motherwell catalog from a 1980s exhibition, inscribed by the artist to a friend. Yes! I let myself look at the others; the earliest was a Thomas Hart Benton. I researched and described them, feeling the old pleasure, though I was still jittery from yesterday in court.

I also knew that I had to go back to Southampton. I had been warned away, but Carew's threat had all the force of a sock on a windless day.

Still not time to go out there yet. At noon I closed up the barn and went back to the house to make a grilled cheese sandwich. Then I went downtown to Port Lewis Books.

BECAUSE IT WAS early in the week, I thought Marty might be there, phoning collectors and gloating over his newest acquisitions. But as I parked in the residents' lot, I remembered that he was at a book auction in Manhattan. A book auction I could have attended if my life hadn't been so chaotic—and I'd had Marty's money.

When I opened the bookshop door, the overhead bell sounded and Susie looked up from behind the counter. Her face was still flushed with new hormones, but her eyes were sad. So Paul had not come around yet. "Delhi. Hi!"

I crossed over to her quickly. "How are you?" I kept my voice too low for the customer in the room with us to hear, a man in his seventies whom I recognized by his fashionable white mustache. He was a retired physics professor from the university who loved World War II books. Our eyes met and I gave him a wave.

"I'm okay," Susie whispered gamely. "Paul doesn't want me to have an abortion, after all."

"Well, good! That's something to be happy about, isn't it?" My feelings about abortion were complicated, but I was sure that for Susie it would lead to years of regret.

She fiddled with the sales pad. "He wants me to have the baby. But—" She couldn't go on.

"But *what*?"

"I can't tell anyone. I promised."

"You can tell me. I've already heard it all."

"Have you? You think so?" She didn't sound scornful, not exactly, but there was an edge of challenge there. "Well, listen to this. Paul says you can get a lot of money for a healthy white newborn. Enough to get our business going."

"What?" So much for not being shocked. "What is he thinking? You can't list babies on eBay!"

"I know that. Do you think I don't know that? But he knows these people, a couple who's been trying to adopt a baby forever, and have gotten frustrated. They both work, they could afford . . . to pay a lot. He says we could have our own baby in a few years."

"Susie, that's crazy." *No, he's crazy.* I thought of Paul Pevney, tall and skinny with his mop of curly hair and granny glasses. He looked like someone who belonged on a college campus and I had been surprised when he had taken the job at Home Depot, though I knew they had needed money quickly. The way he loaded up books at sales had made him seem obsessed, but this went far beyond that. "He does know it's against the law. To buy babies."

"Delhi, it isn't like that." She sounded as if she were trying to convince herself. "This is something private. He says it would be like—you know—me being a surrogate mother. I'd be making someone else happy." Her eyes, behind pale blue-framed glasses, had begun to blur with tears.

"Never mind making someone else happy! You have to make *you* happy. Your baby belongs with you. This isn't about letting someone go in front of you in the checkout line."

"But what am I going to do? If I don't have him . . . Listen, Delhi, I was this big dope in high school, I was fat, I knew that no one would ever want to marry me. But Paul did. He loves me the way I am!"

Even pregnant?

"He says people do this all the time. At least"—she stared down her stomach, which was starting to gently mound—"this way the baby would still be alive." She gave a laugh with little humor in it. "It's kind of sweet, the way he's encouraging me to take vitamins and eat right. To do everything to make sure the baby's healthy."

That seemed more monstrous than anything else she had said. "When is the baby due?"

"Around Christmas." And then her face melted like a wax mask. The idea that she would have to give up her baby during the holidays reached her as nothing else could. She opened her mouth and began to keen like a child who has seen her pet run over.

The retired professor leaped up from the wing chair. "What's wrong—can I help?"

"No, it's fine," I told him, motioning him back into his chair with my hand. I had moved around the counter and was holding Susie now. "She's just upset."

He lifted his eyebrows at me, but returned to his seat.

I stayed on at the shop talking to Susie, insisting on bringing her tea from the Whaler's Arms next door. I moved her back into the small office, where for the first few minutes, all she could do was press her hands against her stomach and sob.

"No one's going to make you give your baby away," I kept repeating. "I'll be here. And you can always go home."

"But Paul—"

"It's his baby too. He'll come around."

I hoped that was true.

BACK IN MY van, I was still shaken as I checked my iPhone. Nothing from Hannah yet. A stab of unease. She was no doubt busy with graduation preparations, but she had always been a communicator, forwarding every adorable cat or dog photo that popped up on her screen. She was the one who had introduced me to Grumpy Cat and other animal videos. I told myself that it had only been since yesterday that I had not heard from her. Right now she was probably at the animal hospital where she had interned. She would be working there for the summer, and could continue to live in her off-campus housing.

Should I try her at the animal hospital? As soon as I made two other calls, I would. I asked Siri for the information and she connected me.

Next I phoned my sister, Patience, hoping she was still at their beach home in Southampton. Once the weather was nice, she didn't always return to Manhattan during the week with Ben and the girls. She owned her own high-powered accounting firm that dealt only in corporate accounts and could work from wherever she pleased.

"Hi, Delhi." Her voice was neutral; her interest in hearing from her twin was tempered by caution about what had inspired me to call. I never called anyone just to chat.

"Hey, Pat. I'm glad you're out here. Are you by yourself?"

"Of course. School's not over yet for the girls, but I have a garden tour committee tomorrow so I stayed."

"Perfect! Do you want to have dinner with me tonight at the John Dory?"

"The John Dory Inn in town? Can you afford it?"

"No."

She sighed.

"It would be early. Around six?"

"Why so early? And why does it have to be there? I know some better places."

"It has to be there."

"Am I allowed to ask why?"

"You don't read *Newsday*?"

"You know I don't."

"Well, find today's paper online. And then meet me."

"Wait, Delhi! What part do I read? You know you can't just show up at the John Dory without a reservation."

A mother and daughter passed me on the sidewalk eating ice cream, so close to my window I could tell that the flavor was mint chocolate chip. *Call Hannah.*

"Just go to the Web site, you'll see right away. And we do have a reservation. That's why we're eating early."

I asked Siri for animal hospitals in Ithaca since I didn't know the name of the one where Hannah worked. Siri produced eight, none of which stirred a memory response. Hannah could just as easily be based one or two towns over, in a town whose name I didn't even know.

No, I'd try her at home tonight. I was sure she was fine, but I couldn't forget Elisa's warning.

I'm okay. Be careful.

Chapter Twenty-Five

THE JOHN DORY Inn resembled a New England governor's mansion, white clapboard with black shutters and a large screened-in side porch. There was even a square widow's walk on top and pansies in the white window boxes. The restaurant was set back from the road, with parking discreetly off to one side. As I walked up the wide steps, I knew my instincts had been right. You couldn't just appear at dinnertime and start asking questions. You especially couldn't ask questions about a couple who had dined there a week earlier and been incinerated afterward, even though it was probably all the staff had talked about for days.

Patience was already in the small waiting room, poised on a delicate chair and looking down at her smartphone. If I had been a stranger, I would have been impressed by her exquisite profile and peach-toned skin, her blond French braid and black Armani jacket. I would have identified her as someone in television production or a gallery owner.

I had only a moment to admire her before she turned on me, appalled.

"Delhi? *What* is going on?" She was so agitated she did not even offer me the usual hug.

"Hey, Pat. Let's get our table and I'll tell you."

The dining room reminded me of Williamsburg, with deep blue tablecloths, white napkins, and gold-framed portraits on the walls. There were only a smattering of diners so far, but the woman I'd spoken to had assured me they were fully booked later on. The hostess brought us to a table for two under the portrait of a gentleman looking over the room with a self-satisfied air.

She handed us menus. I didn't ask her for the Early Bird Special.

Patience ignored the menu she was holding. "What's going on?"

"You read the story?"

"Of course I read the story! I couldn't believe it when I saw your photo. Why are they accusing Colin? The paper made it sound as if he did it!"

"Of course he didn't do it." It made me furious that people would read Louis Benat's story and think it was true. Would the university think it was true? Some of Colin's colleagues must have read it. "The judge *said* they had no case. He said—"

"Good evening, ladies. Would you prefer sparkling water or still?"

Patience glanced up at him, annoyed. "Tap."

The cheerful server didn't blink. "I'll get that for you right away. Your waiter will be here to answer any questions you might have."

Any questions? The square root of 145? Who set the fire in Southampton?

I tamped down my hysteria. "The police have no real evidence." I described Ethan's letter and the boots with the mud from Southampton that the police found under the back porch. I detailed my interview with Agent Olson and Detective Carew, her disregard of my discovery of Kathleen. "They've decided it has to be Colin and they're too lazy to consider anything else. The judge thought it was a joke. I think someone stole the boots, pressed them into the mud out there, then put them back. Would we be dumb enough to leave them there to be found?"

Pat played with her newly poured glass of tap water. "But if the Crosleys are dead, who's left to do that? Elisa's the only one left in the family."

"No, she has a brother. Who didn't get along with them." But it planted the wild thought that maybe Elisa had finally believed what I'd been telling her and become so furious with the Crosleys for changing her life that she had ended theirs. I wasn't sure why she would try to put the blame on Colin though. To divert suspicion from herself? She had been to our house and seen the boots lined up outside. I played out the scene. Elisa had set the fire, returned to Ithaca and then Boston, but decided it wasn't safe. So she had taken what she needed from her room, cashed the check that Ethan had sent her, and was now God-knows-where.

That could also have been why she had let Hannah know she was all right, but had not told her where she was.

But that theory was ridiculous, as leaky as my parents' old rowboat. Elisa had been at Cornell visiting Hannah when the fire happened. It would have taken her over five hours to drive from Ithaca to Southampton. And unless Hannah had been part of it, which I was sure couldn't be true, there was no way that Elisa could have disappeared for ten hours without Hannah noticing.

"May I tell you this evening's specials?" The waiter had introduced himself as Max and was smiling expectantly. I was glad this jaunty young man was waiting on us and not the dour, gray-haired waiter who looked like he belonged in a British country home.

"Go right ahead," Patience told him pleasantly.

In the end my sister and I both opted for the seafood salad, which, our waiter assured us, was made from shrimp, crabmeat, and scallops that had been swimming in the bay that very morning! It reminded me of a dinner in France we had been treated to by a colleague of Colin's. The waiter had gone into raptures over each course in heavily accented English. My favorite had been about a chèvre cheese: "The product of lambs—how you say— gamboling in the Languedoc region. They are treated to a grass found nowhere else on the continent."

"Would you care to see the wine list?"

"No, I'll have a glass of Chardonnay."

Patience and I said it at the same moment, our voices so similar that Max blinked and then grinned. "Sisters?"

"Twins," I assured him. Should I make my move now in this moment of conversation? I decided to do it closer to the tip.

"But why are we eating here?" Patience asked when he left. "Is it to help Colin, or did you just want to see me?"

"Both. The Crosleys ate here the night of the fire and spent over five hundred dollars. I want to know why."

She nodded. "Pricey for two people."

"Whatever I ask, just agree."

AFTER WE HAD told our waiter regretfully that we were not having dessert, he brought the check. I smiled at him. "I understand you had some excitement here last weekend."

"Excitement? You mean about the people who died in the fire?" He kept his voice low.

"We knew them," I whispered back. "Do you remember who they were eating with?"

He nodded. "They were my table. No one."

"No one?" I was stunned. "Someone told me their check was very large."

He glanced around the room as if checking for spies. "They paid for a couple at another table. Now that you mention it, I wondered why they weren't sitting together." He laughed. "I thought maybe the man was going to propose and the Crosleys were treating them to dinner, but didn't want to impose. They sent over several glasses of champagne."

"Did the other people look like family members?"

He thought that over. "Maybe. The woman did. The man was shorter and had black hair. A burly type."

"You remember them very well," Patience complimented him.

"Hard not to. They must have been drinking before they came. They didn't overdo it here, but they could barely get out the door." He nodded at the leather folder. "I'll take that whenever you're ready."

Patience already had her American Express card in her hand and was slipping it inside. "What do you think?" she asked me when Max had left.

"I think the Crosleys were setting them up for the fire. By the way: How much does a Patek Philippe cost these days?"

"You're in the market now? Depends on the model. And the age. Some of the antique watches are priceless."

"No, just an average. Does Ben have one?"

"Of course not!" My esteem for Ben rose, and plummeted only slightly when she said, "He's such a klutz, he'd kill it in no time. I'd guess they start at around twelve thousand. But you can pay much, much more."

I nodded. A minor point, yet it threatened to upend my theory.

If you were substituting another body for your own, why would you destroy an expensive watch when you could be identified by a wedding ring instead? On the other hand, if Ethan and Sheila had been so badly burned that they could not be identified, how had the watch survived so easily that Frank Marselli could identify the brand? That made it sound as if someone had slipped the watch on the man's wrist afterward. Perhaps the Crosleys considered it a small price to pay.

Outside the restaurant, Patience and I hugged for a long time.

"I've never been this scared," I confessed.

"No, no, you'll get through this. You're strong."

I couldn't say anything, just held on to her.

"We'll get the best lawyer in the country. If it even comes to that."

"Thanks." I was glad to have her on my side.

ON THE WAY home I went back and forth about whether I should call Frank and give him this new information. I wasn't going to call Ruth Carew ever again.

Frank Marselli told me that you like to play detective.

Though I tried to get past Carew's comment, it smarted as fiercely as a towel snapped against sunburnt shoulders. Even if it were only her own interpretation, I could hear the words in Frank's quick, dismissive voice. I hadn't been *playing* at anything, I reminded him silently. *I've brought fresh perspective to your investigations, and kept you from making terrible errors more than once. Doesn't that count for anything?*

This time, unfortunately, Frank's usual skepticism at my out-of-the-box perceptions was heightened because I was so personally involved. Still, I didn't think I was that far off.

I left Sunrise Highway at the Manorville exit, and pulled onto the side of the road, across from a farmhouse whose fields lay in darkness beyond.

I had Frank's number on speed dial. Even if he would not share information with me, I would make him listen to what I had to say.

"Marselli."

"It's me." *Miss Marple, your favorite amateur sleuth.* "Before you remind me, I'm not calling you for information. I have to tell you something important."

"Okay . . ."

"Did you see the story in *Newsday* today?"

He sighed.

"What it didn't say was that the judge himself didn't seem to think Colin was guilty. But I talked to the reporter and he told me that the Crosleys' dinner bill came to over five hundred dollars. That's too much for two people, even in the Hamptons."

Silence.

"It turns out that they paid for a couple at another table. A woman who looked very much like Sheila Crosley. I've seen a photo of Kathleen, the Irish woman who's missing, and *she* looks just like Sheila. I think the Crosleys treated her to dinner. Before."

"Who told you all this about the restaurant?"

"Newspaper reporters do a lot of digging. Did you find Will Crosley?"

"Not yet, but—you didn't hear this from me."

"I didn't," I agreed.

"I mean it, Delhi, although it's a moot point now, I guess. Will was picked up in a drug sweep in the South Bronx two months ago. He was dealing, but he negotiated his release."

"How?"

"He offered to give the FBI Art Crimes Unit information about his father's antiquities ring. Ethan Crosley was smuggling artifacts out of archeological sites and selling them to collectors. Will Crosley worked for him making fakes from the originals, and Ethan sold them as the real thing too. Will offered to give them a lot of solid information if they would make the drug charges go away."

"Did they?"

"What do you think? The specifics checked out. The FBI was getting close to an arrest when the Crosleys disappeared to Barbados. Ethan Crosley had already been questioned once."

"That's why they left," I cried. "Not because of some vague threat to prosecute them for kidnapping from me."

"Probably," he agreed. "He was already being tracked by several governments."

"So he wasn't that smart after all. Did you find Will?"

"Not yet. He's deliberately gone to ground."

"Well, I'm thinking that maybe it was his phone Elisa used his phone to text Hannah. It was a 917 number and Elisa said he lived in Spanish Harlem."

"Did you tell Carew that?"

"I just thought of it now." I should have thought of it earlier, but with so much else crowding my mind I hadn't.

At the farmhouse, the porch light went on.

"Do you have the 917 number?" he asked. "It will be on her log of texts received."

"It will? Even on a cheap phone?"

"The kind of phone doesn't matter. It's the server that keeps the record."

Quickly I gave him Hannah's number and told him it was hosted by T-Mobile.

"We'll check it out."

"I haven't been able to reach her today, but I'll try the landline when I get home."

He rang off.

I had just pulled back onto the road when I heard my ringtone. Hannah!

But the identification came up as Louis Benat. Again. So far I had not taken the reporter's calls, two or three of them today, but I considered that he might have some new information.

"Hello?"

"Hi there, Ms. Laine. You're a hard person to get ahold of."

"Just busy. I told you I'd call you when I knew anything."

"Ah, but I bet you already know why the Crosleys' bill was so high."

I sucked in my breath, startled. "I just found out."

"I knew it!"

"If I tell you, will you leave me alone?"

"For how long?" The man was insufferable.

"Two days," I said firmly.

"Deal."

Was it that easy? "They treated a couple at another table. They plied them with champagne."

"Who?"

"I don't know yet. I'm going to find out."

"Me too."

If Frank picked up on trying to identify them, it would be a three-way race.

Chapter Twenty-Six

MY NEED TO reach Hannah had gone from *I'd better talk to her tonight* to *I have to find my daughter now.* I knew I could not rest until I heard her voice.

Driving home, I tried to remember the last names of Hannah's three housemates. Like nearly half of Cornell undergraduates, she lived off campus, in the upstairs of a retired science professor's home. I reminded myself that the girls probably used smartphones whose numbers would be impossible to get from an online directory. There had to be a landline in the downstairs of the home, but I didn't remember the name of her landlord either.

But I had her street address in my book at home.

As soon as I unlocked the kitchen door, I went to the address book I kept on the counter near the phone and brought it to the kitchen table. Then, accessing the Internet on my phone, I typed in Whitepages.com and clicked on "Address." It wouldn't work if the professor had an unlisted number, but a name popped up and a phone number at the address. I told Siri to connect me.

The phone rang.

"Good evening." An older man.

I glanced at the schoolhouse clock and saw it was just before ten.

"Yes, hello! This is Delhi Laine, Hannah Fitzhugh's mother? I can't reach her on her phone and it's an emergency."

"She's not answering her phone?" he inquired politely.

"No! Is she there?"

"We don't usually interfere with the girls. Young women, I mean." He chuckled softly.

"*Please*. And if she's not there, could I speak to one of the other girls?"

"You want me to go upstairs and ask?"

"If you would. It's very important."

"I'll ask my wife to go up." The sound of the receiver being laid gently on a table.

While I waited, my eyes squeezed shut, I did not allow myself the possibility that she might not be home.

Minutes passed before the phone was picked up again.

"Hello?" a voice said.

Not Hannah.

"Hi, Mrs. Fitzhugh, it's Janelle. We met—"

"Yes, I remember. Hannah's not home?"

"I thought she was with you. That maybe you'd come up early?"

I wasn't prepared for the rush of panic that knocked me back against the wooden chair.

With us? "When did she leave?"

"Oh, gee. When did I last see her? You know, it was probably Sunday night when we were brushing our teeth. Everybody's so busy . . ."

Another rush, this time of sadness. This was Tuesday night.

Why didn't Hannah have close friends who would have noticed that she was not around to walk with them to campus, friends who would become worried when she did not meet them for dinner Monday night? Close friends kept tabs on each other and always seemed to know where the other one was. Was this the reason Hannah had become so completely enmeshed in Elisa, finally deciding there was someone she could trust?

Suddenly I resented Janelle and her disregard of my daughter. "Could you do me a favor? Could you go up to her room and see if any of her clothes seem to be gone? Her laptop, things like that?"

"But if she's not with you, where *is* she?"

"That's what I'm trying to find out."

"Hannah wouldn't just—I mean, she doesn't even have a boyfriend."

Of course not.

"Could you please check those things for me?" Unfair, but I wanted to scream it at her.

"Oh, sure. Just a sec."

I wasn't even sure what it would tell me. Had *Elisa* come to Ithaca suddenly and the two of them gone off somewhere?

A too-long wait. And whoever finally picked up the phone was not Janelle.

"Mrs. Fitzhugh? This is Kim Collins. We met at—anyway, I was here yesterday morning when those men came for Hannah."

"*What* men?" I was so astounded I could barely choke the words out.

"I was the one who answered the door. At first I thought they were college officials, they had on suits and all, but when Hannah came back upstairs to get her stuff she said that her sister was in trouble and that they were going to bring her to see her."

"What kind of trouble?"

"She didn't say. I've met her twin, she's really nice. But—aren't you *her* mother too?"

"Yes, but there's no trouble. It must have been a trick to get Hannah to go with them."

"Oh, my God! Who were they?"

Think, Delhi. "What did they look like?"

"Well, I was in kind of a hurry, I was late myself, but one of them was kind of dark like he was Arabian. The other was younger, with glasses. Like a nerd? They were very polite, very nice to Hannah. I never thought . . ."

Then in one of those flashes that seem spontaneous but probably aren't, I knew who the dark man had to be. He had shown up at the 7–Eleven, described as looking like Omar Sharif, but I hadn't made any connection them. Now I was sure he was Ethan's employee who had disappeared from Egypt before he could be prosecuted for antiquities theft. I had read the story online though I didn't remember his name.

"Did she say anything to you about Elisa, where she was?"

"No, just what I told you."

I remembered Kim then, a lanky, freckled blonde who played on the basketball team. "Listen, Kim, if you remember anything else, if you hear from Hannah at all, could you call me? I'll give you my number."

"Okay, sure. Are you coming up for graduation Sunday?"

I hope so.

Chapter Twenty-Seven

WITHOUT MUCH HOPE, I tried Hannah's phone one more time. As before, it went to voice mail, and I left yet another message. "Hani? Kim Collins told me what happened. If you get this, wherever you are, *call me*." It was impossible to keep my voice from shaking and I couldn't think of anything else to say.

Dear God, let her still be alive.

But why had they taken her? I had the wild idea that maybe Elisa wanted Hannah with her, that perhaps Hannah was headed out of the country with the Crosleys too.

At least she would still be alive.

Even if you never see her again?

I was still at the kitchen table when my phone rang.

Unbelievably, Hannah's ID appeared.

"Hani?" I gasped.

"Mom?"

"Oh, my God, where are you? I've been worried sick. Where *are* you?"

"I think we're in a harbor. We're not moving right now."

"You're in a harbor? On a boat? Is Elisa there?"

"No. They promised she'd be and that she had to see me, but she's not! They don't know where she is either. They said to tell you they'll trade me for her."

"But she's not with me."

"They think you can find her. You found her before. But maybe you shouldn't, they're so mad at her. They may try to hurt her." The sound of a slap on flesh, and then a gasp. "Oww!"

"*Hannah*—" My whole body was shaking. How could this be real?

Silence and then a different voice, young, insistent, male. "A twin for a twin. That's fair, isn't it?"

"I don't have her! I have no idea where she is. How can you do this?"

"You're good at finding people," he mocked. "Don't try to call back, we'll be in touch. This phone's going overboard when we're done."

"You can't do that! And if you do anything to Hannah, there's no deal."

The phone clicked off.

I redialed Hannah's number immediately. But it rang uselessly and I imagined the small maroon phone spiraling gently into the water, drifting in a slow dance to the bottom of—where? Narragansett Bay? Long Island Sound? The police could trace where the call was made from, but I knew the boat would be hours away by then.

Nothing made sense. I had to believe that the men who had Hannah were acting on Ethan's orders. The Crosleys had to still be alive. They must have first gone to Boston to get Elisa. Had she been thrilled to find out that the Crosleys were still alive, that her grief had been for nothing? Yet why would she have run away from them? Maybe these men had had an altercation with Ethan and they had then killed the Crosleys to take control of the antiquities operation. Maybe they had gone to Boston and lured Elisa away with promises of taking her to her parents, lured her the same way they had tricked Hannah.

But why? Unless it was some kind of Middle Eastern revenge killing they were planning, or Elisa had something they needed to get?

I turned my attention to where they could be. On a boat, Hannah had said. That might be impossible to trace. Unlike planes, boats did not have to register with the authorities before they set sail. You could leave a harbor with no one knowing your destination, and unless you got into trouble and called the Coast Guard, no one could tell where you were. Even if it was confirmed that the Crosleys had owned a boat, there was no way to track where it was now. There could only be the negative information that the yacht was no longer in its slip.

Besides, if they were dead, this could be some other boat entirely.

Wishing that I had not called him before, I called Frank Marselli's number again. This time he was no longer in his office. The phone went to voice mail, then suggested another detective's extension if it was an urgent matter.

I pressed in that number.

"Rogers."

"Yes, hi! This is Delhi Laine. I need to talk to Detective Marselli right away."

"He's not on duty."

"I know that. I just got his answering machine. But it's about one of his cases and something terrible's happened. My daughter's been kidnapped!" As soon as I said it out loud, I found I couldn't breathe.

"Your daughter's been—you need to talk to a duty officer immediately! Did you call 911? How do you know it was a kidnapping?" His alarm ratcheted up mine. "We need to put out an Amber Alert!"

"Well, she's not a child. Frank Marselli knows all about the case. It's Detective Carew's, but this is something else."

"Are you talking about that arson out east?" His voice turned as guarded as a yellow caution light. What had Frank been telling him about me? Of course they would talk about the case. Last year Suffolk County had had under twenty-five homicides.

"Ma'am, you've got to call 911! I'll give you back to Frank's voice mail so you can leave a message for when he comes in."

"No! It can't wait that long. Can't you at least call him and ask him to call *me*? Tell him they have my daughter Hannah and they'll kill her!"

"You know who they are?"

The world was spinning now, my voice not part of me. "Please, *please*. I'm not crazy! I just need to talk to Frank. He'll know what to do. Just call him and ask him to call me. You can do that."

"Give me your name and number."

I started to say that he knew the number, then did as I was told.

I DREADED CALLING Colin. He had admitted he was glad I had found Elisa, even if it meant his coming under suspicion. But that was before Hannah's life had been put in danger. He would not tolerate another of his children in jeopardy. I shut my eyes and made myself breathe. If I had known ahead of time that I would be risking Hannah's life, would I have set out on this quixotic quest?

Of course not. I would have ignored the note from England, treated it as a missive from hell. I had underestimated how vicious these people were. I had not let myself realize that anyone who would steal a child and murder the go-between would stop at nothing to hang on to the life they had made.

Hannah. What if her captors kept her alive and tortured her, reporting each fresh outrage to me? I had warned her to be careful and not go anywhere alone. But I had not warned her about being tricked.

Dumb bookseller in her dumb little world.

I called Colin next.

But instead of his usual "Hey-lo," the phone went right to voice mail.

I panicked. I didn't know what message to leave, what to say. More than that, where was he? In the past I had never worried when I could not reach him, assuming he was at a lecture or out with colleagues. Now my thoughts ran wild, scavenging hyenas reaching for the bloodiest morsels possible. He had fled the country after all, was driving down through Mexico where perhaps a driver's license would suffice in getting across the border. Or worse. He had become despondent over the possibility of going to prison and killed himself.

Maybe the Crosleys or their killers had tracked him down and killed him—just because they could. There seemed to be no limit to their rage. For that matter, why was I still alive?

Crouched in the wing chair, holding my arms, I willed my phone to ring. Raj came over and put his paws on my leg, his small Siamese face anxious. He could always sense what I was feeling and tried to offer comfort. I wanted to push him away, to refuse any softening that would compromise the edge I needed. I didn't deserve consolation. But I wanted it. Reaching down, I airlifted him and pressed him against my chest, closing my eyes and stroking him hard.

Tell me it will be okay.

But no one could do that, especially not a cat.

I opened my eyes finally and looked at the clock. Nearly eleven! Even if Colin had gone somewhere local, a theater or lecture hall where he needed to turn off his phone, he would be home by now. If Frank had believed my message, he would have called me back.

How could I possibly find Elisa on my own? Was she with Will in the South Bronx? Or had she gone to stay with other friends, young women I didn't even know about. According to Hannah, she had broken up with her college boyfriend in January. But— damn! I should have looked for her address book or other clues when we were in her room. Except, did she even have something so old-fashioned? Everything was probably on her phone. *You should have taken her phone.*

I thought about Nick and Micah Clancy then. Nick was vindictive enough to want to lash out at Elisa, deciding in his twisted way that she was to blame everything. If his mother had not been offered money to kidnap her, his mother would still be alive. I had been shocked to hear that both brothers were in New York. Right where everything was happening.

I told myself to calm down. Nick and Micah were here to film a TV series, not spend time kidnapping young women in Boston and Ithaca, and hiding them on yachts. That suggested a level of local knowledge and money that I doubted they possessed.

There was the sound of tires on the gravel outside. When it stopped I heard a car door slam. Colin had gotten my message.

I was surprised when he knocked on the door. Perhaps he

thought I had locked up for the night. But when I crossed the room and pulled the door open, Frank Marselli was standing outside. He was dressed in a gray sweatshirt and jeans, and looked very grave.

"Oh, thank God, thank *God*" was all I could say. "Thank you so much for coming."

He stepped inside and gripped my upper arms as if I had been about to swoon, his face close to mine. "Delhi, *what* is going on?"

"Oh, God, I don't know. They've kidnapped Hannah and I don't know what to do. Everything I do is wrong!" The tears that had been held back for days came gushing out. "It's all so hopeless! Everyone is going to die!"

He pulled me closer for a moment, then moved back. "I'm here as a friend, okay? I'll do whatever it takes. But you have to calm down. Do you have anything to drink?"

"There might be some beer in the refrigerator." I sniffled. "I can check."

"I mean for *you*."

"There's wine, but I need to stay alert." My voice veered up in more panic.

"No, you need to get a grip. Go get yourself some wine."

I gave him a death-mask smile. "Isn't it supposed to be brandy?"

"Do you have brandy?"

"No."

He waved me off.

In the kitchen I pulled a bottle of Cabernet Sauvignon from the cabinet, picked up two wineglasses, and went back inside. But when I started to pour one for him, he shook his head.

He must think it's really desperate for him to come in person.

Instead of going back to the wing chair I sat down on the

striped couch close to him and set my glass on the antique coffee table.

"This happened *after* you called me?"

I took a sip of wine and realized it had been in the cabinet for a while. "It really started yesterday when I couldn't reach Hannah. I kept leaving messages on her phone. Then when I got home tonight I called the house where she lives and she wasn't there. Someone who lives there told me these two men had come for her yesterday morning. I tried her number once more and this time she called me back." I tried to remember exactly what Hannah had said, taking more slow sips of the Cabernet as if it were medicine. It helped a little. "They said they wanted me to find Elisa; evidently she ran away from them. Then we'd 'trade.' But what if I can't find her and they—hurt Hannah?" My voice was getting shaky again.

Frank put his hand over mine and patted it the way you would to reassure an upset child. "It's not in their interests to hurt Hannah."

"You don't know Sheila Crosley. She'd do anything to get back at me!"

"Delhi, she's dead. She's lying in the morgue. The bodies are just too close to theirs to be anyone else's."

"Then these people are their killers. Maybe they want to kill Elisa too!"

But they'd had the chance, a voice reminded me, and they didn't.

"How did they leave it with you?" Frank asked briskly.

"I'm supposed to find Elisa. They'll be in touch."

"You're sure it was Hannah you spoke to." His hazel eyes watched me gravely.

"It sounded like her. And those men took her from Cornell."

"Do you have any idea where Elisa might be?"

I collapsed back on the couch. "No! Like I said, she might have called Hannah from Will's phone. I guess she could be with him. Did I tell you what her text said? Something like, 'I'm okay. Be careful.' So she knew they were looking for her."

"Okay. I've requested those printouts of Hannah's phone log so we can check the 917 number." He moved to stand up. "We'll have them in the morning."

No, don't go! I can't be alone here! "Can't we get them now?"

"It takes a few hours. You need to get some sleep. It's going to be fine." He brushed my cheek with the back of his hand, then stood up. I got up too. "Come to my office in the morning. I'll be there from eight on."

I closed my eyes against the terror. "I don't know if I can do this!"

He did something then that I never would have expected. He reached out and held me tightly against him for a moment as if trying to impart the confidence he felt. "You're a strong woman, Delhi, you've been through a lot of stuff. It's going to be okay."

Chapter Twenty-Eight

THERE WAS NO way I could imagine sleeping. Sleeping implies that your well-being is more important than the crisis you are involved in, that it can safely be ignored for a few hours. That was not the case here. At midnight I tried calling Colin again, but his phone went right to voice mail. The last time this had happened was when the police had confiscated his phone. Had something happened that Frank had not told me about?

I had to find out. Now. Slipping on a hoodie against the night air, I half ran to my van and drove to his condo. The stars seemed far away, as indifferent as if they had seen this kind of crisis too many times before, as if they were tired of what happened on earth. I had felt the same in Stratford-upon-Avon last December, sitting in front of the fireplace in a three-hundred-year-old inn. Starting at the flames I imagined all the people who had sat there before me, their lives even more difficult than mine. We had been given stony soil and told to create a garden anyway. So we tried.

When I pulled into a space in front of number 47 next to Colin's BMW, I was relieved to see he wasn't on the road to some faraway place. But if he was here and okay, why hadn't he answered his phone? *What fresh hell is this?* Climbing the fieldstone steps, I pressed the buzzer for a long moment.

Nothing. Then the light beside my head flared on. A moment later, the black enameled door opened. Colin stood there in a navy T-shirt and briefs, staring at me.

"Why aren't you answering your phone?" I demanded.

"My—oh, God, I forgot to turn it back on" He closed his eyes at his own forgetfulness. "I shut off the ringer for a graduate seminar and didn't think of it again."

"I didn't know where you were!"

He pulled the door wider and I stepped inside. "Where did you think I was?"

"I don't know. On your way to Mexico?" I tried to make it into a joke, but my voice sounded shaky.

"I don't have my passport, remember?"

Had the thought of flight actually crossed his mind?

"What's happened?" He took my upper arm and pulled me into the tasteful Asian setting.

I sank into a black lacquered chair, too weak to stay on my feet any longer.

Colin sat down opposite me on the couch. "What's the matter?"

"It's Hannah. I hadn't been able to reach her since Sunday night. Then when I called her house tonight, it sounded as if she was being—detained."

Tell him the truth. It's his daughter and she's in terrible trouble! But I couldn't. I couldn't say the words "kidnapped" or "hostage."

"Detained?" He frowned at the formal word, a word with political overtones. "Detained by who?"

"I don't know! Whoever it is had Elisa. She ran away from

them, and now they want her back. They think she came to us. So if we give her up to them, they'll exchange her for Hannah."

"Delhi, you're not making sense."

"I already talked to the police. Frank Marselli. He's going to find Elisa in the morning and get Hannah back."

I could see that Colin was trying to process what I was saying. Probably he had been asleep. "But what if Elisa's not willing? You said she already ran away from them once?"

I was haunted by what Hannah had said. *They're so mad at her. I'm afraid they'll hurt her!*

But I pushed it away. "It'll only be for a few minutes, the police won't let them keep her. They'll arrest whoever it is as soon as Hannah's safe."

"Hannah's supposed to graduate Sunday," Colin said as if it had just occurred to him. "We're going up to Ithaca."

I nodded.

He bowed his head, hand shielding his eyes. "Dear God, will this ever end?"

I STAYED AT Colin's condo for the rest of the night. He retreated to his bedroom and I lay on the couch, but I was filled with a dread so deep I felt frozen there. If I lifted my face, the brocade upholstery would come away too. It had been a terrible tragedy to have your child drown at two years old—or believe that she had—but it was unthinkable to lose a daughter at twenty-one. You had spent nearly half your life with her, knew her plans and dreams, the life she deserved to live. In both cases, my fault. Yes, I had been tricked in Stratford, but if I hadn't been inattentive it couldn't have happened. This time I had underestimated Ethan and Sheila Crosley again and the lengths to which they would go to have what they wanted.

Had Elisa finally recognized them as the criminals they were and wanted no part of them? Or was it that she was refusing permanent exile, a life of having to move from country to country no matter how luxurious the surroundings? Because if they were alive, the Crosleys would be guilty of far more than an ancient kidnapping and murder in England. Ethan was facing charges of antiquities theft and counterfeiting as well as the murders in Southampton. This time there would be concerted efforts to track them down.

And if the worst happened—if Frank was unable to protect Elisa—could I justify sacrificing her for Hannah? It was true that they were equally my daughters, but lying in that dim room that might have been in China, I couldn't escape the difference. I had no history with Elisa. She didn't need me the way Hannah did. I pushed the question aside. I had to concentrate on not letting that happen.

Get some sleep. I pushed up off the couch and moved toward the door of what I thought was Colin's bedroom. The door was not fully shut and I pushed it gently.

"Delhi?"

"Yes."

He threw back the covers of the double bed and I climbed in next to him. Then we were holding each other. Not moving, just holding on tightly as if only together would we be able to face whatever was coming.

WE GOT UP around 6 a.m. and Colin went into the tiny kitchen to make coffee. He brought two cups out and sat across from me, this time in the ebony chair. I leaned forward on the sofa and faced him. If the English are strengthened by a cup of tea, coffee does it for me. With the first sip of its dark promise I felt more hope—not anything like calmness, but as if there was a chance for this not to end in more tragedy.

"I'm coming with you," Colin said. "To the police."

"Do you think—I mean, they still have a case against you." I waved my hand, helpless. *Don't draw attention to yourself!*

Colin set down his cup. "Do you think I'm just going to go about my day, teaching and acting normal, when Hannah is missing? What do you think I am?"

"It's not that. It's just—okay, come if you want. I don't know. I don't know anything anymore."

But he was shaking his head. "Well, they can't blame me for *this*. If it means Ethan and Sheila are alive, there goes their whole case. If someone else is responsible, same thing."

"If they believe it's them." Carew had scoffed at my theory about the Crosleys faking their own deaths; why would she believe my claim that they had "kidnapped" my adult daughter? Like an icy hand reaching out to grasp my wrist, I realized that I had nothing to corroborate the story, not even an e-mail. They had made Hannah call me using her own phone. They had sent nothing over the Internet.

If Frank hadn't known me, the police might have thought this was a ploy we had concocted to shift the blame from Colin to someone unknown. They might not even have investigated! I imagined myself going in cold and trying to convince Carew that something had happened to Hannah. I shivered and took another sip of coffee.

Colin was nodding grimly. "Stanton says I'm still their prime suspect. God knows what else they'll try to come up with. They just want to close their fucking cases any way they can. No wonder so many prisoners were released when they started using DNA.

Okay, I'll stay away but leave my phone on. You'll call me as soon as there's *anything*."

"Of course."

It was still too early to go to Frank's office.

Colin gestured at the flat-screen TV. "Put on the news if you want."

The news? How could I watch the news? I had no room left for any more tragedy.

Chapter Twenty-Nine

FRANK MARSELLI'S OFFICE was located in Hauppauge, a name that most outsiders routinely mispronounce as Hap-a-gue rather than Hop-og. Hauppauge is more of an idea than a physical town, a place that Gertrude Stein would have characterized as having "no there there." The low-lying brick buildings that hold the police offices are on Nesconset Highway, another Indian name, though one more easily pronounced.

As I pulled into the parking lot, I felt as if I had been awake for hours, running for miles. A white buzz circled my head, a sensation that took me back to sleepless nights with squalling babies that had left me sleepwalking through the next day. How could I face today's challenges if I was not alert? I'd left Colin's condo early and gone home to take a shower and put on fresh clothes, black jeans and a pale green cotton blouse. Even as I'd outlined my mouth in soft pink lipstick, I'd thought what a silly thing that was to do. Yet if I looked confident and prepared, it might help me act that way.

I went through the formalities of admission in the lobby on autopilot, not remembering afterward how I had gotten to Frank Marselli's office. It was as utilitarian as I remembered, though the photo of the two grinning boys in Cub Scout uniforms tape to a metal cabinet door seemed new. They were adorable towheads. I knew nothing about Frank's personal life except that he was divorced.

Frank was already behind his desk, papers fanned out in front of him when I burst in. I think I was hoping that the problem might have resolved itself overnight, that Frank would have magically gotten the answers we needed while I slept. But as I sat down in the chair opposite him, I knew that couldn't be true.

He looked up and smiled sympathetically. "You doing okay?"

"Better. I guess. You didn't find out anything?"

"You'll be interested in this." He glanced down at what looked like pages from a fax machine. "We heard from Rhode Island about the DNA."

I jerked back. No amount of makeup and clean clothes could have kept my stomach from clenching. A drawstring pulled it excruciatingly tight. What was I afraid of? Nothing—except everything. Was I ready to know who the enemies I was facing were?

"They got a court order to collect DNA in the house, so they went there yesterday afternoon. The house was empty."

Well, not a total surprise.

"I mean, it was completely empty. No furniture, no dishes, nothing even to take evidence from like hairbrushes or toothbrushes. No coffee mugs in the sink. The Crosleys told their next-door neighbor they would be traveling for the next few months and were putting everything in storage."

"Where's the stuff now?"

"Good question. But all the surfaces were wiped clean. The guys who went in said you could smell Clorox a mile away."

I remembered what Mairee had said about Sheila's mania for having everything spotless. "What does Ruth Carew think?"

The twist of his mouth at her name told me nothing. "She doesn't think it's that unusual. She still doesn't believe the Crosleys could have found substitutes to match them. The size of the bodies is very close to the height and weight of the DMV information. To say nothing of Dr. Crosley's medical condition, the heart stents."

That was where my theory broke down. "But she can't still be blaming Colin."

"She can believe whatever she wants, it's her case. The first case she's handled on her own. I may not agree with her, but she gets a lot of things right."

"But why is she so sure it's *him*?"

Frank gave the pages the slightest shake, the sound of a mouse crossing the desk.

"She likes the way the facts fit."

"But what about people like Nick and Micah Clancy? Or Will Crosley? If the FBI was closing in on Ethan, there have to be other people who were afraid he'd implicate them. Besides, she can't blame Colin for kidnapping his own daughter."

"She doesn't know yet; she hasn't come in. No doubt she'll point out that we have no objective proof that a kidnapping actually occurred. There's only your word for it."

I jerked as if my chair had been electrified. "Can she *stop* it?"

"Easy, Delhi. Of course not. I'm treating Hannah's kidnapping as a new investigation. This is my case. I have Hannah's phone log, we put a rush on it and requested Will Crosley's records, which just came in. There's been no activity in the last twenty-four hours."

"Do you think he still has his phone?" What if Will had ditched it the way Elisa did hers?

"Probably. Smartphones are expensive, you don't just toss them away." Frank reached for his desk phone and turned it around to me. "Why don't you call his number?"

I didn't pick up the receiver. "Won't the ID come up as the police? That would spook him." I reached into my bag and brought out my own phone, then turned it on.

Frank dictated the number.

I pressed it in and sat with my eyes closed, waiting for it to ring. My whole life depended on something as tenuous as whether a phone was answered. If the gods were ever with me, if I had been granted just one more answered prayer, I prayed it would be now.

"*Hola!*" The voice was good-natured, slightly ironic.

"Will? Will Crosley?"

"Who is this?"

"You don't really know me, I'm Delhi Laine. I'm looking for Elisa—"

His phone clicked off.

I looked at Frank, feeling as if the room were dissolving around me. "He hung up! I mentioned Elisa and he hung up. Isn't there any way to find where he is?"

"It will take a few hours."

"We don't have a few hours!" I started to press redial, then stopped. "Maybe I should text him. He'll have to read that."

Frank nodded, giving nothing away.

I pressed redial but instead of letting the phone ring, I keyed in letters: *Tell Elisa Hannah's in trouble.* I added my cell number, then sent the message.

"If she cares about Hannah at all, she'll call me," I said. "Even if she's not willing to do anything, she'll want to know what happened. They've been inseparable since they met. Much closer than my twin and I ever were."

"You're a twin?"

How could he not know that about me? But maybe he did. Maybe he was just filling in the time until we heard something back.

"You think he knows how to reach Elisa?" Frank asked.

"I hope so! He's her brother. She said he sometimes calls her for money, so he has the number."

Then I remembered her cell phone lying abandoned on a dresser in Boston and wanted to weep.

Chapter Thirty

After another excruciating minute there was a ding, indicating a text message. I looked down at the phone still in my hand:

What kind of trouble?

"He wants to know what kind of trouble," I said to Frank. "I don't know what to say!"

"Tell him you have to talk to Elisa."

"But what if—"

"We're not going to get anywhere otherwise." He was firm, years of experience behind the statement.

"Okay." I sat back in my chair. *I need to talk to Elisa*, I wrote.

Time passed, then another ding. *This a trap?*

I typed, my fingers falling over each other. *No trap. I need her help. Pls call me!*

And then my phone rang.

"Hello?"

"You're Elisa's real mom?"

"Yes." My throat choked up immediately.

"Okay. This is Will. What's happening?" His voice was crisp, unaccented. But he'd had the same privileged upbringing as my daughter.

"Someone—maybe the Crosleys—kidnapped my daughter Hannah. Elisa's twin sister. They want to trade her for Elisa or they say they'll kill Hannah." *Stay strong.* "And I know they will." *If it's the Crosleys they'll want to make me suffer for the rest of my life.*

"Hang on." Silence.

Finally, "Delhi?"

"Elisa? Is that *you*?"

"This is the last thing I wanted to happen! I thought they'd go after you. I mean, I didn't want that, but I made sure not to call you. And I knew Will would help me. What have they *done* to Hannah?"

"Nothing yet. But someone went up to Cornell Monday morning and told her you were in trouble and had to see her. So she went with them. She wasn't answering her phone until last night, I finally reached her. She said she was on a boat."

"*The Beautiful Past*, probably. Oh, God, I should have warned her more! I should have known."

"They want to trade her for you." There was nothing to do but say it flat-out.

"To trade—you mean they'll let her go if *I* go with them? But I can't! Oh, God, this is all my fault. She only wanted to help me. Where are you right now? Are you—it doesn't matter, they're probably watching you wherever you are."

"Who? Who is?"

"You don't know them. Are you home?"

"No, I'm at the police station. They know all about it. Even if we set up a trade, it would only be for a few minutes. The police would be right there to arrest them."

"You'd need a lot of police," she said darkly.

"They have a lot of police." I looked to Frank for verification and he nodded.

"Elisa, are your *parents* alive?"

"No, but it's complicated. But I'll have to do this. For Hannah. She's the only innocent one."

"The police will be there to protect you," I promised.

"Okay. Call me back when you know more."

And she clicked off.

I lowered the phone. "She'll do it. She said she'd do it." I closed my eyes, but opened them fast. "That's what she says now. But—we have to set it up now."

Feeling desperate, I pressed in Hannah's number and listened to the ringing. Her cheerful voice finally telling me to leave a message was unbearable.

"Hani? I don't know if you'll get this, but if you do, I've found Elisa. We'll get you home soon." I could do nothing about the tears flooding my eyes.

Frank stretched out his hand and held my wrist. "They said they'd contact you, didn't they? Doing this is in their own interests. Go home and wait."

"No!" I wasn't going to move. How could I leave his office for a world too dangerous to live in? "What if they think it will take longer and don't call? What if she changes her mind?"

"Delhi." His smile was warm. A friend. "They want what you want. When they know you have Elisa, they won't hurt Hannah. We'll get her back safely."

"Really? You think so really?"

"I do. I'll speak to Carew, bring her up to speed."

"Okay. I'll go home." I pushed out of the chair and headed for the door, startled when I passed the wall clock and saw it was not even 9 a.m. This day had barely begun. Sometimes at home when I got up early and began listing books, I was pleased to check the time and see it was only eight or nine, with hours still ahead of me. Not today.

The parking lot was on a rise from the brick precinct buildings. I climbed the steps between banks of grass, grass that was still fringed and as delicate as the growth on a Chia Pet head. Elisa had said they were watching me and I examined the cars I passed. But I saw only one patrolman in standard navy blue walking toward the building. Crazy ideas swamped me. If I had a megaphone, I could shout the news that I had Elisa and I was ready to trade. If I had notepaper, I could leave a message under every windshield wiper of every car parked here: *I have Elisa. Call me!*

When I reached my van I waited by the driver's side door in case anyone wanted to approach me.

Nothing.

Then, as I was unlocking the door, my phone rang.

Colin wondering why he had not heard from me? But when I retrieved the phone from the bottom of my bag and looked down the screen showed "Private Caller."

My heart began jumping like a child promised ice cream. "Hello?"

"You have the girl?" It was the voice from Hannah's phone last night.

"Yes! I mean, she says she'll come."

"Where is she?"

Right. Of course I'm going to tell you so you can go get her first. "How is Hannah?"

If you've done anything to her. . .

"Not very cooperative. But she's okay."

"Are you watching me?"

He laughed. "You'll never know, will you? Do you know Fire Island?"

"A little. What part?"

"Take the 3:30 ferry from West Street in Patchogue to Watch Hill. Just you and Elisa. Don't bring your police escort. *Don't ask her any more questions.* You won't live to regret it if you do."

Gangster talk. But the command about not asking questions jarred me. Had he somehow heard our conversation? Could you tap an iPhone? Not physically, of course, but by some electronic method? "What do we do when we get there?"

"Bring your phone." He clicked off.

I looked down at the brick police station. This was a book I had already read. The initial shocking call, getting the ransom together, waiting for instructions. Since I would be carrying my own phone, I would not be racing from telephone booth to telephone booth, but I would probably be given directions designed to lose any police surveillance. If *you hadn't promised Elisa an immediate rescue, you wouldn't even need the police*, a voice nagged.

Wrong. Elisa's my daughter. I'd never let them keep her.

Meanwhile, I was still confused about who was doing this. I had been sure that Kathleen was the victim. She had disappeared, after all. And who—and where—was the other man from the restaurant? I had been imagining him just as innocent as Kathleen, not suspecting that the flutes of champagne that arrived at their table from their new friends had probably been laced with Rohypnol. Now I didn't know anything.

I looked back at the police precinct. If I were being watched and had been warned not to involve the police, it would look suspicious if I went back inside. No, I would have to call Frank and let him know the plan.

But carefully. *You won't live to regret it if you do.* For the first time I realized that I was a target as well. As long as I could be used to find Elisa, I was safe. But once they had her and I had been lured out on the sand on Fire Island, shooting me would be as easy as knocking over a traffic cone.

Don't think about that now.

And don't phone anyone from the van. It would have been easy for them to plant a listening device underneath it while I was inside talking to Frank. They knew where I lived; they had probably tapped the landline as well. And my iPhone? I started to ask Siri if a smartphone could be bugged, then stopped. Why let them know what I was thinking?

I started the van, drove down the slope to the traffic light, and turned east on Nesconset Highway. Where could I safely call from? Progress had done away with most public phones. Besides, they would see me and assume I was calling the police anyway. I tried to remember where I had seen an inside pay phone. Probably at Smith Haven Mall, but everything was out in the open there. There was a landline in Port Lewis Books, but what if they had gotten to that phone as well? I told myself I was being paranoid, but paranoia wasn't always wrong.

Chapter Thirty-One

It was still before 10 a.m. so I parked in the residents' lot in Port Lewis and stopped to buy two cappuccinos in the Whaler's Arms.

Susie was already inside Port Lewis Books and unlocked the door for me. "Oh, you're a darling," she said when she saw the coffee. "Coffee's one of the things I haven't gone off yet."

Her face was rosy and cheerful once more, her navy overblouse already pushing out slightly. I did not think I could handle another pregnancy crisis without saying something I would regret, but it appeared that for now things were calm. Then Susie said, "I told Paul we're keeping the baby no matter what."

"Good for you! What did he say?"

"Nothing. But I think he's starting to realize that it's part of *him* too. That sounds so obvious, but I think he was thinking of the baby as this—I don't know—alien. We'll see. Have you been out mailing books already?"

I groaned, thinking of the unwrapped orders in the barn. One of the things I promised was fast service. "No, I still have to wrap.

I just wanted to check in here and make some calls." I thought of something. "Do you have a cell phone I can borrow?"

"Sure. But I thought you had a better one."

"Dead battery." I made my face rueful. "I'm bad at charging things." That much was true.

"Me too," Susie agreed. "But I keep my phone with me in case Paul has to reach me. He won't use the bookstore phone." She moved behind the counter and brought up a maroon Nokia. I could see that it didn't do any tricks.

"What's going on?"

"I'll tell you when it's over."

She glanced up from the counter, admiring. "Your life is like something out of a book."

One I never hope to read again.

I started to walk back to the small office, then hesitated. Could the whole store be bugged? "I'll be right back," I assured Susie.

Stepping outside into a crisp May day that promised untold delights—to someone, somewhere—I started back to the Whaler's Arms, then stopped. It would look suspicious after I had just walked out carrying two cups of coffee. Instead I turned in the other direction and crossed the street to the Port Lewis Library, which stood a little way up the hill. The white columns in front made the building look grander than it was, but they had a good collection. I knew the library frowned on cell phone use, but I could go downstairs and find a secluded area near the restrooms.

I smiled at the clerk behind the desk, an older woman I had known for years, then went to the stairs in the rear. Certain that I was being overcautious, I pushed open the door to the ladies' room and went into a stall. Then I took out the paper with Will's number and pressed it in rapidly.

"*Hola!*"

"Hi, Will, this is Delhi."

"Okay." He didn't sound happy about it and my heart began to pound. I realized I did not trust him.

"Can I talk to Elisa?"

"I'll give her a message."

"*Please?*"

He sighed, loud enough to make sure I understood his displeasure. "Liss?"

After a moment she was on the line. "Delhi?"

"Are you around here? Don't tell me where. They want us to take the 3:30 ferry to Fire Island, to Watch Hill, from West Street in Patchogue."

Silence.

"I know it's asking a lot. Probably too much."

"Oh, no, I'll do it. I'm the one who got her into this. Besides, all those animals need her."

I gave a shaky laugh. "Do you know Patchogue at all?"

"I've been there."

"West Street. Meet me on the Watch Hill dock a little after three." I considered telling her to meet me somewhere else, like the Patchogue Library parking lot or outside Friendly's Ice Cream, but couldn't guarantee there would be other people there for protection. "Don't let anybody see you before. Walking down the street or anything."

"Okay." Her voice was flat.

"One more thing. Don't stay where you are now. I don't know if they tapped my phone, I'm using a different one now, but if they did they heard our first conversation. I don't know if they can trace where you are from Will's phone. Just to be safe."

"To be safe," she agreed.

"And Elisa? I'm sorry."

"I'll see you at three."

Someone came in and went into the stall beside mine. I pushed up against the opposite wall to try and see underneath the partition. Whoever it was had on navy pants and matching navy wedgies. A librarian? I waited, listening to her pee. Finally the stall latch was pulled back and I heard the sound of water, then the soap dispenser. Probably a librarian, though everyone in Port Lewis took the posted notice to wash your hands seriously.

As soon as the outer door wheezed shut, I pressed in Frank's number.

"Marselli."

"Yes, hi. They called me when I was in the parking lot. They want us to take the 3:30 Fire Island ferry from West Street in Patchogue to Watch Hill." I was talking so fast I had to stop and take a breath. "They'll give me instructions when we get there."

"Watch Hill on Fire Island. Three-thirty ferry. We'll be there."

"But not—you know—they said—"

"You won't know we're there."

"I borrowed my friend's phone to call. I don't trust mine."

"Good. Only call if there's a change."

"Okay."

I hung up as the bathroom door opened again. This time it was a harried mother escorting several toddlers.

Chapter Thirty-Two

RATHER THAN TRY to make another phone call, I decided to drive over to the university and find Colin. I had five hours to fill before I had to be in Patchogue.

On my way out of the library I picked three books from the shelves in the new releases room and checked them out. I barely noticed the titles. They were my alibi, to explain to anyone watching why I had gone into the library.

After returning Susie's phone, I retrieved the van and drove the ten minutes to Stony Brook University. I did not know Colin's teaching schedule, but if he had a class I would wait in his office until he returned. The university had been part of my life for so long that I turned off Nicolls Road at the main entrance without thinking. I barely saw the cement buildings, useful but without charm, and parked in the multilevel garage near the humanities building. Since I had last been here they had finished the on-campus Hilton Garden Hotel across the way.

I entered the brick social sciences building. Having eaten nothing since the coffee from the Whaler's Arms, I felt too weak to climb the stairs and took the elevator to the fifth floor. I try to eat regular meals, but life often gets in the way. Now I saw lunch as a way to eat up some time.

Although Colin taught archeology, he was part of the larger anthropology department. Leaving the elevator, I began turning corners to reach the Institute for Long Island Archaeology. I turned into the hall where the offices were, but stopped abruptly. Colin, in profile, was explaining the bulletin board photographs to a graduate student. He had his hand companionably on her shoulder and I could tell he was instructing her in the warm, erudite way he used to dazzle young women. She was taking it all in eagerly, studying the wonders of his face as much as the board.

That girl was me. She was the entranced sophomore I had been twenty-six years ago, believing that this man, and this man alone, could give me the life I craved. He could teach me everything and show me the world I had known only from books. Not just that: He was bright, charming, witty, and adored me.

Standing in the shadow, I didn't suspect that there was anything going on between Colin and this particular young woman. I was seeing instead how ordinary I must have been, just part of that year's parade. Would he have even thought of marrying me if Jane hadn't been on the way? Maybe it had simply been time for him to settle down and have a family. For me there had been no question, of course. I had been ready to hand my life over to him like an empty blue book.

The realization was so stunning that I stepped quickly back around the corner before he could turn and see me. Any words would have stayed clogged in my throat. There had been exciting years in the beginning, I reminded myself, the times when the children were very small and we traveled to exotic countries and guest lectureships. We had never been equals, but our roles had seemed time-honored. But then in Stratford the family had been shattered and I had become someone who could be blamed for everything that went wrong.

This time I did not wait for the elevator, but hurtled down the cinder block–lined staircase and ran all the way to the parking garage. Only when I was in my van, leaning back against the seat, did I feel safe. But safe from what? No one was chasing me, nothing but the thoughts I had unleashed like lurking demons in medieval paintings. What had changed was a view of myself. Too much of me had remained an idealistic and naïve college girl instead of a woman who had given birth several times, sorrowed through the deaths of her parents, and established a good-enough business completely on my own.

I was an adult who should have embraced that life years ago. Was this what Colin had been trying to teach me by his slow fade-away? If so, I had been a slow learner.

A slow learner who had picked the worst possible time for this epiphany. *By the way, Colin, I've lost our daughters, and I don't want to be married anymore.*

Then I realized he still did not know what was happening. I reached for my iPhone. Even if the line had been compromised, it wouldn't matter. It would seem suspicious for me to suddenly stop making calls. Besides, I wouldn't be saying anything to Colin that they didn't already know.

As promised, he answered immediately.

"Delhi? What's going on?"

"I found Elisa. She'll do it."

"You found her? Where *is* she? What about Hannah?"

"They said she's okay. A little uncooperative, but . . ." My throat was clogging.

"What happens now?"

"They want us to go to Fire Island. Elisa and I are supposed to take the ferry from West Street in Patchogue. No police, no one else."

"What about me?"

"They said no one else."

"But I'm her father!"

"I know, but—" But what? "You can be there, but—come after four. We'll be coming back to that dock."

He sighed. I knew he wasn't happy being sidelined. "I'll be there."

Chapter Thirty-Three

PATCHOGUE IS A village that has yet to find itself. Or find itself again. Located on the South Shore of Long Island, it was a prominent seaside resort in the late nineteenth century, even known as "the land of a thousand hotels." Trolley tracks ran from the Long Island Railroad station down Ocean Avenue to the Great South Bay. Vacationers could enjoy raw clams and oysters, vaudeville acts, and sailboat rides in the fresh air.

The gigantic houses that were once hotels and inns have been turned into nursing homes or multifamily dwellings. I arrived in Patchogue much too early and drove slowly down South Ocean Avenue. Unfortunately the early industries of shipbuilding, lumber milling, and paper making died away shortly after the vacationers moved on. When the last vestige, the Old Lace Mill, burned, it stood as a ghostly brick ruin for years. The village is finally making a comeback as an arts center.

From South Ocean Avenue I drove over to West Street. I had assumed the pier would be at the end of the street jutting into the bay, and nearly passed the rustic chocolate brown sign announcing "Fire Island National Seashore." I jerked the van into the large lot, surprised at the number of cars and trucks already there, and parked three rows from the building. It was too soon to go inside so I sat in my van and obsessed over what would happen in the next few hours.

No other cars had come into the lot after me, but that did not mean I wasn't being watched. Knowing I would end up here, they could already have parked and be watching everything I did.

Where was Elisa? Could I blame her if she didn't come?

It was nearly 3:15 when a black sports car pulled into the row behind me and I saw two doors open. Elisa climbed out of the passenger side, dressed casually in jeans and a dark green hoodie, her hair pulled back from her face. The driver was a fair-skinned young man in stylish sunglasses and a red golf shirt. Could that be Will? I had formed an image of him as the cliché of a Hispanic drug dealer, someone short and swarthy with a ponytail, his arms inked with sinister designs. This young man could have been modeling his clothes.

When they had almost reached me, I climbed out of the van and locked the door. I stood facing them.

Elisa and I didn't hug, though I wanted to. The mood was too businesslike for that.

"Will?" I asked.

His face, boyish in a prep school way, didn't smile. "She's not going."

Elisa gave me a look of appeal. Did she want me to understand his concern or was she letting him speak for her?

"We can't talk out here," I said. "It's safer inside."

I moved quickly toward the modern tan building facing the water. Except for a long, narrow photograph showing Fire Island,

Haldimand County Public Library
CALEDONIA BRANCH

the facade gave nothing away. The hall we stepped into was dim and cool, opening up to display two counters flanking the entrance to the pier. The only decorations were several photographic posters on the walls and the iconic Red Flyer wagon, used on the island to transport groceries since no cars were allowed.

As I moved closer, I saw that this wagon was filled with shells sprinkled on sand and some larger artifacts—a horseshoe crab, a bottle holding a message, a child's blue plastic shovel. It was a vignette promising travelers a fantasy of ocean and beach.

We paused deep in the entryway between two backless benches on facing walls.

"Thank you for coming," I said, then winced at the party hostess words.

Elisa turned her pretty face to Will. She was carrying a large compartmented leather bag, the purse Hannah had talked about.

"You want to put her in danger," Will accused me.

"No, of course I don't! But she's going to be well-protected."

"You don't know them."

I stared into his amber eyes. "No, but I knew the Crosleys. I knew them before you were born. These people can't be any worse."

"You don't know them," he repeated.

"Will, it's going to be okay." Elisa put her hand on his upper arm. "I told you, it'll only be for a few minutes."

I realized they must have been having this conversation all day.

"I know you want to protect me, but I have to get Hannah back."

He gave his head an angry shake. "It's too risky. You take too many chances, Liss. You always have to show that you're braver than anyone else!"

She opened her mouth to protest, then closed it again.

He moved closer until his face was a few inches from hers.

HiZimand County Public Library
CALEDONIA BRANCH

"You just met this Hannah. You've known *me* all my life! Doesn't that count for anything?"

Sibling rivalry? Was he actually jealous that Elisa had a twin she was worried about? Would Hannah lose her life because Elisa's adopted brother felt put out?

"We have to get our tickets," I broke in. I had been watching both doors as we talked, frightened that someone would storm in and take Elisa by force. If they had a gun, what could we or the young woman behind the ticket counter do? Perhaps going to Fire Island was just a ruse to get us into an unprotected place.

I reached out and took Elisa's upper arm gently to move her toward the counter. A beat later Will grabbed her left wrist and started pulling her toward the doors.

"Oh, for God's sake." Elisa tried to shake us both off. "Delhi, let go of me! Will, I told you I'm going to do this and I am."

I dropped my hand immediately, but Will did not. Furious, she wrenched her arm away. Yet when she spoke to him, her voice was mild. "Stay here, I'll be back. We'll be eating fried chicken and drinking cerveza tonight. Many beers, I promise."

"No, don't expect to see me again. I'm asking you not to do this and you're doing it anyway."

"Now you're being ridiculous." She turned and walked rapidly to the accommodations counter with me in tow. I bought two roundtrip tickets, then we stepped outside onto the pier. I didn't look back at Will. I half expected him to move around the side of the building and try and pull her away. There was still a chance he would keep her from going. The only thing that would keep him in check was her fury.

"Liss?" He was suddenly at the doorway to the pier. "At least remember what I told you!"

"Don't worry. I will."

He nodded, his mouth an angry line, and disappeared back into the building.

As if Elisa could tell what I was thinking, she said, "He'll be okay. He promised not to screw things up. It's just, he hates anything to do with my parents. They've said terrible things to each other, things that you never get over or forget."

"You *know* I don't want to put you in danger."

Yet that was exactly what I was doing.

Seven or eight other passengers waited on the raised deck with us. I looked them over. Two young women in T-shirts and capris were sprawled on one of the benches, laughing at their whispered comments, tote bags and a six-pack of Blue Point beer at their feet. The one with dark curls periodically looked down at her smartphone, then up, without losing a word of conversation. A couple in their thirties with a rambunctious four-year-old watched fondly as he ran in crazy circles. A burly man in a Long Island Power Authority uniform sat facing the sun with his eyes closed.

The last passenger was a woman holding the leash of a small dog with wavy brown fur, a breed I could not identify. She stood by the railing with a chartreuse-dotted tote bag by her side.

I decided the LIPA worker had to be the undercover cop.

Looking at the dock, I pictured it packed with excited families laden with camping gear, and vacationers headed for rentals at the eastern end of Davis Park. Across the narrow canal from us there would be the activity of people climbing on and off the boats in the slips, sunning themselves or getting ready to push off into the bay. Today nearly every slip was filled, which meant that few people were out on the water.

But where was the ferry? It was after 3:30 and the pilings in front of us were still empty. What if it had been canceled and the kidnappers didn't realize it? I looked around at the other people waiting to board, but they seemed unconcerned. Perhaps the boat was always late. Perhaps they knew something I didn't.

Beside me Elisa fidgeted with the zipper of her sweatshirt. It had a white pocket logo for a ski resort in Vermont.

"You should have called me," I whispered.

"I couldn't. You're one of the first places they'd look. Someone's probably been watching you for days."

"Really? But who *are* these people? And why do they want you?"

She gave me an oblique look and didn't answer. Instead she put her head back against the wood and closed her eyes as if to nap. Or pray.

Chapter Thirty-Four

I STOOD UP and moved to the wooden deck railing to see if I could see the ferry approaching. Finally I saw the boat gliding slowly down the canal, its outside upper deck a crowded mass. The ferry moved with the stateliness of a parade float, but as it came closer the mass broke into a jumpy collection of small children and adults. A field trip to the Sunken Forest or the dunes? No doubt it had taken time to make sure everybody was safely on board.

Offloading the crowd was a slow process. After the side of the ferry bumped against the pier several times like a friend making insinuations, a young woman jumped off to secure a rope around the pilings. It was another few minutes before a metal gangplank was stretched across and the children disembarked. I saw that they were no more than five or six years old. A kindergarten class? I watched one of the girls in a pink sweatshirt, blond hair in pony-tails, talking eagerly to her mother. The sharp pain it brought me, a knife to the gut, was so unexpected that I gasped.

"Are you okay?" Elisa whispered.

I nodded. I would have to think about what it all meant later.

Then it was our turn to board. Everyone climbed the skinny metal stairs to the top deck except for the man in the LIPA uniform who ducked into the inside cabin. *Wait a minute. You're supposed to be protecting us!* Elisa and I sat on wooden benches painted the pale yellow of beaten eggs, with our backs to the wall. Maybe nothing would happen on the ferry. The young women and their beer camped farther down on our side, the family and the woman with her dog sat across the way from us, their backs to the boat slips. A low metal structure separated us from them.

I watched the moored boats as we navigated slowly up the canal. Most were facing us, but a few were angled enough so that I could read their names: *Dream Wave, Fuzzy Logic, Doing Better Now.* The sun was warm on my face. I sniffed, hoping for salty air, but picked up only the fumes of diesel oil.

I began to obsess over what we would find on the other side. "Have you been with Will all this time?" I whispered to Elisa.

"Uh-huh, but moving around. He knows lots of places to stay."

"What was your plan? You didn't go to the police?"

"That's what they thought we would do. But Will didn't think—we figured they couldn't stay around, they'd have to leave. I had no idea they'd do something like this."

But who are these people? I wanted to demand. Why wouldn't Elisa tell me?

I had the prickly feeling of being watched then, but when I looked up I saw it was just the lady with the dog. Yet she was staring intently, as if there was something she wanted to tell me. I had been surprised when I first saw her, I hadn't known that you could bring animals on the ferry. But why not, if you weren't disturbing other passengers. This dog was settled calmly at his owner's feet, his curly head resting on one of her white sneakers.

The woman's brown hair was nearly the same shade as her dog's, scraped back and clipped at an odd, fashionable angle. She wasn't noticeably pretty, wasn't wearing lipstick, but she had a good white-teethed smile, which she bestowed on her puppy. Then she looked back up at me and gave her head the slightest jerk.

Definitely a signal. I pushed up from the bench, nearly losing my balance as the ferry lurched. We had just entered open water and the boat was speeding up, starting to bounce. The American flag on the hull crackled in the wind out here, threatening to snap apart. I reached for the metal center railing, then made my way around. Squatting down beside the dog, I said, "I've been watching him. He's so cute!"

"You can pet him. He's very friendly." She reached down to straighten his red-studded collar affectionately and her hand pressed against mine. I realized I was holding a small piece of metal. "His name's Sir Love-a-lot."

"That's really cute." I gave him several more strokes, then pushed back to my feet with my free hand.

As I moved by her, she said in the lowest voice possible, "See that she wears it."

Without saying anything, I moved to the front of the boat and stared out at the strip of land that expanded as we moved toward it. Then I brought my fist to the front of my waist and opened it cautiously. I was holding a smooth gray circle, the size of a quarter, though thicker. Some kind of tracking device that I would have to get to Elisa as soon as possible.

I felt a moment of calm before anxiety overtook me again. The police were doing their job; it was up to me not to jeopardize everything.

THE BUILDINGS WE docked in front of were more whimsical than the no-nonsense headquarters, odd angles of wood sticking out like the arms of beach chairs. The boats moored in the slips surrounding them were grander, most of them yachts, few names visible. Perhaps the Crosleys' yacht was one of them, anchored here to watch us get off the ferry. As we tied up, I studied the fifteen or twenty people lined up at the barrier waiting to board for the ride back. None of them looked threatening, but that meant nothing. What meant more was that Elisa didn't seem to recognize any of them.

We were the last to disembark. Looking at my watch, I saw that the ride had taken nearly thirty minutes, longer than I expected.

"What do we do now?" Elisa's voice held the fear of someone entering a hospital who knows a procedure will be painful.

"They're supposed to call and tell us." The metal tracking device burned hot against my palm.

"It doesn't make sense!" She was suddenly angry.

Then my phone rang.

The identification still came up as "Private Caller."

I pressed the button. "Yes?"

"Follow the signs in the direction of Davis Beach until you get to the stairs that go up over the dunes. Don't go up them! Just turn right and continue along the walkway."

"Okay. But—"

The phone clicked off.

"We need to start walking."

We started up the sloping path past the office and general store. The walkway was a combination that changed back and forth from cement to wooden cross-slats, raised slightly from the sand. There was a wooden rise like a shallow bridge, then we were on concrete again.

"Elisa," I said very low. "I'm going to give you something that you have to hide somewhere on yourself. I'm going to drop it on the cement. Bend down and retie your shoe, then pick it up."

I let the metal circle dribble out of my fingers and kept walking. She crouched down and fiddled with her shoelace.

When she caught up with me, she whispered, "What is it?"

"Some kind of tracking device, I think. The woman with the dog gave it to me."

"*Really?* How did you know she had it?"

I looked around before saying any more, but we seemed to be truly alone. Still I kept my voice low. "I thought *someone* on the ferry had to be from the police. And she kept looking at me."

"Cute dog."

It was so incongruous given everything, we both laughed.

Beyond the walkway the sand was covered in low green growth, beach plum, bayberry, and an evergreen vegetation I did not recognize. Where was Hannah right now? Was she waiting in a house in Davis Park? Out on the beach? She had been on my mind every moment, covering my thoughts like a deep gray sky. She had been there even when I was worrying about whether to use my phone to call Colin and whether my van would be safe in the parking lot in Patchogue. Just because I had done everything I was told didn't mean they would spare her.

After several minutes we came to the stairway that climbed to the beach. Though the dune was too tall to see the ocean on the other side, I could hear a continuous drone like lawn machinery several houses away.

"Turn here," I told Elisa.

Where had the other people from the ferry gone? Although they should be walking ahead of us, they had disappeared into air.

I looked behind me, but could see no one there either. Could they have all been from the police? No. Surely no parents, even police officers, would risk putting a small child in danger.

We kept on walking, passing several shingled homes. This part of Fire Island was not exactly the Hamptons, though I knew that other areas like Cherry Grove and The Pines were fancier. Although it was nearly summer, this landscape felt empty. I shivered, imagining its desolation in January.

"Where are the police now?" Elisa whispered.

"They have to stay out of sight."

As we walked toward Davis Park, the smattering of houses and sheds vanished. Here there was only the same low growth. We might have been on some alien planet.

My phone rang.

"Hello?" I hated the shakiness of my voice.

"Turn around and walk back to the stairs over the dune, then go up them to the beach."

This time I clicked off.

"We have to turn around."

"They're playing with us!" The whites of Elisa's eyes flashed like a frightened colt's. "This is crazy!"

And then I finally felt like her mother. Her mother, her protector. This was my *child*. I had known it intellectually, of course, from the moment I saw her on St. Brennan's campus, but I was finally viscerally feeling it. The momentary stabbing pain I had felt when the ferry was unloading was now steady and unbearable. I grasped her upper arm. "When I saw those children getting off the boat with their parents I couldn't stand it. All I could think of was the time I had missed with you. A whole lifetime we can never get back."

"Did you think about me a lot?" Her blue eyes searched mine.

"All the time. But thinking about you as if you were dead. I had to stop myself just to get up in the morning and do what I had to for the rest of the family. It was worse around the holidays and your birthday, I'd picture what it *would* have been like, you and Hannah."

"But she said you never talked about me."

Why were we talking about this now, her existence threatened again. My existence, Hannah's as well. Pushed to the edge, we finally could.

"Why didn't you ever talk about me?"

I sighed. "Colin thought—we thought it would be too sad for the children to grow up with your death always there. But we *should* have. If we had, we might have picked up more clues from people and found you earlier."

"But you didn't." I couldn't tell from her soft voice if she was sorry that hadn't happened. She had only known one life, after all.

Then the pain, the knifing, was so intense that I had to stop walking and press my arms against my belly. The deep agony that I had never allowed myself to feel was finally overwhelming me. All the sick regret, the *if onlys*, all the unfathomable things I could not take in. The idea that my bright and enchanting baby would never grow up to experience life, I had had to push it aside. I had been about to give birth, then I had a new baby, other little children with constant demands, If I had given in to the terrible loss that was there, I would not have been able to move from my bed.

Excuses, excuses.

"I don't blame you for loving them more than me," Elisa was saying bravely.

That was so far from what I was feeling that I could only stop and stare at her. "Is that what you're thinking? Because it's not true. You were the tragedy of my life! Now that I've found you how could I love you any less?"

And saying it, I realized I didn't. But I said, "We have to go."

I did not want to be having this conversation. There was too much finality to it, too much a sense of summing up to say goodbye. As if we would never see each other again.

I began to walk quickly.

And then the wooden stairs came into sight. The way they loomed looked for a moment like the steps to a gallows. Whatever was going to happen would happen on the other side.

Chapter Thirty-Five

WE STOOD AT the bottom of the steps without moving, as if gathering the strength we would need for what was to come. I was anxious to see Hannah, desperately anxious, but I reached out and pressed Elisa against me, holding her as if we had all the time in the world. She hugged me back hard. "It's going to be fine," I whispered. "You and Hannah and I will be together in a few minutes. It's going to be fine."

I wanted to believe it.

My daughter gave a soft laugh.

And then we were climbing slowly, the gritty sand from other people's sandals against our soles. The sound of the Atlantic slapping the shore was louder now, the afternoon sun making us squint. I thought about my sister, Patience, perhaps staring at this same ocean right now, and realized she didn't even know about Hannah. The most terrible event in recent history, even worse than Colin's arrest, and it hadn't occurred to me to call her. My daughters were ready to risk their lives for each other because of an unbreachable bond. Would Pat and I be willing to give up our lives for each other now that we were grown?

I batted a black fly away from my eyes, already on an emotional overload. *Don't think about it now.* Patience and I would never let each other come to harm. Neither of us would ever find herself hungry and on the street. *Leave it there.*

I could feel Elisa beside me, hear the scuff of her sneakers on the wood. We stopped at the top of the stairs as the beach spread out before us. Sugary sand, the ocean the deep sea green that Winslow Homer favored. Small waves like the ruffles on a toddler's dress. Here the noise of the Atlantic blended with the shrieks of gulls, the whir of a helicopter in the soft blue sky. There were no lifeguard stands in this section of the beach. Two women with a flock of children were stationed under an umbrella near the water. Two men were lying on a blue plaid blanket. One of them stood up slowly, lifting his arms to the fading sun. He did not lie back down. The second man was starting to push up too. I had the sense they had seen us come.

But I did not see Hannah. Where was *Hannah*? Had we been tricked? Would we get to the bottom and be told to turn around and climb back up?

I looked at Elisa and she gave an uncertain shrug. We started down the steps, some thirty or forty of them.

My phone did not ring.

At the bottom we stepped onto the sand and looked around uncertainly.

Then from under the shadow of the stairs a few feet behind us, there was a sense of motion. And a familiar figure stepped out. I pulled back as if I could not believe Sheila Crosley was real. I had pictured her blackened body so often that it did not seem possible that Sheila was standing here in white slacks and a navy shirt, her black hair tied back with a red-printed scarf. And Elisa had said she had died. Was this some kind of elaborate trap?

I jerked my head around to Elisa. She gave hers a small shake. *I'll explain later.*

Where was Hannah?

Sheila stepped closer. "You've always done what you were told, haven't you, Delhi. "Never an original idea in your head. I could have predicted the life you'd lead, the way Elisa would have been if she'd stayed with you."

"Where's *Hannah*?"

"A perfect example of what I'm talking about." She gave her red mouth a small twist, the scorn I remembered all these years later. "You claimed that money couldn't buy happiness. I've spent my life proving you wrong."

"Where's my *daughter*?" I was ready to cross the sand between us and grab her throat. Choke her. *Why didn't you burn to death?*

A mock sigh. "You really want that fat slug back. You didn't do a great job with her. We did much better with her twin."

I realized that she was stalling. But why?

"Where is Hannah?" I repeated.

Elisa stepped away from me. "Where is she, Mom?"

"Now I'm 'Mom' again?" Sheila taunted.

Then I felt the vibration in the air, a subtle change, before I heard the clattering.

I felt as if I were vibrating as well. I took a step toward Sheila, my foot sinking lower in the sand than I expected, momentarily startling me.

Sheila gave a quick glance toward the water, then back under the stairs. "For God's sake, get over here. Now."

She stretched out her hand like a magician impatient with a slow assistant, and Hannah lurched into view, landing against Sheila for balance. "Oh, good Lord, help me." Sheila moved away and positioned Hannah upright on the sand. Hannah looked at me, looked at Elisa then. She did not seem to recognize us.

Over the noise of the ocean and wind, I heard a sound like slats falling, the whine of an engine, and whirled to stare. Beyond the corner of the beach to my left something large and white was settling down on the sand, halfway in the water.

Sheila Crosley was the first to react, grabbing Hannah's shoulders and giving her a shove toward me, then reaching out her hand. "C'mon, Liss! The boat's waiting for us."

Elisa seemed to move closer to her, but turned to make sure I had Hannah in my grasp. Then she veered away in the direction of the helicopter. She was running toward it even as a door opened and several metal stairs dropped down. The official-looking white helicopter had a string of official numbers and "SUFFOLK COUNTY POLICE" in large blue letters on its nose.

Thank God, thank God. I hadn't imagined them doing it this way, but Elisa would be safe with the police. Unless Sheila pulled out a gun, Hannah and I would be safe too.

But Sheila began running after Elisa instead, as if she were trying to reach her and tackle her to the sand. Elisa was athletic and faster. She got to the metal steps and was up them seconds before Sheila was close enough to touch her. I thought Sheila would turn and run then, run for her boat, but momentum carried her up the steps too and into the plane. Did she still believe she could pull Elisa out?

The two men who had been on the blanket were streaking across the sand and had almost reached the helicopter.

Then like a snake's tongue retracting, the stairs disappeared and the door slid closed. A moment later, the helicopter lifted noisily toward the sky.

I turned my attention to Hannah. "See, Hani," I crooned, "everything's all right. Elisa's safe. The police have her."

Hannah stared at me, dazed. "*Mom*"

I looked back into her blue eyes, as blank and empty as a doll's. They must have drugged her. Sheila couldn't take the chance that Hannah would break and run. I prayed they hadn't caused permanent damage.

"Hannah, you're safe now," I cooed, as if she were three years old again. "Elisa's safe. Nobody's going to hurt you now."

"You okay?" It was one of the two men from the blanket. The second was here now too, turned away from us and speaking urgently into a cell phone. I saw that they were older than the boys I had imagined them to be. Police, of course.

"They gave my daughter something. She's out of it." I tried to keep my voice from quavering. Sheila was vicious enough to have permanently destroyed her mind.

"We'll have her checked out." He smiled at Hannah.

Someone was clattering down the stairs. *Frank Marselli and Ruth Carew.*

All I could think was that Carew would have to believe us now, believe that Colin had never been involved. We were all safe now.

Frank, dressed informally in a light blue shirt and chinos, gave us a quick, appraising look. "This is Hannah?"

"They drugged her." I squeezed her shoulder tighter against me. *Hannah, say hello to the nice policeman.* "But I think it's wearing off."

"Where's the other girl? Elisa?"

"She's safe too, thank God. The police helicopter picked her up."

Frank turned to Ruth, who shook her head, then gave me an odd look. "What police helicopter?"

Chapter Thirty-Six

HADN'T THEY TOLD him? "The police helicopter that landed on the beach by the water. Elisa ran to it and they picked her up. Sheila got on board too; *I* think she wanted to pull Elisa off. But they closed the doors before she could."

"How did you know it was a police helicopter?" Ruth demanded. Her face looked flushed against her white blouse, her eyes glittery.

Well, duh. "It said Suffolk County Police in big blue letters on the side. There were a lot of official numbers on the tail."

"But was the undercarriage dark blue?"

What was she talking about? "It said Suffolk County Police," I repeated.

She turned to Frank as if I was too stupid to live.

"What are you saying, that it wasn't from the police?"

Frank turned back from the other two men. "We have four units in Suffolk County, used mostly for medevac. None of them were deployed."

"But whose was it then?" I *was* too stupid to live. No wonder

Sheila had scrambled aboard. "You mean the police don't have Elisa?"

Nobody seemed to hear me.

"We've contacted MacArthur-Islip," the shorter, swarthier cop was telling Frank and Carew. "We've put out an alert for anything trying to land in a public strip. Does the device work in the air?"

"I don't know." Frank turned to me then. "Do you remember any of the numbers on the helicopter?"

I closed my eyes to conjure up the copter but saw no numbers. "Ethan has some kind of plane," I added dully. "Elisa said she used to skydive from it."

Ruth scowled at me. Her excitement had faded; now she looked like a disgruntled raccoon. *You need to get more sleep.* "A plane is not a helicopter. Unless he had one of those too and the girl was in on it."

I pressed my hand against my waist to keep from giving her an angry shove. *How dare she?* "Of course she wasn't 'in on it'! She saw that the copter said Suffolk County Police. What else was she to think? You promised to protect her and you didn't!"

Carew gave me a black look and turned her back deliberately, making the huddle of police a closed circle.

The catastrophe of what had happened made me want to collapse on the sand and wail. The unthinkable had happened; they had Elisa. How would we ever get her back? I was holding on to Hannah as if I were the one unable to stand, but I said, "How are you feeling now?"

"Uhh." She turned to me like a patient waking from ether. "They kept making me take stuff, they had a *gun*.Where are Elisa and the police?"

"We're trying to find that out." I suddenly remembered Will, probably waiting back at the ferry terminal, hanging on to Elisa's promise that she would see him for dinner tonight. He would kill me.

Frank moved back to us and gestured toward the steps. "Let's go."

But I didn't want to leave this contained place. It made no sense, but once we did it meant that we had abandoned Elisa, that she could be anywhere in the world.

Ruth Carew turned to us too. "How's she doing?" she asked, eyeing Hannah with concern. "She was drugged?"

"She says they gave her stuff. But it seems to be wearing off. A little."

She nodded. "We'll have her looked at as soon as we get back."

I sighed. Just when I was ready to write Ruth off completely she did something human.

Then she was business again. "Who else was on the beach?"

"Sheila Crosley." *I told you.*

"That's impossible."

"You think I'm making it up?"

"No, but—"

"We're going. Now." Frank's voice overrode our conversation.

I waited until Hannah was holding the railing and climbing, then caught up with him on the stairs. "Do you really think we'll find her?"

"A helicopter's not that easy to hide. Small craft aren't required to file a flight plan if the weather's good and they're flying under VFR conditions. Visual flight rules. They're supposed to set their transponders to a certain frequency so they can be tracked on radar, but if they don't, they don't . . . Radar doesn't work below a certain altitude anyway. And helicopters can fly very low."

"You mean no one can *see* them?" The stairs tilted under my sandals and I reached for the wooden rail.

"We'll find them if they go through Islip's airspace. Or Republic's in Melville. Everyone's been notified." He sighed and looked back out across the beach. "Everything was set up for a boat. Or if they tried to hide out here, that's what the device was for. But a copter?" Frank shook his head.

Lack of imagination. Lack of thinking outside the box. And not just on their part either.

We climbed each step slowly, a tired procession. The sun was disappearing for the day and Fire Island was already chilly. Once it was dark it would get very cold. I needed to hurry, but I felt weak as a tissue doll. When I looked back to Hannah, she seemed exhausted too.

When we were nearly to the dock, Ruth Carew said to me, "The police launch will take you back to Patchogue. That's where your car is, isn't it?"

"Where are *you* going?"

"Same place."

I nodded. She didn't need to know that I had no intention of climbing in my van and driving home.

As soon as we had boarded the white launch and were settled on the seats inside, I called Colin. When he answered, I handed the phone to Hannah.

"Daddy?" I heard her say. "Yes, it's really me. I'm with Mom. No, I'm okay. But we can't find Elisa! She's in a helicopter but we don't know where."

She listened, then said, "No, I'm not coming home with you. Mom—we need to find Elisa!" A pause. "No, I'm fine. We're with the police. Love you, Dad." She clicked the phone off and handed it back to me. "He doesn't get it."

Hannah was returning to herself.

But my phone rang immediately. "Delhi? You're coming in at West Street?"

"That's where my—"

"I know, I'm here. And I'm taking Hannah home."

"You're at the dock?"

Colin sighed at my surprise. "Where else would I be? You told me where you were leaving from. I'm looking at your van right now."

"We're just crossing the bay. We'll be there soon."

I put my phone away. My arm still around Hannah, I said, "Dad's at the pier. He'll be hurt if you don't go home with him."

"But *Mom*—"

"We don't know what's going to happen, how long it will take. And I don't want you anywhere near those people again!"

The police launch, smaller than the ferry, skimmed the water so rapidly that some of the time I felt we were airborne. When we had slowed enough to enter the canal, Frank came from the front and hopped down to the benches where we sat.

"Can you tell me what happened?" he asked Hannah.

She nodded. "These men came to my house and kept asking me where Elisa was. Then they said that she was in trouble, that she needed to see me." A quick, guilty look at me. "I know. How could they know she was in trouble if they were asking me where she was? And I shouldn't have gone with them after Elisa warned me. But I was *worried*."

"Do you know who they are?" Frank asked urgently. "Was Dr. Crosley there too?"

She frowned. "But he died in the fire."

"Give her more time, she's still confused."

Frank ignored me and leaned closer to her. "Did they use any names? Did they say why they wanted your sister?"

"No-o." It came out as a wail. "No!"

Frank may have thought it was his questions upsetting her. I knew she was starting to understand that things were very wrong with Elisa.

"You were on a yacht the whole time?" Frank asked.

"I think so."

"How did they treat you?" I demanded.

"Okay. They just wanted Elisa back."

And now, God help us, they had her.

THE CONFRONTATION I had expected with Will at the ferry terminal did not happen. When the police launch arrived at the dock a moment later, the building was already locked for the night. Hannah and I climbed off shakily and walked around the grassy side to the parking lot. At every moment I expected Will to appear, to rush at us demanding to know where Elisa was. But it was Colin who ran toward us, who stopped short and held out his arms for Hannah, enveloping her in a fearsome hug. They held on to each other like people reunited after a catastrophe who hadn't been sure they'd see each other again.

I couldn't help myself. I moved over and pressed my body against theirs, hating the tears that ran down my face in streams. I hadn't let myself think fully about Elisa, but now I couldn't help myself. "Never again," I sobbed. "Never again," though I had no idea what I meant.

When our family hug ended, Hannah said to me anxiously, "You're coming home too, aren't you?"

"Soon," I said. Frank and Ruth Carew were already at the edge of the parking lot, about to cross the street to a police cruiser.

"Wait!" I shouted. Colin and Hannah jerked, startled, but I motioned them on.

Frank and Ruth turned to their right to stare at me as if in a choreographed dance.

I beckoned them urgently. After exchanging a look, they moved toward me.

When they were close enough, I pointed and said, "That's Will Crosley's car."

The black Mazda sports coupe sat forlornly in the row behind my van in the deserted parking lot.

Ruth Carew gave me a so-what? blink.

"He brought Elisa here, but he didn't want her to go through with it. He was waiting for us to get back. So where is he?" I couldn't account for the bleakness that enveloped me when I looked at Will's car. It was true my emotions were raw, but this was something else.

"Maybe he went to get a drink," Frank suggested.

"And risk missing us? He was completely opposed to Elisa's going. It was almost this macho thing, as if she was disobeying his orders."

Frank walked over to the car, peered in, then took a pair of vinyl gloves from his pocket and opened the door. We leaned in behind him. The car was empty, but a set of keys dangled from the ignition. The sunglasses tossed on the passenger seat seemed ominous.

"Shit," said Frank, pressing his lips in a disappearing line and looking heavenward. "Shit, shit, *shit*."

"What?" demanded Carew.

"You don't go off and leave your keys in the ignition in West Patchogue. Not with this kind of car. Not if you're as street smart as he was supposed to be." He turned to me. "Do you remember what he was wearing?"

"Yes." I closed my eyes a moment. "A red polo shirt like a golf shirt, jeans I think. And the sunglasses."

"Who's in the squad car?" Frank asked Carew.

She gave him two names.

"Good. We'll take the car and they can search this area."

He jerked his head and she started to walk.

I followed them.

Ruth Carew must have sensed me behind them because she turned at the curb. "Ms. Laine, go home. Police personnel only."

"Wait a minute." I was ablaze with a fire I had been keeping under control. "I promised Elisa the police would keep her safe and you didn't. Now I don't know if I'll ever see her again. I'm not going home until you find her!"

We faced off in the shadow of an elm tree.

Carew appealed to Frank. "She can't come with us. This is an official investigation."

"She knows who the perps are."

"They're the people in that chopper." Her pale face was reddening. "We don't need her. You may have seniority, but this is *my* case."

Frank gave her a flat, unfriendly stare. "I do have seniority. And this kidnapping case is mine. Let's just go."

Her eyes shifted to me, furious. But then she looked back to Frank and I saw not the anger I was expecting but a flash of desire.

Wonderful. I wanted to tell her that he and I had only recently become friends. Just friends. But my feelings were so overwhelming right now, my need to see Elisa so strong, that I couldn't tell what I was feeling for anyone. Even though I had been sure earlier that my marriage was over, holding on to Colin on the dock had weakened that idea as well.

AND THEN WE sat, crowded uncomfortably in the squad car, waiting for any direction, any information. Frank was tense in the driver's seat, Carew fiddling with the GPS and tracking screen, me hunched in the back. I saw a blue-uniformed policeman appearing and disappearing in the woods beside the parking lot. Would he find Will's body? The Crosleys had to know he had given them up to the FBI. Perhaps they had been looking for him all this time too. I couldn't escape the horror of Will lying motionless on his back, a blood-edged hole on his forehead like a red scar. If they knew he had been hiding Elisa as well, what reason was there to let him live?

Chilled, I turned my attention to the gray bungalow we were parked in front of. It had probably been built in the 1930s judging from the fat-columned porch and crumbling stone flowerpots. I half expected to see a metal box for milk deliveries by the front door.

I didn't know how much longer I could sit and wait. There was no point in driving around blindly until we had some idea where the Crosleys had gone, but this was getting unbearable. Carew had already informed us of what I had guessed, that Elisa's device wasn't tracking.

When the news came it was not from the screen, but a crackling voice from the radio. "Aircraft down. Aircraft down!"

I leaned forward in terror.

"Give me the coordinates." Frank's voice was calm.

A pause, then the voice rattled off numbers. The second time Carew finished punching them into the GPS device.

"Helicopter?" She leaned toward the radio.

"Affirmative."

"Did it land?"

"Crashed."

"Oh, no!" It was my voice that filled the car in a wailing protest. Ruth jerked, startled.

"Where did it crash?" Frank asked.

What did crash *mean*? Just a hard landing? Or . . .

Ruth turned to the second, smaller screen. "Eastport."

Eastport? They were flying *east*? I had pictured the helicopter heading in the opposite direction, toward JFK, the Crosleys abandoning it in a nearby lot and, and boarding a commercial flight out of the country. But perhaps *The Beautiful Past* was moored in Southampton and they had been heading there to lie low for a few days. In a week or so, when surveillance had eased up, they could have left the country with forged passports, slipping away forever.

And now?

Frank had already pulled the cruiser away from the curb and into traffic. I could hear the siren he had turned on and imagined the red and blue lights flashing.

I pressed forward. "Can you find out how—bad the crash was?"

Frank's eyes locked on mine in the rearview mirror. "Do you really want to know?"

"I *have* to know."

He nodded toward Ruth Carew. A soft sigh, then she spoke to a dispatcher who patched her through to an officer at the crash scene. The officer's voice crackled as he identified himself.

"Carew here. We're on our way. How bad is it?" She lowered her voice to where I could barely hear her.

But his answer was clear enough. "No survivors."

I pressed back against the seat, too stunned to breathe in. Was this how my life would finally end? I knew I would never recover this time. *Thank God Hannah isn't here.* She would be inconsolable. The thought of her arriving at the scene and seeing Elisa's body . . . She would never survive that. I doubted that I could.

Hold it together. Don't scream. Think about what you do now. Yet I couldn't stop the thought that knowing Elisa again had been like a visitation from an angel. I had been given the rare chance to find out what my daughter would have been like as an adult, given time to make peace with her, and say a longer good-bye. Thank God I had had a chance to tell her how much I loved her and had missed her all these years.

But it was not a visitation, not a dream. It was a nightmare.

Chapter Thirty-Seven

I found I was sitting with my fists clenched, eyes closed and my body rigid as a board with the effort not to think. Not to feel.

In the front seat there was a beeping.

I opened my eyes and saw Carew give her head a shake. "What am I getting here?"

Frank veered onto the median shoulder. We had just entered Sunrise Highway and rush hour traffic was clotted around us. "What? Where is it?"

"Not in Eastport. It's closer to us, in East Moriches. It could be anything, of course."

"No. It's a discrete signal. Key it in."

I tried to picture the distance between East Moriches and Eastport. They bordered each other, but Moriches came first. So Elisa's transmitter couldn't be from the debris. Had they discovered the device on Elisa and tossed it out? Could you open a window on a helicopter? I thought of incidents on commercial airlines where passengers had been sucked out of planes by air pressure. But helicopters weren't pressurized. Or planes.

What if . . . I thought of something so crazy that I nearly kept quiet. But I could never keep quiet, especially now. "Can you radio and ask how many people there were in the crash?"

"Why?" Carew said, then as she understood it added, "That's not a bad idea."

She did something I couldn't see, then said, "Carew and Marselli, we're on our way. How many vics and ages?"

The cop on the scene didn't have to check. "One male, one female, mid-forties."

"That's it? No one ejected nearby?"

"We've secured the entire area."

"Okay. Roger."

I put my hand over my mouth as if I were going to be sick. I had suddenly remembered the movie *The Good Shepherd*, where a young woman had been deliberately thrown out of a small airplane, cartwheeling down to her death. *Dear God, no.*

But helicopters didn't fly that high. She could still be alive, just badly hurt.

If that was even what had happened.

We were moving again, siren screaming. Other cars were veering onto the shoulder, but it was still taking much too long. Maybe she was only hurt. We had to save her! I cursed a silver SUV that blocked our path until Frank pressed on the horn as well. Sitting forward, I craned to see the screens. Our sedan was a blue arrow. Then Ruth zoomed out beyond street names and I could see something round and red throbbing in the distance.

Breathe in. Breathe in.

We had just passed the green DOT sign for Mastic Beach and Shirley at William Floyd Parkway when the radio came to life again. A static voice reported, "Crash scene, helicopter crash scene. ME is here. Vics died on impact, but the pilot was shot in the chest first. Could be why the craft went down."

"Any sign of a weapon?"

"Still checking."

Ruth and Frank exchanged a rapid look. Not in their playbook. Not in mine either. But I was in an emotional red zone and couldn't consider anything else.

We screeched off the highway at Center Moriches and raced north on Old Schoolhouse Road. By looking over Carew's shoulder, I could track our progress to the pulsing red object. *Hang on, Elisa, hang on.* Carew pressed a button and the screen switched to a satellite view, trees and open farm fields. Could that tiny quarter-sized piece I had pressed on Elisa be this powerful?

"Here. Stop here!"

Frank swerved onto the side of the road, spewing dirt and pebbles into an irrigation ditch he nearly drove into.

"In there." Ruth pointed at the field. "It's in there. Somewhere."

"Okay. We'll find it."

I had a moment of panic when I couldn't open my door. Locked in the backseat like a criminal. Would they make me wait in the car? I wouldn't, of course. I saw myself climbing into the front seat, freeing myself, and running after them. But Frank came around to pull the door open. He took my arm and helped me out, my legs weak and stiff.

I had hoped that the field would be hard brown earth so that we could see across it, find Elisa faster. Despite no evidence, I was convinced she was here. But as we started in, Ruth holding the screen close to her chest, knee-high cornstalks started blocking our way. They were almost low enough to see over—but not quite.

"Over here!" Ruth was peering at the screen.

The ground kept getting softer, my sandals sinking into mud. We pressed on. Then to the right I saw a large piece of white cloth splayed out and crushing the cornstalks, as if a family of giants had spread a picnic cloth. Was some metal device attached to it that had fooled us into thinking it was Elisa's? *I can't bear this.*

Then Marselli just ahead of us was kneeling down. "Here!"

Pushing closer, I realized that the cloth was a parachute. There was a body still attached to it, a body that did not move.

"No!" I wailed.

"Easy, it's okay, she still has a pulse." Then Frank was on his radio, calling for medical help.

I WAS KNEELING behind her, resting her head and upper shoulders on my knees when she opened her soft blue eyes and stared into mine. Carew had objected, but I had been careful not to disturb Elisa's back.

"You found me," she whispered.

I couldn't help the tears streaking down my face. "I promised—I promised you'd be okay."

"I need to sit up." She pressed her hands into the dirt, and I helped her the rest of the way.

Carew gave a cry. "You can't move yet," she commanded. "We don't know about your injuries yet."

"No, I'm okay, I just landed wrong. My father taught me how, but I'd never jumped out of a helicopter before and I think I banged my head. I was afraid of hitting wires. What—happened to the helicopter?"

"It crashed in the next town," Marselli said briskly. He was still kneeling at her right side, his khaki chinos ruined.

"It crashed?" She jerked with surprise. I steadied her, my arm around her.

"Can you tell me what happened?"

"Can't it wait?" I asked. "She's still in shock."

"Just a few things. We need to know a few things *now*." He looked up at Carew. "Why don't you wait out on the road so you can show them in?"

She looked at him as if he had suggested she lie down and roll around in the mud. "This is *my* case."

"When I saw the copter on the beach, I thought it was the police," Elisa started. "Even when I got closer and saw that the letters that said police were just stuck on and were peeling, I got in anyway. Then I saw Youssef and knew it was a trick. I tried to get out, but he wouldn't let me." I felt her body sag against me and held her tighter. "As soon as we took off I tried to get to the parachutes."

"How did you know about the parachutes?" Carew interrupted, skeptical.

"I knew there had to be some. I'd skydived out of my father's Cessna before, when Youssef was flying it. But when I started to strap the chute on, my mother pulled a gun out of her bag and pointed it at me. She doesn't even know how to shoot! But she was close enough to kill me."

"You're sure it was your mother?" Carew interrupted again. She was the only one standing, looking down on us.

"Well, not my *mother*." A flick of her eyes at me. "I mean the witch who passed herself off as my mother all those years. Anyway, I grabbed the gun from her and it went off. She fell back and I thought it had hit her, but Youssef cried out so I guess it hit him. I kept the gun pointed at her, but she was all over him anyway. So I strapped in, and opened the door."

"Where was Dr. Crosley?" Marselli asked.

"Dr. Crosley, my *father*?" Elisa was bewildered. "But I thought you knew—he died in that fire. They burned him to death." Her eyes filled with tears that ran down her muddy face. "He was the only good one," she sobbed. "Will said he had done some bad things, but I don't believe it!"

"Wait a minute. Sheila Crosley killed her husband?" Carew was incredulous. I was just as stunned.

"I didn't even know it. When she and Youssef came up to Boston to get me, I was so excited that they were still alive. When I asked where Daddy was, she said in Barbados taking care of some stuff. I *believed* her, he was there a lot. She told me that a couple renting the house had died in the fire. I believed that too." She gave her head a shake, possibly at her own naïveté. They took me to *The Beautiful Past* to wait for a phony passport so we could join Daddy. But then—"

She lowered her head to her arm, which was across her knees. More tears. I held her tightly.

"You were on the yacht," Frank prodded.

She looked up, her blue eyes large. I reminded myself how young she was. "The next morning I started to open the door to my parents' cabin. I wanted to tell her that I was still upset that they'd put me through all that. I'd mentioned it before and she'd just laughed. Like thinking they were dead was nothing! Anyway, she and Youssef were in bed, so wrapped up in each other they didn't even hear me.

"I went up on deck and talked to Craig, he does the computer stuff, he's worked for my father for years. He didn't want to tell me, but I kept pushing him and he's always—liked me. Finally he said that they had started about three years ago. He couldn't believe I hadn't suspected anything. But my father had finally guessed and was threatening to turn Youssef over to the Egyptian authorities.

"Then—Sheila came up with the idea about the fire and convinced my father that she would disappear with him, without Youssef. Craig said the FBI was about to arrest him! If they thought he'd died in a fire, they'd leave him alone. But my father never thought he *would*." I thought she would start crying again, but she said, "Anyway, when Craig told me what had happened to my father, that's when I ran away. So then they had to find me and get rid of me before I told anyone what they had done."

"So why didn't they just go into hiding in another country?" More skepticism from Carew.

Elisa gave me a who-*is*-this-woman? glance. "Because Youssef didn't want to hide. He wanted to continue the business and live it up on my father's money. They figured when he introduced Sheila as his wife, no one would connect her with someone who died in a fire in America. They've probably moved the money somewhere safe by now."

"No, we've monitored the bank accounts and credit cards for activity." Carew straightened smugly. "There hasn't been any."

Elisa's look at her was scornful. "Do you think those accounts were the only ones they had? People like that? Those everyday accounts are *nothing*."

But I could tell she was tiring. "Anyway," Elisa said more faintly, "my father—Ethan—thought the plan was to use this other couple to die in the fire. But Youssef came up behind him and strangled him. They put him on the bed with the woman and doused them in kerosene. They still had my father's stand-in there, unconscious, so

Craig said they beat him up to make it look a drunken fight, then dumped him in the woods somewhere."

"The vic in Mecox Woods," Frank said grimly to Ruth.

"My God!"

"But how did you get away from them?" I asked Elisa.

"That was the easy part. They didn't know I knew anything. We went on shore that night for dinner near the marina. I went to the restroom and then ran. I called Will, I knew he'd help me. Will!" Her eyes flared open. "I have to let him know I'm okay!"

The sun had gone in and darkness was creeping across the green field. It was getting colder as well. I didn't want to think about Will.

Frank pushed up from the ground. "Just one more thing. Was Craig on the helicopter?"

"No. He must be in Southampton with the boat."

"What is it called again?"

Elisa sighed. "*The Beautiful Past.*"

Chapter Thirty-Eight

I STAYED SILENT on the ride back to Patchogue to retrieve my van, terrified of what we would find in the parking lot. In my rush of feeling at finding Elisa alive, I had forgotten Will. I'd watched enough police procedurals to know if they had found his body in the adjoining woods there would be flashing lights, a white canopy erected, everyone milling around. Elisa would see Will's abandoned car and *know*. Would his death, on top of Ethan's, push her beyond the point of recovery?

As we passed Bellport and were moving into East Patchogue, I tried to think of a way to have Frank take me to pick up the van alone. But my mind was a jittery adolescent, too overwhelmed by everything that had happened to focus on any one thing. I had been right about Sheila, but wrong about Ethan. As soon as I'd heard about Kathleen I'd felt she was the victim, but had never been able to explain why the man's body matched Ethan's so perfectly, down to the two stents. Poor Kathleen! Her American odyssey had ended in being sacrificed. For nothing. What was not surprising was that Sheila, given Ethan's lack of sexual ability, had fallen into an affair with a man as handsome as Youssef. I doubted that he was her first.

If Ethan traveled a lot, just indulging themselves might have been enough. But Youssef no doubt had had ambitions beyond taking orders. When the opportunity to have it all came up, he and Sheila had seized it.

I held my breath as Frank turned down West Street and then into the parking lot. There was a spotlight on the long narrow photograph of Fire Island on the front of the rustic building, but the area lay otherwise in darkness, No activity of any kind.

Will's car was gone. Had it been towed away as evidence? I waited for Elisa to wonder where he was, but she didn't seem to notice.

And then we were finally home and I was in the kitchen making the pasta I fell back on when we needed comfort: linguini with onions, capers, anchovies, garlic, red pepper flakes. Colin and the twins were in the living room, wine easing their sometimes incoherent conversation. When we'd come into the house, after the twins had grabbed each other tightly and finally let go, Elisa and Colin had looked at each other. There was so much they needed to say. Then Colin opened his arms the way he had with Hannah on the dock, and Elisa moved into them. I saw she was crying again.

There was a conversation Elisa and I needed to have before the police interviewed her again. I'd wanted to give her a chance to decompress, to be with Hannah and let the wine relax her, but suddenly it seemed urgent. What if Frank or Carew decided to stop by now?

I went to the living room doorway. "Elisa, could you help me with something?"

Surprised, she pushed up from the striped couch. There was

a momentarily silence, then the murmur of Colin and Hannah talking again.

In the kitchen I pointed to a chair at the oak table and Elisa sat down opposite me.

"I know you've been through hell. But I have to know what really happened before you talk to the police again."

"But I told you."

"No, you didn't. Not about what happened on the helicopter."

I could see her teetering on the edge of trusting me. On the drive back to Port Lewis from Patchogue, she had told me a few things. She'd known she was going to die when Sheila boarded the helicopter and started screaming at her. "She told me I would fall out trying to escape. She said—she told me, 'Now I'll be free of all of you, my pathetic attempt at a 'normal' life. I should have given it up years ago!' Then we took off and it was too noisy to talk."

"It was Will's gun, wasn't it?" I said now, keeping my voice low. "Not one that your mother pulled out of her bag. You had it with you the whole time. That's what Will didn't want you to forget."

She nodded. "He wanted me to be able to protect myself. He was *right* not to trust them. But I wasn't going to shoot her, I just wanted to get away. She tried to grab me, she clawed at my arm with her nails, then Youssef turned around with a knife in his hand. He wasn't close enough, but he tried to make my mother take it and she started to reach for it. So I shot him."

"And you left the gun on the helicopter?"

"Why not? Will had it when he worked for my father, he just kept it when he left. It's registered in my father's name. That's what they'll find out. That's what I *want* them to find out."

What they would never find out was how extraordinary my daughter was.

THERE WOULD BE rocky days ahead. The case against Colin was withdrawn in court, but Elisa deeply mourned Ethan and there was no way we could console her. After the police returned the Patek Philippe watch to her, she had it cleaned, sized to fit her, then wore it constantly. It had survived the fire only by chance. According to Craig, Youssef had removed the watch from Ethan's wrist, intending to sell it, but Sheila pointed out that it was engraved on the back from his father and could raise red flags. There had been an argument, but after the bodies were burned the watch was replaced. It suffered only minor damage in the second fire.

Once, when I asked Elisa if she was going to return the stolen archeological artifacts to their countries, she flared like a gasoline fire. "My father never stole anything. He didn't need to. He paid for everything he owned!"

Yet Fire Island and its aftermath brought us together in the way no amount of polite visits could. It had allowed me to tell her how much I loved her and had missed her, and let her know that this time I *would* put my life on the line to keep her safe. Perhaps it had also let her know what a mother loving her felt like.

According to Frank, Craig had been captured while he waited on *The Beautiful Past* for the others to return the leased helicopter and take a taxi back to Southampton. Although he had been the one who had handled the negotiations with me, he insisted that he never would have hurt Hannah. He had actually been in the parking lot and had watched Elisa and me board the ferry. He had been instructed by Sheila to kill Will Crosley if he brought Elisa there. But he couldn't.

"I mean, I *knew* Will," he'd told them earnestly. "We'd worked together for Ethan, I couldn't just shoot him. I'm a computer geek, not a killer! He said he wouldn't tell the police what Youssef and

Sheila had done. I gave him the money I had with me to seal the deal. It was plenty because we were leaving the country that night. We left his car open to make it look like someone had ambushed him and shot him. I even took his wallet as proof to show Sheila."

Craig also detailed the antiquities theft empire that Ethan had commanded. "The countries never missed the stuff because they didn't even know about most of it. The stuff left the sites immediately. Collectors paid a lot because there was no record of it being stolen. And he had Will forge some of the easier stuff. Ethan was a weird guy, that's for sure. It was like he was trying to get revenge on the whole world."

Elisa tried calling Will and leaving messages. He finally called her back several days later. But he was lying low, afraid he could still be charged in the antiquities scam. Their evening of cervezas and fried chicken would have to wait for a while.

I even had a call from Micah Clancy after the whole story was reported in the *Times* and *Newsday*—by Louis Benat. Micah's TV series, *Jamaica Blues*, was set to air in September, and he said he was loving New York.

"I've already brought the wife and kid over; maybe we'll stay. We should get together, I'd like to meet your daughter *now*."

I said I'd call him.

Meanwhile, we were feeling our way. Hannah's graduation was a watershed, a way to be together as a family that seemed a manual for the future. Everything has been a watershed. I had dinner with Frank after we got back, an evening that ended in an intense kiss but nothing more. We made plans for the next weekend.

I also admitted to myself the ways I had fictionalized Colin, first by my hero worship, then by playing him for laughs, making him sound more outrageous than he was. Now I can see him as gifted in many ways, but still a man. I didn't explain that part of it to him, but I let him know that I was not the girl he married. I thought he would be relieved that I had finally realized what he had been trying to tell me, but he is not quietly fading away Perhaps, now that we are complete again, he is ready to be a family man.

I'm not sure about that. We'll always have the children, of course, and the sunsets we shared over the places I dreamed about as a girl. New Mexico, Machu Picchu, Morocco.

The Beautiful Past.

Acknowledgments

It's TIME, AS they say, to round up the usual suspects:

Chelsey Emmelhainz, my amazing editor, who can coax cardboard into living, breathing characters.

Agnes Birnbaum, my tireless agent who, if life were a boxing match, would be always in my corner offering support, wise counsel, and Band-Aids.

Andrea Hackett, my publicist, who works tirelessly finding ways to tell the world about my books.

Eleanor Mikucki, my copy editor, whose eagle eye saved me from much embarrassment.

My trusted first readers who work hard to make my books what they should be: Tom Randall, accomplished husband; Robin Culbertson, insightful daughter-in-law; and Adele Glimm, dear friend and writer herself.

Some new faces: Ellen Stein and Tom McVetty, retired Nassau County detectives, who kept the police activities on track; Toby Speed, expert pilot, friend, and author of *Death Over Easy*, who vetted the helicopter information; Andy Rich, financial planner and mystery aficionado and fount of great ideas. Linda Levering, Pam Crum, and Eleanor Hyde for their ceaseless support, and Liz Randall and her Retired Teachers' Book Club. Also the Setauket Meadows Book Club, who served Yellow Tail Chardonnay at their reception because it was what Delhi liked to drink. And my New York City Writers Group, always.

Finally, the stellar family of writers and agents I am fortunate enough to spring from: Tom Randall and Andy Culbertson; John Chaffee and Heide Lange; Jessie Chaffee, Brendan Kiely, and Joshua Chaffee; David Chaffee and Deborah Hess.

Andrew, Emily, Charlotte, and Regan, you have a tradition to step into.

Not ready to stop sleuthing with Delhi Laine?

Read on for an excerpt from Judi Culbertson's

A Photographic Death

Now available from Witness Impulse

An Excerpt from

A Photographic Death

Nineteen years ago, Delhi Laine's two-year old daughter disappeared. After a frantic but inconclusive search, authorities determined that she must have drowned, her body washed away from the picturesque English park in which she was playing.

Delhi's heart has never healed, yet her family has since soldiered on. But when a mysterious letter arrives containing the ominous words, YOUR DAUGHTER DID NOT DROWN, their lives are once again thrown into turmoil. With her family torn between fighting for the past and protecting the future, Delhi is caught in the middle. For a mother, the choice to find her daughter seems easy. But for a family left fractured by the mistakes of the past, the consequence, and the truth, may be infinitely more costly.

"ARE YOU COMFORTABLE, Jane?"

Karl Lundy looks at my daughter with the smile of a chef about to garnish his favorite piglet. It makes me want to grab her wrist and head for the door.

Yet Jane looks comfortable enough, her hair golden against the navy worsted fabric of the chair, her mouth slightly open in anticipation. Dr. Lundy seems excited too. His gray eyes keep blinking behind gold-rimmed glasses. His hand plays with a paperweight on his desk, a rose trapped under glass.

When I approached him last week and told him what we wanted, he explained that he rarely did one-offs, that he hypnotized people over the course of months for therapeutic reasons. But he didn't refuse. Jane must be an interesting change from people trying to stop smoking or lose forty pounds.

"You need to understand that hypnosis is serious business, Ms. Laine."

"Call me Delhi. And I'm happy to hear you say that."

Yet I'm still uneasy, shunted off to one side on a straight chair like a husband in a dress shop. Is it too late to say we have another appointment and walk out? What if Jane is about to be traumatized for life? Whatever we learn is going be a shock, I know that. We will find out either that my youngest daughter, Caitlin, may still be alive, or that Jane stood on the riverbank and watched her drown nineteen years ago. *The lady or the tiger. Dear God, don't let it be the tiger crouching behind the unopened door.*

Restless, I search the room for clues as to what's going to happen, but it is a typical doctor's office that gives nothing away. The vanilla scent is meant to be calming, as are the paintings on the walls— country scenes of red barns and golden haystacks, mountains reflected in turquoise lakes. I wonder if someone Dr. Lundy knows painted them. The bookcases hold the kind of academic volumes that I, as a book dealer, have little interest in. I would not rescue *them* in case of fire.

"Jane, I'm going to put you in the light trance I told you about, and we'll gradually regress you to the age of four. You'll be back in the park in England on the last day you visited there." He looks to me for confirmation and I nod. "Is there anything else you'd like to work on in your life?"

She laughs. "You mean like getting up early and going to the gym every day? Or not spending so much time in clubs?"

"Any area of your life you'd like to improve."

"You can tell me not to buy any more expensive purses and shoes. Seriously," she adds, seeing his expression.

"All right. Now sit back and get as comfortable as possible."

Dr. Lundy has been standing behind his desk all this time. Now he moves to the chair on Jane's left. They can glance at each other, but don't have to. He is as bland and comforting as the vanilla cookie scent of his office, from his gray-and-sky-blue argyle sweater to his solid gold wedding ring. His soft Midwestern voice reminds me of Garrison Keillor telling a story.

In the pre-hypnosis interview, he gave me the facts meant to reassure me: That Jane would not be unconscious or asleep. She would be alert and attentive, able to bring material from the past into awareness. He promised he would not cross-examine her or make any suggestions he knew would be contrary to her wishes. If she became uncomfortable, she could raise her index finger and he would move away from what was upsetting her. He managed to make hypnosis sound as interesting as watching water boil.

It was what an apprehensive mother needed to hear.

"Do you want me to close my eyes?" Jane asks.

"If that makes you feel relaxed, certainly."

"Okay." She does, pressing deeper into the chair.

"You're becoming very relaxed," Dr. Lundy drones. "When you're completely relaxed, your right arm will feel as light as air. The lightness will start in the fingers and spread up through your wrist toward your elbow. The arm will become so light that it will lift into the air on its own."

Oh, sure, I think. And for two or three minutes nothing happens. But then her arm eerily starts to rise, the gold bracelet sliding back against the cuff of her sweater. My stomach jumps. What have I gotten us into?

Her arm floats in space until Dr. Lundy says, "As you go deeper and deeper, your arm will gradually lower back to the chair rest. When that happens you will be fully in a trance state, ready to explore the things that have happened to you in the past."

He continues to make the same suggestions, stating them in slightly different ways. My own lids start to droop and I have to fight not to sink into the past with Jane. Both she and my other daughter, Hannah, have the ability to close their eyes and be immediately asleep, napping until a change in the atmosphere startles them. I used to be the same way.

Then I am jerked awake, as surely as if Dr. Lundy had slapped me. Before my eyes, Jane is turning into a little girl. It's in the way she twists in the chair, mouth slightly open in wonder. Her eyes are open now too, but they are not seeing the room we are in.

"Where are you now, Jane?" Dr. Lundy wants to know. "Are you in the park?"

"In the park," she confirms. "We brought bread to feed the ducks. They ate all of it!"

"Who is in the park with you?"

"Mommy. And the twins. And the new baby. But we can't see her yet."

Dr. Lundy tenses. "Why not?"

"She's still in Mommy's tummy." None of us knew then that the baby would turn out to be Jason.

Dr. Lundy smiles sheepishly, gets Jane to tell him where everyone is in the park, then summarizes for her: "So your sister Hannah is asleep and Mommy is taking photos of people in boats on the river, and you and Cate are playing. What happens next?"

"That lady comes."

What lady? I don't just tense, I pull back in the chair, galvanized, electricity running haywire through my body. I actually lean toward Jane before I remember that I am forbidden to interfere.

"Jane, I want you to look at this lady and tell me about her. What kind of clothes does she have on?"

"Her nurse clothes. She always wears her nurse clothes."

What could she be talking about? Jane sounds as if she is used to seeing this woman in the park—how could I not have seen her, not even once?

"Does she have on a white dress like a nurse?" He waits for her to nod. "What color are her shoes?"

"Her shoes, her shoes." She actually seems to be looking down at someone's feet. "Her shoes are brown like Daddy's shoes. But she has on these funny stockings. With bumps."

"Is she as old as Mommy?"

No answer.

As old as Grandma? I want to demand. *What kind of funny stockings?* My hands are gripping the metal seat edge as if I am high on a ski lift with no restraints around me. He's not asking her the right questions! I lift an urgent hand to catch his eye, but he is focused on Jane.

The smell of vanilla in the room is making me nauseous.

"Is the lady talking to you?"

"She says—she says, 'Go pick that yellow flower for me and I'll give you a toy from the carriage.' "

So the nightmare begins.

About the Author

JUDI CULBERTSON draws on her experience as a used-and-rare-book dealer, social worker, and world traveler to create her biblio-phile mysteries. No stranger to cemeteries, she also coauthored five illustrated guides with her husband, Tom Randall, starting with *Permanent Parisians*. She lives in Port Jefferson, New York, with her family.

Visit Judi online at www.judiculbertson.net.

Discover great authors, exclusive offers, and more at hc.com.